Mouthwatering Pr█████████████████**es**

Death Bee Comes Her
"Personable characters and lots of honey lore."
—*Kirkus Reviews*

"Sprinkled with delightful notes on honey and its various uses, this debut novel in the Oregon Honeycomb Mystery series is a fun introduction to a new cozy series. Everett, the Havana Brown cat, is an animal delight, often proving to be smarter than the humans around him."
—*Criminal Element*

"The author writes a captivating story with interesting characters. Naturally, Everett [the cat] contributes to the solution. A charming read."
—**Reviewingtheevidence.com**

"This warmhearted book is fast-paced, with realistic dialogue and a captivating plot."
—*Mystery and Suspense Magazine*

Have Yourself a Fudgy Little Christmas
"Two nasty murders, charming surviving characters, plenty of Christmas cheer, and enough fudge recipes for a major sugar rush."
—*Kirkus Reviews*

Forever Fudge

"Nancy Coco paints us a pretty picture of this charming island setting where the main mode of transportation is a horse-drawn vehicle. She also gives us a delicious mystery complete with doses of her homemade fudge . . . a perfect read!"
—*Wonder Women Sixty*

Oh, Fudge!

"*Oh, Fudge!* is a charming cozy, the sixth in the Candy-Coated Mystery series. But be warned: There's a candy recipe at the end of each chapter, so don't read this one when you're hungry!"
—*Suspense Magazine*

Oh Say Can You Fudge

"Beautiful Mackinac Island provides the setting for a puzzling series of crimes. Now that Allie McMurphy has taken over her grandparents' hotel and fudge shop, life on Mackinac is good, although her little dog, Mal, does tend to nose out trouble. . . . Allie's third offers plenty of plausible suspects and mouthwatering fudge recipes."
—*Kirkus Reviews*

"WOW. This is a great book. I loved the series from the beginning, and this book just makes me love it even more. Nancy Coco draws the reader in and makes you feel like you are part of the story."
—**Bookschellves.com**

To Fudge or Not to Fudge
"*To Fudge or Not to Fudge* is a superbly crafted, classic, culinary cozy mystery. If you enjoy them as much as I do, you are in for a real treat."
—**Examiner.com** (5 stars)

"We LOVED it! This mystery is a vacation between the pages of a book. If you've never been to Mackinac Island, you will long to visit, and if you have, the story will help you to recall all of your wonderful memories."
—*Melissa's Mochas, Mysteries and Meows*

"A five-star delicious mystery that has great characters, a good plot, and a surprise ending. If you like a good mystery with more than one suspect and a surprise ending, then rush out to get this book and read it, but be sure you have the time, since once you start, you won't want to put it down."
—**Mystery Reading Nook**

"A charming and funny culinary mystery that parodies reality-show competitions and is led by a sweet heroine, eccentric but likable characters, and a skillfully crafted plot that speeds toward an unpredictable conclusion. Allie stands out as a likable and engaging character. Delectable fudge recipes are interspersed throughout the novel."
—*Kings River Life*

All Fudged Up
"A sweet treat with memorable characters, a charming locale, and satisfying mystery."
—**Barbara Allan**, author of the Trash 'n' Treasures Mystery Series

"A fun book with a lively plot, and it's set in one of America's most interesting resorts. All this plus fudge!"
—**JoAnna Carl**, author of the Chocoholic Mystery Series

"A sweet confection of a book. Charming setting, clever protagonist, and creamy fudge— a yummy recipe for a great read."
—**Joanna Campbell Slan**, author of the Scrap-N-Craft Mystery Series and the Jane Eyre Chronicles

"Nancy Coco's *All Fudged Up* is a delightful mystery delivering suspense and surprise in equal measure. Her heroine, Allie McMurphy, owner of the Historic McMurphy Hotel and Fudge Shop (as much of a mouthful as her delicious fudge), has a wry narrative voice that never falters. Add that to the charm of the setting, Michigan's famed Mackinac Island, and you have a recipe for enjoyment. As an added bonus, mouthwatering fudge recipes are included. A must-read for all lovers of amateur sleuth classic mysteries."
—**Carole Bugge (Elizabeth Blake)**, author of the Jane Austen Society Mystery Series

"You won't have to 'fudge' your enthusiasm for Nancy Coco's first Mackinac Island Fudge Shop Mystery. Indulge your sweet tooth as you settle in and meet Allie McMurphy, Mal the bichon/poodle mix, and the rest of the motley crew in this entertaining series debut."
—**Miranda James,** author of the Cat in the Stacks Mystery Series

"The characters are fun and well-developed, the setting is quaint and beautiful, and there are several mouthwatering fudge recipes."
—*RT Book Reviews* (3 stars)

"Enjoyable . . . *All Fudged Up* is littered with delicious fudge recipes, including alcohol-infused ones. I really enjoyed this cozy mystery and look forward to reading more in this series."
—**Fresh Fiction**

"Cozy mystery lovers who enjoy quirky characters, a great setting, and fantastic recipes will love this debut."
—*The Lima News*

"The first Candy-Coated Mystery is a fun cozy due to the wonderful location filled with eccentric characters."
—*Midwest Book Review*

Books by Nancy Coco

The Oregon Honeycomb Mystery Series
Death Bee Comes Her
A Matter of Hive and Death

The Candy-Coated Mystery Series
All Fudged Up
To Fudge or Not to Fudge
Oh Say Can You Fudge
All I Want for Christmas Is Fudge
All You Need Is Fudge
Oh, Fudge!
Deck the Halls with Fudge
Forever Fudge
Fudge Bites
Have Yourself a Fudgy Little Christmas
Here Comes the Fudge
A Midsummer Night's Fudge
Give Fudge a Chance

GIVE FUDGE
A CHANCE

Nancy Coco

Kensington Publishing Corp.
www.kensingtonbooks.com

KENSINGTON BOOKS are published by

Kensington Publishing Corp.
119 West 40th Street
New York, NY 10018

Copyright © 2023 by Nancy J. Parra

All rights reserved. No part of this book may be reproduced in any form or by any means without the prior written consent of the Publisher, excepting brief quotes used in reviews.

To the extent that the image or images on the cover of this book depict a person or persons, such person or persons are merely models, and are not intended to portray any character or characters featured in the book.

This book is a work of fiction. Names, characters, businesses, organizations, places, events, and incidents either are the product of the author's imagination or are used fictitiously. Any resemblance to actual persons, living or dead, events, or locales is entirely coincidental.

If you purchased this book without a cover you should be aware that this book is stolen property. It was reported as "unsold and destroyed" to the Publisher and neither the Author nor the Publisher has received any payment for this "stripped book."

All Kensington titles, imprints, and distributed lines are available at special quantity discounts for bulk purchases for sales promotion, premiums, fund-raising, educational, or institutional use.

Special book excerpts or customized printings can also be created to fit specific needs. For details, write or phone the office of the Kensington Sales Manager: Attn.: Sales Department. Kensington Publishing Corp., 119 West 40th Street, New York, NY 10018. Phone: 1-800-221-2647.

The K and Teapot logo is a trademark of Kensington Publishing Corp.

First Printing: June 2023
ISBN: 978-1-4967-3555-3

ISBN: 978-1-4967-3556-0 (ebook)

10 9 8 7 6 5 4 3 2 1

Printed in the United States of America

Chapter 1

"Are you entering the cornhole contest?" my best friend, Jenn, asked. She sipped a decaffeinated slushie. She switched everything to decaf once she found out she was pregnant. I don't know how she stands it but she says she enjoys the flavor.

"I've got fudge in the candy contest," I said. "That's enough competition for me." Unlike Jenn, I wasn't coordinated enough to even consider trying to toss a beanbag through a hole a few yards away.

It was August, and that meant the Mackinac County Fair was in full swing. Usually, the fair was held on the Upper Peninsula, but this year they had moved the fair onto the island as they renovated the regular fairgrounds.

Tents and booths filled every inch of Marquette Park, which was a large lawn at the base of Fort Mackinac. Exhibits were scattered throughout the island. Some of the exhibits were in the school a few blocks away, while others were located in the senior center and the community center.

As winner of the fudge festival, I had moved on to the county fair, hoping to qualify for the state fair. The more recognition I received for my fudge, the better the publicity for the McMurphy Hotel and Fudge Shop. The McMurphy has been in my family for over a hundred years, and I was the current owner and operator. With my friend Jenn's help, we'd had a successful second season, and I wanted to continue that success.

The air was rich with the scent of funnel cakes and animal tents, as well as the sound of people riding rides.

"Oh, it's the haunted murder mansion!" she squealed. "Let's go inside."

"But we have a haunted house on Main Street," I pointed out.

"Yes, but this one is new," she said. "I've already been through the one on Main Street twice."

"Fine," I said and gave the ticket guy my tickets. "You love these things, don't you?" I asked Jenn as we walked through the dark entrance and into a spooky, green-lighted foyer.

"They're so much fun!" Jenn's eyes glittered in the strange light. The soundtrack began with loud, spooky laughter.

"Enter if you dare," the soundtrack went on.

"Look, a bloody handprint on the door," Jenn said. "It's going to be great."

We stepped inside, and a mannequin in a monster mask jumped out at us with a knife in his hand. We both screamed and ran to the next doorway. We entered a funeral home scene with the corpse rising out of the coffin. Ghostly music played as the coffin lid lifted and closed.

We continued to a man in a jail cell reaching for

us. Jenn laughed and ran across the room. But he grabbed my arm. "Help me, there's a murderer on the loose," he said. "Be careful, or they'll get you, too!" I broke free from his grasp, and he called out. "Wait! Please let me out!"

"What was that?" I asked Jenn. "He grabbed me." Then a mechanical monster pushed out of a closet. We ran through the next door into a room where a man lay on the ground half in and half out the door to the outside. It looked like we would have to step over him to go out. "I'm not stepping over that," I said. "I don't want him to grab my leg."

"But it's the only way out," Jenn said. "Just tell him not to grab you." She walked up to the pretend corpse. "Look, I've got a dress on and I'm pregnant, so you'd better not grab me." Then she took a big step over him and opened the door wide letting in the bright sunshine. Light flooded the room, and we could see bloody handprints on the floor next to the corpse. Curious because he didn't even blink at the light, I squatted down to see if he was even real.

Oh, he was real, all right. A big pool of blood grew under him. "Those are some effects," I said to the guy. Nothing. I snapped my fingers close to his face and still he didn't flinch. My heart beat faster. "Mister," I said and shook his shoulder. His head lolled to the side.

"What are you doing?" Jenn said. "Just step over him. He clearly isn't going to grab you."

I frowned and touched his neck. "He's cold."

"As in 'not alive' cold?" Jenn asked. "Because if he's a mannequin, then I need to get my eyes checked."

"As in 'dead human' cold," I said. I'd found my share of dead bodies enough to know one when I saw one. "Don't move," I instructed Jenn, who held the door open.

Standing, I pulled out my phone and called nine-one-one.

"Nine-one-one, what is your emergency?"

"Hi, Charlene," I said. "You'd better call Rex." Charlene and I had never met in person, but we knew each other well, and Rex Manning was the lead police officer on the island and my boyfriend.

"Are you okay?" she asked.

"Yes, we're fine," I said. "We're at the back of the haunted house."

"The one on Main?"

"No," I said and blew out a breath. "The one in the carnival on the makeshift fairgrounds."

"Right," she said. "Got it. Don't worry, the police are on the way."

"Have him come quick and bring Shane." Shane was Jenn's husband and the county crime scene investigator. "There's a dead man near the back door."

"They're on their way," she said. "You said you were at the murder mansion attraction. My husband and I went through that last night. Are you sure it's not just a prop?"

"I'm sure," I said. "It's a very real dead man."

"Stay on the line with me until the police get there, just in case something happens. Is there anyone with you?"

"Yes, Jenn Carpenter is with me," I said. "I think we're safe. I don't see anyone else around."

"Stay on the line anyway," Charlene replied.

"Will do," I said and looked back at the corpse to see if I could recognize him.

"Does Charlene want you to stay on the line in case we're in danger?" Jenn asked as she held the door open.

"Yes," I said. "It's standard—"

"Hi, Charlene," Jenn called into my phone. "Allie and I are safe. I'm outside, holding the door open and no one else seems to be around."

"Tell her I still need you to be on the line until the police get there," Charlene said.

"We need to remain on the line," I repeated to Jenn.

"This is kind of exciting," Jenn said and hugged herself as she held the door with her back.

"A man is dead," I pointed out.

"Oh, come on." She shook her head at me. "You love murders. You practically live for solving them."

"I'd rather make fudge." I straightened, glanced out the open door, and caught two people having an intense argument next to the corn dog stand. "Is that Hazel Green and Isabel Frank?" I pointed toward the two women. Their hands were flying a mile a minute as they tried to make their points.

"It is," Jenn said. "The argument looks pretty heated."

"I heard Hazel was into parkour," I said. "And she was jumping onto Isabel's balcony to get to the roof of the next building."

"Parkour?" Jenn frowned. "Is that where they train by jumping from thing to thing?"

"They challenge themselves to get from one place to another as quickly as possible. It's crazy. You should look it up," I said. "But I bet that's why they're arguing."

The sound of ambulance sirens grew closer. Motorized vehicles had been banned from Mackinac Island for nearly a hundred years, but when it came to emergency vehicles, they were state of the art.

Rex and Officer Charles Brown came up on bicycles. The ticket taker from the front of the haunted house came around the back with them.

"What's going on?" the ticket taker asked.

"We discovered a dead man," I said.

"It's a haunted house," the ticket taker said. His name tag read Smith.

"With a real dead body," Jenn said and pointed at her feet. I held the door open and illuminated the body.

"That's the employee exit only," the ticket taker said.

"Well, we saw the daylight and thought it was the way out," Jenn said.

Rex squatted down and felt for a pulse. "The body is real," he said and looked up at me. "And very dead."

Easy Dark Chocolate Mint Fudge

Ingredients

- 3 cups dark chocolate chips (I use Ghirardelli dark chocolate chips, 70% chocolate.)
- 1 14-ounce can sweetened condensed milk
- 2 tablespoons unsalted butter
- 1 teaspoon mint extract

Directions

Butter an 8x8x2-inch cake pan. In medium saucepan, mix chocolate chips and sweetened condensed milk. Heat mixture over medium heat and stir until chips are melted. Remove from heat and stir in butter and mint extract. Pour into buttered pan and let cool. Cut into 1-inch pieces and enjoy! Makes 64 pieces.

Chapter 2

"**O**nly Allie can find a real dead body at a haunted house," Rex said.

"Are you kidding me?" Jenn laughed. "If Allie hadn't checked on him, there's no telling how many people would have gone through and left him just like I was going to. It's a good thing Allie has become a magnet for all things murder mystery."

We were eating chicken salad on the rooftop of the McMurphy. I had placed several bistro tables and chairs up there so people could sit and enjoy the view. Rex and I had hard apple cider while Jenn drank sparkling soda.

The breeze blew in the familiar scent of lake, fudge, and horses. "At least you were able to identify the body quickly," I said to Rex.

He sipped his cider. "Yeah, Mike Sanders was a good guy and didn't deserve to die that way."

"Any idea who did it?"

"Not that I'm going to tell you," he said. "Just

because you found him doesn't mean you should investigate."

"Fine," I agreed. There was a sudden loud *plop* on the rooftop deck. It was Hazel. She was dressed in a white T-shirt, workout leggings, and athletic shoes, her red hair pulled back in a ponytail.

"Don't mind me," she said. "I'm just rooftop hopping." She ran to the edge of the deck and leapt to the top of the Old Tyme Photo Shop next door.

"What was that?" Rex asked as we watched her continue her daring trek across the rooftops.

"Parkour," Jenn said. "Allie told me all about it this afternoon."

"She's lucky if she doesn't break her neck," Rex said.

"There's no law against it, so there's nothing to be done but watch," I said and took a bite of my chicken salad.

"There should be a law," Rex said. "Or we'll have a bunch of kids on the rooftops."

"I suspect Isabel will be going to the city council soon," Jenn said. "We saw her fighting with Hazel at the fair."

"Speaking of the fair," Jenn said, "I'm suddenly craving funnel cake."

"Just don't tell me you want to eat it with pickles," I teased.

"Oh, that sounds good. I can text Shane and have him bring us all funnel cakes," Jenn said and got out her phone. "I think the baby wants one."

"He's still at the fair?" I asked. It had been close to five hours since we found the dead guy. Rex had closed the crime scene nearly an hour ago.

"He had to take his stuff to St. Ignace. You know evidence, chain-of-custody stuff. Now that it's at the lab, he's just getting off the ferry," Jenn said as she let her thumbs glide across her phone. "Shane said he'll bring funnel cakes."

"Yum," I said. "I've got some ice cream that we can put on top."

"That is a dessert I can get into," Rex said.

"Say what about that guy in the fake jail cell?" Jenn asked.

"What guy?" Rex paused between sips.

"Oh, remember I told you there was a guy behind bars at the haunted house. He grabbed me and begged me to let him out," I said.

"Oh, that was Paul Patterson," Rex said. "According to the ticket guy, he's an employee who was supposed to be watching the exit where we found the dead guy. You know, scare people away from the door."

"What was he doing in jail?" Jenn asked.

"It seems he heard a noise that wasn't right and went to investigate. They were getting kids destroying the displays. When he turned around, someone had locked him into the jail with the fake mummy," Rex said.

"He must have seen the murderer," Jenn said.

"Or kids locked him in as a joke," Rex said.

"If you haven't already, you should talk to him. I think he knows something," I said. "Because he grabbed my arm and told me there was a 'murderer on the loose'."

"I spoke to him already," Rex took a sip of his cider. "But he didn't mention anything about a murderer on the loose."

"Then he lied," I said.

"Maybe he was just trying to scare you," Rex said.

"Yeah," I said. "He did a good job of that. Still, you might want to make him a person of interest. He was there, and he has to know something."

"There you go, case closed," Rex said.

"Oh, please, nothing is ever that easy," I said. "And why lock yourself in a display? If you're going to murder someone, the last thing you want to do is stick around the scene of the crime."

"Unless you want to make people think you *didn't* do it," Jenn said.

"Do you think he's a person of interest or not?" Rex asked. His blue eyes twinkled.

"Okay, fine, I'll stop trying to do your job for you," I said. "But that doesn't mean you shouldn't question him again."

"Allie . . ."

"I know." I sighed. "Let you do your job."

If only it was that easy.

Chapter 3

"**G**ood morning, Allie," Isabel said as she entered the lobby of the McMurphy dressed in a sundress and sneakers, but with a full head of steam.

"Good morning, Isabel," I said as I stood beside my general manager and dear friend Frances Devaney. "What can we do for you?"

She strode straight across the lobby and right up to the reservation desk, where Frances worked. "I need you both to sign a petition. I need two hundred signatures before I can get it in front of the city council."

"Sure," I said. "What are we signing for?"

"To keep people off the roofs unless they are working on them."

"Ah, you mean Hazel and her parkour," I said.

"She might be the first, but unless we enact a law, she won't be the last," Isabel said. "Can you imagine the danger we would all be in? What if someone slipped and fell? They could kill themselves and someone on the street. Not to mention the noise and the invasion of privacy when they come scampering over your balcony."

"I'll sign," Frances said. "I agree, it's pretty dangerous." She picked up a pen and scrawled her name.

"Allie?" Isabel asked.

"I'll sign, too," I said. "My insurance is already high due to the rooftop deck. I'd hate to see what would happen if people used the roofs as a walkway." I signed my name.

"Thanks, ladies," Isabel said and took back her clipboard and pen.

"Did you hear about the dead man at the fair's haunted house?" I asked.

"Yes," Isabel said. "I heard you found another body."

"It was Mike Sanders," I said. "Did you know him?"

"I know his sister, Hailey," she said and shook her head. "Terrible thing, losing a brother like that."

"If you see her, give her our condolences," I said.

"Will do." Isabel turned on her heel and strode out of the lobby as fast as she'd come in.

"I hope she gets all the signatures she needs," Frances said. "That roof stuff is dangerous. Hazel ought to know better."

Frances was in her early seventies with brown hair, cut in a short bob. Today she wore a T-shirt and maxi skirt with a flower pattern. Frances had been a teacher who worked the summers for my Papa Liam. But then Grammy Alice had died, and Frances retired from teaching to take a full-time job at the McMurphy. With Papa Liam's death, I was lucky that she'd stayed on. She knew all the nuances of running a hotel during the high season on Mackinac.

It was 10 a.m., and I'd finished making fudge to stock the shelves. The fudge shop was in the lobby of the McMurphy. I'd enclosed it in glass because I had two pets that roamed the building. My bichon-poo pup, Mal, who had just turned one a few months ago, and my calico cat, Mella. I was downstairs in full fudge-maker uniform because I planned a fudge demonstration at 11 a.m. It brought people in off the street and into the shop to taste and buy fudge.

My new fudge assistant, Madison, walked in dressed in black pants and a white polo. She was working the summer season and would be going back to college next month. My original summer assistants had been with me a few weeks, then gotten full-time jobs off the island, and Madison had saved the day.

Working a fudge shop by yourself was hard, but during high season, it was impossible.

Mal jumped up from her dog bed beside the registration desk and ran over to greet Madison. "Good morning," Madison said cheerfully. "How are you guys this morning?"

"Hey, Madison," I said. "Do you know anything about parkour?"

"Oh, yeah, I know some guys from school who do it. It can get pretty crazy for some. They seem to fling themselves around. Anyway, I wouldn't do it. Why?"

I shrugged. "We signed a petition to keep people off the rooftops."

"Oh, wow, yeah, rooftop parkour is really hardcore," she said. "Even the guys I know wouldn't try that."

"It is one way to get around the crowds on Main Street," Frances said.

"Not a good way," I said. "Come on, Madison, let's get set up for the fudge demonstration."

The bells on the lobby door jangled, and Mal barked and went running. The scent of horses and lake followed Rex inside. "Allie, do you have a minute?"

"Sure." I waved Madison toward the fudge shop. She knew what to do. "What's up?"

"There's been a development in the case," Rex said as he took off his hat and tucked it under his arm.

"Should we go upstairs?" I asked.

"That's probably for the best," he said.

"I hope it won't take long," I said over my shoulder as we took the stairs to the fourth floor, where my office and apartment were located.

"Not too long," he said as I unlocked my office door and we walked inside.

"Can I get you some coffee or something else to drink?" I asked as I moved toward my desk.

"No, thanks," he said and stood while I sat down behind my desk. "Listen, what do you know about Ralf Smith?"

"Who?"

"Ralf Smith, the carnie ticket taker working the haunted house?"

"Nothing, why?" I sat up, put my elbows on the desktop, and rested my chin in my hands.

"I understand you have some of the carnie workers staying at the McMurphy. Is he one of them?"

"Oh, no," I said with a shake of my head. "The carnie workers are all staying off the island at St. Ignace. Why?"

"He didn't come to work today," Rex said. "The fair manager thought it was odd and wanted me to check on him."

"I hope he's all right," I said.

"Then you don't have any of the fair employees staying with you?"

"No, we have a wedding party and two rooms of ladies who are showing at the fair. And speaking of the fair"—I checked my watch—"I've got to get my eleven o'clock demonstration done because I have to be at the judging tent at noon to watch the candy judging. I've got fudge in the candy contest, and I'm hoping for Best in Show."

"Congrats on that," Rex said. "Thanks for the info." He opened my office door, and Jenn stood on the other side.

"Oh," she said. "I didn't know you two were in there."

"Hi, Jenn, how are you feeling?" Rex asked.

"I'm good," she said. "Not even showing yet. But nearing the end of the first trimester."

"I heard you don't show until at least six months along," I said. "For your first child, anyway."

"Which is fine by me," she said. "I hear you feel like a whale your last trimester, and I'm not rushing into that."

"Don't let her kid you," I said to Rex. "She glows, doesn't she? I mean, some women just look gorgeous pregnant, and I think Jenn's one of them."

"Oh." Jenn blushed. "No, I think it's the slushies I've been drinking."

"Well, slushie or not, you look good," Rex said. "Take care, ladies."

Rex walked down the stairs, and Jenn and I watched his cute backside until it disappeared.

"What was that all about?" Jenn asked.

I shrugged. "The ticket guy at the haunted house didn't show up for work. Rex is trying to hunt him down."

"Oh," Jenn said. "I certainly hope nothing bad happened to him."

"Me, too," I said and headed down the stairs. "Me, too."

Chapter 4

The candy judging tent was warm, and I worried how the fudge would hold up. There were five stations of judges and two rows of chairs where the people who entered waited with their candy in hand. I glanced over. There was a lot of fudge, but then again, Mackinac was the fudge capital of the world. I worried for the others who were showing divinity, peppermints, almond truffles, taffy, and chocolate-covered cherries.

Carol Tunisian was showing off her truffles. She waved at me from her seat to my left. I waved back. In the fudge category, I was showing my deep chocolate mint fudge. Emma Prince, who worked for JoAnn's Fudge, was showing chocolate cherry. Ethan Albert was showing walnut caramel for Murdocks, and Bryce Shelton was showing milk chocolate praline for Mays. There was a smattering of home cooks in the fudge category, but all the main fudge shops were represented. As far as I was concerned, Emma was the one to beat.

"Allie, first time showing at the county fair?" Emma asked me.

"Yes," I said.

"Don't worry. Even if you make it to Best in Show, you won't win," Emma informed me.

"Why?"

"Christine Keller's caramels have won Best in Show for the last twenty years," Emma said and pointed with her chin toward a woman in the front row with a smug look on her face and a plate of caramels in her hands. "For Mackinac being the fudge capital of the world, fudge hasn't won Best in Show here since Christine started showing her caramels."

"Maybe the judging will be different this year," I said and looked down at Emma's plate. "You make fantastic fudge."

"So do you," Emma said with a soft smile. "But try telling the judges that. I swear, Christine puts something addictive in her caramels."

"Well, that would be cheating, now, wouldn't it?"

"It's not like I wouldn't try it if I thought it would work," Emma said with a sigh.

"Best of luck," I said and took my place. I was surprised that Emma thought Christine would automatically win Best in Show. They brought in judges from far and wide to ensure there were no locals with preconceived ideas of who should win.

Chef Rick Burns was from New York City, and Chef Morgan DePaul was from Chicago. They were the two judging the fudge category. I was familiar with Chef DePaul from my days at the Culinary Institute of America in Chicago. He was a tough cookie to please. I had no idea what Chef Burns was like.

"Allie McMurphy," the coordinator, Cathy Lund, called my name.

I got up and plastered on my best smile. "That's me."

"Chef Burns will judge your fudge now." She pointed me toward the chef, a short man with a bald spot on the top of his round head.

I presented my plate of fudge and took a seat across the table from him. He studied it thoughtfully, his expression unreadable. "Flavor?" he asked.

"Deep chocolate mint," I replied.

"'Deep chocolate'?" He questioned me, not sounding at all pleased. "What exactly is 'deep chocolate'?"

"It's seventy percent dark chocolate," I said, "with a coffee base to richen the dark undertones."

"I see," he said and cut a small piece. He eyed it as if it were something suspicious, and my nerves started jumping. I bit my bottom lip as he put a small taste on his tongue and then started writing on his judging sheet.

He wasn't talking. I could hear Chef DePaul going on about the mouth feel and texture of Ethan's fudge. His tone was encouraging. Meanwhile Chef Burns was completely silent. I couldn't tell if he approved or disapproved.

"Thank you, you may go," he said and waved the coordinator over to give her my score sheet. "Next—"

I got up and walked out, leaving my plate of fudge with Cathy, who was collecting them. If I made the top-ten candies, I would then be part of Best in Show, where all top ten were judged by one person. But I was pretty sure I wasn't going to make it. Emma was sitting with Chef Burns, and he was talking to her about mouth feel and flavor.

"How'd you do?" Carol asked me as I left the tent.

"I don't know. He didn't say much," I said. "How'd you do?"

"I got a blue ribbon," she said proudly. "Not up for Best in Show, but hey, a blue ribbon is a blue ribbon."

"How did you know so quickly?" I asked.

"My category is over," she said. "I was one of the last. It looks like they're still judging the fudge."

"I'm surprised he didn't tell me my ribbon when I was finished," I mused. "Aren't you supposed to be judged based on your fudge only, not compared?"

"In the first round, yes," Carol said. "Maybe you just didn't hear him."

Emma came out of the tent with a smile on her face.

"How'd you do?" Carol asked her.

"Blue ribbon," she said.

"He told you?" I asked.

"The coordinator, Cathy, told me," Emma said. "How'd you do, Allie?"

"I don't know. I guess I'll go ask."

"They are putting the ribbons on the plates now," Emma said. "The top three will go for Best in Show in the candy division."

"Excuse me," I said, curiosity filling me. I hopped back inside the tent to see the ribbons on the plates. I glanced through them until I found mine and saw it had a purple ribbon. My heart beat fast with joy. My plate of fudge was being pulled out to be judged for Best in Show.

Chef Eric Swainsden was the judge for Best in Show, and I watched as he pursued the top-ten candies. I stuck my head outside the tent. "Carol, they're judging for Best in Show now."

"Are you in this round?" Carol asked.

"Purple ribbon," I said with a nod. "Sorry, Emma."

"Oh, I'm not mad," Emma said. "I'm sorry you're up against Christine's caramels." Both Carol and Emma stepped inside the tent, and we watched as the judge tried all the candies. I held my breath. Getting a purple meant I could show at the state fair, but Best in Show was for yearlong bragging rights and a ribbon in the shop window.

"And the winner for Best in Show," the judge said, "is Allie McMurphy's Deep Chocolate Mint Fudge."

The crowd gasped, and all turned toward me. Christine sat down hard, as if stunned.

"Go up and let them take your picture," Carol said with a gentle push. "Everyone's going to want to know how you beat Christine."

I stepped up while the crowd erupted in applause as I took the Best in Show ribbon and shook the judge's hand.

"Best fudge I've had in years," Judge Swainsden said. "Good work."

"Thank you," I said.

"Face the camera," Cathy said, and I turned toward the crowd, my hand still in the judge's hand.

"Smile!" the photographer said. I smiled, and the flash went off. In the split instant between the smile and the flash, I noticed that Christine sent me a look that, if it were a weapon, would have killed me. After the flash, I blinked away the dot in front of my eye only to see that Christine was gone.

"I'll take that," Cathy said and took the ribbon from my hand. She placed it on the plate of fudge. "These need to be displayed for the duration of the fair. You can come back later to pick up your plate and your ribbon."

"Thanks," I said and stepped back toward the tent entrance.

"Congrats, Allie," Emma said with a big smile. "You just redeemed all of us fudge makers."

"Congrats, Allie," Carol said and walked me out of the tent with her hand on my shoulder. "I bet Christine and her gang are going to be quite upset over this."

"As long as no one dies, I think it will be alright," I said.

"I promise a lot of people will be happy to know you've knocked Christine down a peg or two. She usually dominates the fair in whatever she enters."

"I'm glad no one knew she was supposed to win," I said.

"It's why we get fudgies to judge," Carol said. "They don't know that Christine is the reigning candy queen."

"I hear we have a new Best in Show champion," Liz said as she met us at the edge of the temporary fairgrounds. Liz McElroy was the owner and reporter at the Town Crier newspaper and a dear friend. "It's going to be the biggest deal of the season. I'll be making it front-page news."

I felt the heat of a blush rush over my cheeks. "Thanks, but it's just the county fair."

"Which hasn't been won by anyone except Christine for twenty years. Now we might finally get more people to enter the contest. Christine has been dominating it for so long that people have given up entering."

"That's sad," I said. "But I have to say, it feels good to win."

"It certainly is a new day," Emma said. "I'm off to work. See ya!" She moved past us toward JoAnn's Fudge.

"Who do you think you are?" came a screeching voice behind me.

I turned to see Christine stomping up. She looked madder than a wet hen. "I'm sorry, what?"

"I asked, who do you think you are, beating me at Best in Show? What did you do, bribe the judge?"

"No," I said and drew my eyebrows down. My heart rate picked up at the sneering tone in her voice. "I won fair and square."

"Nobody beats me," she all but screamed as her face grew red and her hands clenched. "You had to have cheated."

I took a deep breath. "I didn't cheat," I stated. "I didn't have to."

"Oh!" Her face turned a shade of purple. "Are you saying my caramels weren't twenty-year winners? Because I have the ribbons to prove it."

"I'm not saying anything of the sort," I said, staying as calm as possible. "I'm simply stating a fact. I didn't cheat."

"Well, we'll see about that, won't we," Christine said, then turned and stormed off toward the judging tent.

"Oh, I feel sorry for the coordinator right about now," Carol said. "I bet she's getting an earful."

"It won't change the outcome," I said.

"No, it won't," Liz agreed. She patted me on the shoulder. "Congrats again. I've got my front-page headline."

"You don't have to make it a headline," I suggested as we walked toward the McMurphy. "I'm sure there are a lot of grand champions."

Liz grinned. "It doesn't mean that I don't want to rub Christine's snooty nose in it."

Carol laughed. "She was due a comeuppance, wasn't she?"

"She certainly was," Liz agreed.

"She's going to come gunning for you at the state fair," Carol warned.

"I'm sure it will be fine," I said. "I won't be mad if she wins. I got Best in Show here."

"You certainly did," Carol said.

I glanced at the time on my phone. "Oh, I've got to go. I'm due for my two p.m. demonstration."

"Oh, before you go," Carol said, "any headway on the murder investigation?"

Liz's ears seemed to perk up.

"Now, Carol, just because I found the body doesn't mean I'm investigating," I said.

"You say that a lot now that you're dating Rex." Carol pouted. "I like helping you with investigations. Why do you suppose Mike Sanders was murdered?"

"I don't know," I said. "But I'm sure Rex will get to the bottom of it."

"Has he made any further discoveries?" Liz asked. "For the front-page news, of course."

"He hasn't," I replied. "As far as I know."

"Shoot, Allie, everyone knows he needs our

help," Carol said. "You should set up a murder board."

"I've got to go, Carol." I patted her on the shoulder. "We'll talk murder later." I had almost told her to set up a murder board, but I didn't want to encourage her. Carol could get into a lot of trouble quickly if she didn't have supervision. And right now, I didn't have time to supervise her.

"Don't think I'll forget, Allie." She waved me on. "I'll be over later with my list of suspects."

"Bye, Carol. Bye, Liz," I said and hurried into the McMurphy, leaving them on the street to speculate how the investigation was going. The aroma of funnel cake followed me into the shop. I'd made a promise to Rex not to investigate any more murders unless it directly involved a friend of mine. So far, no one I knew knew anything about the murder, and I certainly hoped it stayed that way.

Champagne Fudge

Ingredients
    3 cups dark chocolate chips
    1 cup heavy cream
    Pinch of salt
    ⅓ cup champagne (or sparkling wine—
        fizzy or flat will work)

Directions
    Butter an 8x8x2-inch pan. Microwave on high for 1 minute the chocolate chips, cream, and pinch of salt. Stir and microwave for 30 seconds and stir until melted. Remove and whisk in the champagne. Pour into pan and cool. The fudge should spring back slightly. (Hint: If it is too wet, put back into a bowl and add powdered sugar one tablespoon at a time until it reaches a firmer consistency.) Pat back into pan. Cut into 1-inch pieces. Makes 64. Enjoy!

Chapter 5

I had to go straight into the fudge demonstration with my assistant, Madison. And it was nearly an hour later before the crowd in the fudge shop dwindled. I stepped out and unbuttoned my chef's coat. My pup, Mal, gave a quick bark and ran toward me, then slid into my legs. I picked her up for puppy kisses.

"I heard you have good news," Frances said.

"Word travels fast," I said. "I would have told you myself, but I was late for the demonstration."

"What news?" Jenn asked as she came down the stairs. "Did you solve the murder?"

I tried hard not to roll my eyes. "My fudge won Best in Show in the candy contest at the fair," I said.

"Well, of course it did!" Jenn said and gave me a quick hug. "Why wouldn't you? Your fudge is fantastic."

"Apparently, it's a big deal," I said and put Mal down on the floor. She walked over to her bed next to the reception desk, turned around twice, and laid down.

"Christine Keller has won Best in Show for the last twenty years," Frances said, not looking up from her computer. "Your win is quite the accomplishment."

"Oh," Jenn said. "Wow. Twenty years. I bet she wasn't happy about losing this time."

"She was furious," I admitted. "She even went so far as to accuse me of bribing the judge."

"Now, that's just crazy talk," Jenn said. "No one would ever believe that."

"Christine's friends might," Frances said and looked up at me with her big brown eyes blinking behind her trifocal lenses. "But you don't have to worry about them."

"I won't," I said. "I was just surprised and happy to win."

"As you should be," Jenn said. "Now you can put a sign up in the window telling everyone you won Best in Show."

"I will," I said with pride.

"That's my girl," Jenn said. "Oh, and get ready for sales to go up. Everyone is going to want to taste the fudge that beat a twenty-year candy-contest winner."

"Really?" I raised my right eyebrow.

"Oh, I'm sure of it," Jenn said. "Just wait until everyone finds out. You'll be swamped."

I certainly hoped so.

The next morning, when the paper came out, things took an interesting turn.

"Allie," Carol said as she walked into the McMurphy after my first fudge demonstration had ended. "We've got a bit of a problem." She tossed the newspaper on the top of Frances's reception desk.

Frances looked up from her computer. "Hello, Carol, how are you today?"

"How I am doesn't matter." Carol waved her hand dismissively. "What matters is that this article has riled up the island."

"What? How?" I asked.

"It seems Christine had a bigger following than we knew." Carol poked her finger at the headline. "This has half the seniors upset."

"It's not like I wrote it," I said. "I told Liz not to make it a headline."

"I haven't heard anything about people being worked up," Frances said and studied Carol through her glasses.

"Then you haven't been at the senior center this morning," Carol said.

"True, I've been working," Frances said. "But I didn't think there was a problem with the article. It lists all the Best in Show winners—including how you beat Christine for Best in Show in quilting."

"I know," Carol said and puffed up. "I was quite proud of that myself. Christine has won far too many Best in Show ribbons. I worked hard, and it paid off."

"So did I," I said and put my hands on my hips. "Who all is riled up about it?"

"Well, remember when they started selling ribbons so that the town could choose between you and the Jessops?"

"That was a silly, onetime thing," I said.

"We're back there again," Carol said. "Millie Wadsworth was telling everyone that you cheated, and Alma May started arguing with Irene, and someone suggested we wear ribbons to show whose side we're on."

I rolled my eyes. "That's ridiculous. Are they all upset about you, too?"

"I'm afraid so," Carol said. "Part of the problem with beating a longtime winner. I heard that Christine and her cohort canvassed the island this morning with a petition to boycott the newspaper for backing cheaters."

"Oh, for goodness' sake," Frances said. "The judges judged fair and square, I'm sure. Most people will see that's a frivolous petition."

"I heard some of the advertisers are pulling out of their work with the *Town Crier*," Carol went on.

"What can we do to stop the madness?" I asked, my hands on my hips. "The judging is done, and neither of us cheated. People must know that on some level."

"I say ignore it, and it will calm down on its own," Frances advised. "If you get involved, it will only fan the flames."

"How did you fix the problem last time?" Carol asked.

"I made peace with Trent," I said and smiled at the memory. "That's when we started dating."

"Well, I'm not dating Christine," Carol said.

"That would be silly," I agreed. "You're a married woman. Maybe we can invite her for coffee and have a civilized talk."

"Oh, that woman doesn't have a clue how to be civilized once she's angry," Carol said. "She once waged a war on Sally Frost that lasted ten years."

"Ten years? That's a lot of energy and anger," I pointed out. "What finally ended the feud?"

"Sally died," Carol said, her chin up slightly.

"Oh, boy," I said as I sighed.

"My advice stands," Frances said. "Let her do what she will. You can't control her, and if you react, you're just fueling the flames and creating an even bigger feud."

"Who's feuding?" Douglas asked as he walked down the stairs with a wrench in his hand.

"Christine Keller," Carol said. "She's on a rampage because Allie beat her for Best in Show in the candy category at the fair."

"You beat her, too," I pointed out.

Douglas shook his head. "Some people have nothing better to do than get their noses out of joint. I finished fixing the leaky sink in room 201."

"Thank you," I said.

"You're welcome. Good to know there are problems I can actually fix." He kissed Frances on the cheek. "I'll be in the workshop if you need me." Douglas had a workshop in the basement of the McMurphy. It was where he kept his tools for all things handy at the McMurphy.

"I still think we should start our own petition," Carol said.

I shook my head. "I agree with Frances on this one. Let's just ignore it, and it will go away."

"Alright, but I think you're wrong on this one," Carol said. "The seniors like a good drama."

"I'll take them a plate of fudge," I said. "That really seems to calm them down. It's been a while since I've been to the senior center."

"That's because you aren't investigating that murder," Carol pointed out. "They all know you only come around when you need help investigating."

"That's not true," I said, aghast. "I always come out for the fund-raisers."

"We know you're busy, but older people like young people to come out and visit from time to time," Carol pointed out. "You only see me as much as you do because I'm feisty and get around easier than most."

"You and the rest of the seniors are always welcome to stop in and get a cup of coffee from the coffee bar," I said. "Isn't that right, Frances?"

"That's what I've told them," Frances said and continued with whatever she was doing at the computer.

"I'll remind them," Carol said and looked at her wristwatch. "Speaking of reminding, I'm supposed to meet up with Irene. We've got a jog through the park scheduled. See you, ladies."

Carol turned on her heel and strode out. She was a smaller woman, but her strides ate up distance like a tall person's.

"I've got some inventory to order," I said. "I'll be in the office." I strode up the stairs, and Mal went with me as I went in and sat at my desk. Mal jumped up in my lap. I gave her pets, then put her down on the dog bed beside my desk. "Time to get some work done, baby."

Two hours later, I'd finished my office work, showered, and changed into a sundress. I selected a variety of the day's fudge, including the grand-champion deep chocolate mint, and carried a plate over to the senior center. Waving hello to Mrs. Shoemaker, who was out sweeping her porch, I noted a shadow flitting from rooftop to rooftop. I glanced up and shielded my eyes from the sun. "Hazel?"

"Hi, Allie." She bounded onto the roof of a porch and then onto a porch rail and onto the ground beside me. "Is that fudge?"

"Yes," I said and lifted the covering. "Want a piece?"

"Which one is your Best in Show flavor?" she asked as she looked the various pieces over.

"The deep chocolate mint," I said and pointed to the darkest piece.

"I'm dying to try it." She took a piece and popped it into her mouth. "Oh, yum," she said through her full mouth and then finished the piece. "I can see why it won. Does it have coffee in it, too?"

"It does," I said.

"Well, you need to walk around and give out samples. It would quell the rumors that you cheated."

"I did not cheat," I said, frustrated.

"Oh, I know," she said with a grin. "I'm just saying it would quell the rumors." She glanced at her phone. "Oops, gotta go. See you!" She bounded up another porch rail to a porch roof and took off across the rooftops.

"That girl is going to get herself killed," Mrs. Shoemaker said behind me.

I turned. "Hopefully we can convince her to stop before she does. Would you like a piece of fudge?"

"Can I try the Best in Show flavor?" she asked. Mrs. Shoemaker was my height but rounded by middle age. Her hair was an unnatural dark color. Her eyes were still a pretty blue.

"Sure," I said and pointed. "I guess I should have brought a plate full of that flavor."

"You should have." She toasted me with the fudge and popped it into her mouth. "Oh, that is good."

"Thanks," I said. "Tell people to come to the shop. I'll give out free samples to anyone who asks."

"Oh, I will," she said and started sweeping the sidewalk. "I will."

I arrived at the new senior center in time for the bingo game to start.

"Allie, are you going to play?" Irene asked from two tables away. She had five cards in front of her and an ink stamp in her hand. "It's five dollars a card."

"Sure," I said. Then I addressed the room, "I brought fudge."

"Cheater fudge?" Mrs. Pupkin grumbled.

"Trying to bribe us like you bribed the judge?" Mr. Hatfield asked.

"Not a bribe," I said and sent him a tight smile. "Just a treat."

"Don't mind if I do," Mr. Campbell said and swiped two pieces off the platter.

"Get your bingo cards. The game's about to start," Irene said as she snatched a piece of fudge and sat back down.

I walked over to the reception table. "Two cards please," I said and took a twenty-dollar bill out of my pocket.

"No change," Mrs. McPherson grumbled, snatched my twenty, and handed me four cards. "We don't like cheaters here."

"I'm not a cheater," I told her firmly and snagged a card marker off the table.

"You have to sit on the right side," Mrs. McPherson said, pointing to the right side of the room. "That's your side. The left side is Christine's side."

It was then that I noticed there was a big aisle down the middle of the room. Irene and Carol sat on the right. Ten other people on the left all gave me a suspicious look. I sighed and walked over to sit beside Carol. "This is silly," I said as I laid out my cards.

"Christine's here," Carol said and pointed toward the buyer's table. I glanced up to see Mrs. McPherson handing Christine two cards and a ten-dollar bill.

"She told me she didn't have change," I muttered.

"Don't worry, girls," Mr. Campbell said loudly. "I'm coming over to sit with you."

"Thank you," Irene said and patted the chair next to her.

"Best fudge I've ever had," Mr. Campbell declared. "This gal didn't need to cheat."

"I didn't cheat," I protested.

Christine stared daggers at me while Mrs. McPherson shushed me. "The game has started."

The caller began. "I-9," she stated and continued to roll the little balls and pull them out one by one.

Carol leaned over toward me as I checked my cards. "I started a murder board," she half-whispered.

"B-fifteen."

"I'm not investigating this one," I whispered back. "It's probably one of the carnival workers. Rex will figure it out."

"What if it's not?" Carol insisted. "The killer could strike again."

"N-24."

"They most likely won't," I said.

"N-12."

"Bingo!" Irene called.

There was a collective grumble and uproar from the other side of the room. Mrs. McPherson came over and checked Irene's card. "As much as it pains me to say this, she is a winner," the older woman said.

"Whee!" Irene said and got up to follow her to the front table to pick out her prize.

"Well, that was all the money I had," I said and stood.

"You shouldn't spend it all at once," Carol advised.

"Mrs. McPherson wouldn't give me any change," I stated and glanced at my phone. "It's okay. I need to get back for my four o'clock fudge demonstration."

"You should just let Madison do it," Carol said. "You're all cleaned up now."

"She isn't ready to do a demonstration on her own," I said. "Thanks for the thought, though." I turned to leave when Carol touched my arm.

"The murder board is ready whenever you are. I've already got a couple of suspects."

"You do? Do you have motives?"

"You'll find out when you start investigating," Carol said.

I sighed as she got up to purchase new bingo cards. I glanced over to the other side of the room. Christine was holding court over a group of now fifteen people. What could I do to stop this nonsense? Maybe Frances was right. Maybe ignoring it was the best answer.

Chapter 6

"How's the investigation going?" I asked Rex as I poured us both a glass of wine. It was evening, and he'd stopped by with takeout.

"Not so well," he said. "The carnival people are a close-knit group."

"Did you find Ralf Smith, the haunted house ticket taker?" I handed him his glass and set mine down on the table. I'd set the table with my pretty blue-and-white place settings. He sat across from me and doled out the food.

"Yes, his grandmother lives on the island," he said and filled my plate with rice, beef, and broccoli.

"Oh, I thought you knew everyone who grew up on Mackinac," I said and put my napkin in my lap.

"He didn't grow up here," Rex said and took a sip of his wine. "His mother left the island and married. He was raised near Grand Rapids."

"Huh. How'd he get into the carnie business?"

"I was curious about that myself," Rex said and

took a bite of the beef. "He's an adjunct professor and works the fair circuit during the summers."

"Wait, he's staying with his grandmother?"

"Yes," Rex said. "I told him we were worried because he hadn't reported in to work, and he said he had a stomach bug. Paul Patterson and Mike actually owned the attraction, and Paul has opted to shut it down early as we advised." He paused. "That's enough about the investigation. How was your day?"

I sighed. "People are getting riled up because my fudge beat Christine Keller's caramels for Best in Show. Carol told me they were taking sides, so I took some time to go to the senior center and see if I could smooth the waters."

"How's everybody doing?" he asked.

"They're good," I said. "But Christine is stirring them up. I even brought fudge, and still only a handful sat with me to play bingo. They'd actually divided the chairs—one side for my supporters and one side for Christine's."

Rex laughed. "Sorry," he said and waved his hand in front of his face. "I know it bothers you, but the seniors really do love their drama."

"I know they'll get over it," I said and rested my chin on my hands. "But I really hate to be thought of as a cheater just because I beat their friend in the candy contest. I mean, talk about being poor sports."

"I get it," he said and took my hand in his. "I do, but it sure must have been a shock for Christine to lose. I'm sure they'll find something else to talk about very soon."

As he said that, we heard a loud noise outside.

We both got up and rushed to the window. Luckily it was still twilight outside, and we could see.

"Oh, no," I said and covered my mouth in horror.

"Call nine-one-one," Rex said and went out my back door and down the steps.

I punched the speed-dial number.

"Nine-one-one, what's your emergency?"

"Hi, Charlene, it's Allie."

"Who's dead?" she asked.

"Send the ambulance quickly to the back door of the McMurphy. It looks like Hazel's fallen off the roof," I said.

"Oh, good Lord, hang on," Charlene said and put me on hold long enough to call the ambulance. "Was anyone else hurt?"

"Let me double-check." I looked out the window. "No, it looks like just Hazel. Rex is with her now."

"I've got first responders on the way," Charlene said.

"Thanks." I hung up, grabbed a blanket, and hurried out the back door, careful to keep my pets inside, then rushed down the stairs. "How is she?"

"Not good," Rex said as he squatted beside Hazel.

I noted the odd angle of her limbs and the trickle of blood coming from her mouth. "I brought a blanket to help with shock."

"I think it's too late for that," he said grimly, then took my blanket and covered her up. "She's dead."

"Oh, no," I said and bit back tears. "I was just talking to her today."

Rex stepped back to look up at the roof of the McMurphy. "I'm going around to the front. Stay here with her until the ambulance gets here. Oh, and tell Charlene to call Shane."

"Wait, you think she might have been murdered?"

"I think we need to rule it out," he said. "She was too good at her game to have simply slipped and fallen from a flat deck on the roof."

"But no one should be up there but our guests," I pointed out.

"That's even more troubling," he said. "Watch the back door. I'm heading through to the front."

"I'll call Frances," I said. "She'll want to be here to check on the guests."

Rex disappeared into the McMurphy and I called Charlene back. As I dialed the non-emergency number, I heard the ambulance sirens. On an island that had no cars, the sight and sound of a motorized vehicle stood out.

"This is Charlene," she said as she picked up.

"Hi, Charlene, it's Allie again," I said. "Rex said to have you call Shane."

"Oh, dear," she said. "Is the ambulance there? Have they helped Hazel?"

"They're arriving now," I said. "Please call Shane, thanks." I hung up and waved down Officer Brown on his bike. "Over here."

He stopped a few feet away from me and the blanketed body and got off his bike. "What happened?"

"It's Hazel," I said. "She fell from the roof. Rex had me cover her with the blanket. He went around to the front door."

"Megan is on her way," Charles said. Officer Lasko had become a friend over time. "She was getting coffee when the call came through."

The ambulance drove up the alley, and its siren cut off. George Marron stepped out and grabbed his kit. "What happened?"

"Hazel fell from the roof," I said. "We rushed out to help her, but Rex said she died instantly. I covered her with a blanket."

George nodded solemnly and squatted down to pull back the blanket and check for a pulse. Office Megan Lasko came down the opposite side of the alley on her bike. When Charles stopped her and said something, she nodded. I watched as he went inside, presumably to find Rex.

"Heck of a thing," George said and stood. "Rex was right. She must have died instantly." He glanced up. "Four stories is quite a fall."

"Was she a guest?" Megan asked with her notebook in hand.

"No," I said. "It's Hazel Green. She's local. She's been practicing parkour and traveling on the rooftops. She's dropped into the McMurphy before. But I never thought she'd fall. She seemed so good at it."

"Did you see anyone or hear anything suspicious?"

"No," I said and clutched my throat. "We just heard her fall. Rex rushed out and had me call nine-one-one. He got out here first and knows more than me."

"Got it," she said and looked at the crowd that had started to form at the ends of the alley. "I'm on crowd patrol," she told George.

"I'm staying with her if you need to call anyone," George said to me.

"Thanks. I already asked Charlene to call Shane. But I do need to call Frances. The guests must be worried." I glanced up to see people sticking their heads out the windows to see what was going on. I stepped under the stairs and out of sight as I dialed Frances.

"Allie, what's wrong?" Frances answered.

"Can you come back to the McMurphy?" I asked. "Hazel has fallen from our roof, and the guests need someone to wrangle them."

"I can be there in fifteen minutes," she said. "I'm sure Rex will want to talk to them all. I'll have Douglas stop at Doud's and pick up some cookies or something to help calm the nerves."

"We do have chamomile tea in the coffee bar," I said. "I can make tea and coffee."

"Good idea. See you soon," Frances said, then hung up. I put away my phone and watched as Shane pulled up on his bike. He took out his crime scene kit and put on some gloves, then walked over to Megan. I waited patiently until he was briefed before going over to him.

"Shane, is it okay if I go into the McMurphy? I'm sure my guests are a mess."

He studied me through his horn-rimmed glasses. "Did you touch anything?"

"No, I covered her with the blanket, then waited beside her until Charles arrived."

"Okay," he said with a nod. "Go on in. I can handle it from here."

"Great." I turned on my heel with relief and opened the back door. I could hear the guests talking and milling about in the lobby.

"Allie, what's going on? Did someone fall from the roof?" Mrs. Forge asked me as I stepped out into the lobby.

"There's been a dreadful accident," I said. "Please, everyone, stay put. I'm sure the police will want to know if you saw or heard anything."

"Like what?" Mr. Everett asked.

"I'm sure the police will know what they need," I said. "Now, I'm making fresh coffee, and we have hot water for some soothing tea, if that's what you prefer. I also have some fudge that I'll put out."

"Is that your Best in Show fudge?" Mrs. Aster asked.

"I do have some of that left from today's sales," I said. "Please try to relax. You can go back to your rooms if you prefer, but please don't go on the roof or leave the building until the police have cleared the scene."

Thankfully, my pets were still up in the apartment. I'm sure this many distressed people milling about would have made them crazy. I love them, but they tend to pick up on the energy in a room, and right now this room was full of energy—energy that wasn't particularly positive.

I made a fresh pot of coffee and showed several guests how to use the hot water spigot to make tea. Thankfully, Frances arrived, along with Douglas, who carried two boxes of bakery cookies from Doud's.

Frances took over crowd management while I went into the fudge shop to dish up some different types of fudges. I made a separate plate of the last of the deep chocolate mint. I would make more tomorrow. It really had become popular since it had won Best in Show.

"I have fudge, too," I said as I navigated through the crowd and placed the platters on the coffee bar.

As Frances fielded questions and concerns, I motioned to her that I was going upstairs. She nodded. I stopped at the apartment and checked on my pets. Mella was in the window watching the scene below in the alley, her tail twitching at the ambulance lights. Mal got up from her doggie bed, stretched, and came over to say hi.

"Hi, babies," I said. "Are you alright?" I petted Mal, then quickly put the meal away in the fridge and cleared the table, leaving our wineglasses on the counter. Then I gave them both treats and left, closing and locking the apartment door behind me.

The stairs to the rooftop deck started on the third floor so that the owner's apartments would be isolated. I hurried down to the third floor, said hello to a couple of guests hanging out in the hallway, and headed up the stairs. Charles met me at the top.

"Hi, Charles," I said and looked around him at Rex, who was studying the deck.

"Sorry, Allie, but no one comes up here until Shane does his thing, and he's still in the alley."

"Okay," I said. "Do you guys need anything?"

"I don't think so," he said and turned. "Hey, Rex, do you need anything?"

Rex looked up. "We'll need to get statements from each of the guests."

"I figured as much," I said. "We're keeping them inside and entertained." I glanced at the railings on the deck. "Was it a bad railing?"

"Your railings are secure," Charles said.

"Okay, good." I put my hand on my heart. "I'd hate to think it was a maintenance issue."

"Oh, I don't think there was anything you could have done," Charles said.

"Then it was just an accident?" I asked.

"No," Rex said. "Allie, I think this was murder."

Chapter 7

"Are you going to investigate now?" Carol asked me as I did double duty at the reception desk in between batches of fudge.

It had been another sleepless night as the investigation dragged on to 1 a.m. We finally got all the guests taken care of by two in the morning. I told Frances to come in later than her usual 8 a.m. shift, and then I took a two-hour nap before rising to make the morning's first batches of fudge.

"Good morning, Carol," I said. "You're here bright and early." A glance at my phone told me it was eight thirty in the morning.

"I wanted to hear all the info on Hazel's death," Carol said and helped herself to coffee from my coffee bar. I didn't bother to tell her it was for guests. It wouldn't have made a difference.

I fielded two cancellation calls for the day and worried there would be more once word got out that someone had died at the McMurphy.

"I'm sure Liz has printed a story about it in the

morning paper," I said and took the key cards from Mr. Felcher as he and his wife checked out.

"It was quite an exciting night," Mr. Felcher said. "Don't know that I've ever had the occasion to be interviewed by the police."

"It's too bad we couldn't be of any help," Mrs. Felcher said. "Our room faced the front, and we didn't even know anything was going on until we heard a commotion in the hallway."

"I'm sorry about last night," I said and printed out a detailed receipt for them. "We've never had to interview the guests at the McMurphy before."

"Too bad you didn't see anything," Carol said as she approached the reception desk stirring her coffee. "Murder investigations are tragic, but quite fascinating."

"Murder?" Mrs. Felcher clutched her throat.

"No one knows if it was murder," I said and gave Carol the stink eye. "What we do know is that it's a terrible tragedy. Hazel was a young woman with her whole life ahead of her."

"Oh, right," Carol said. "Sorry."

"We need to go," Mr. Felcher said briskly. "Don't want to stick around a crime scene. Come on, Erin."

"Oh, dear," Mrs. Felcher said. "Oh, dear."

Her husband pulled up the handles to the suitcases and rolled them through the lobby and out the door. Mrs. Felcher followed, her face pale and her arms crossed.

"Thanks, Carol," I said with a sigh. "You're frightening the guests. Who told you it was murder? I don't think the police have given a formal statement yet."

"With you involved, it has to be murder," Carol said with a shrug, then sipped her coffee. "Besides, like you said, Hazel was a young woman. I hardly doubt she suddenly lost her footing."

"Why don't we keep our speculation to ourselves for now," I said. "I've already had two cancellations this morning just from the local news, and they haven't said anything about murder."

"Who got murdered?" Madison asked as she walked in from the back door and snagged a clean apron off the hook in the hallway.

"We don't know if *anyone* got murdered," I stressed. If there was one thing I knew, it was that Rex liked to play his cards close to his chest. He'd not be happy with us talking murder before he made an official statement.

"Hazel Green fell to her death last night," Carol said. "She fell right off the top of the McMurphy."

"Oh, my goodness," Madison said. "She fell off the McMurphy? Aren't there rails around the deck?"

"There are rails," I said, "and they are safe and secure. I'm going to have Douglas put up 'no climbing on the rails' signs."

"Like they have on the fort," Madison said.

"In my day, people were smarter than to climb around on things that weren't meant to be climbed on," Carol said. "Hazel was smart and athletic. That's why she had to have been murdered. Do we even know if it was the fall that killed her?"

"Wow," Madison said. "I go home, and all the interesting stuff happens."

"We were up late last night, so Frances won't be in until ten," I said. "I'm running the front desk and making fudge. Would you mind setting up the ingredients for the fudges I have listed?"

"Sure thing, boss," Madison said.

"As for you, Carol"—I looked her straight in the eye—"let's not run off any more of my guests, okay?"

"Okay." Carol held up her hands and shrugged. "I was just wondering if you're going to investigate this one since it happened on your property."

"How about we talk about this, this afternoon," I said. "We can go get tea or something."

"Wonderful!" Carol's eyes lit up. "I'll be back after your four o'clock demonstration."

"It's a date," I said. After all, Carol and the seniors were a big help whenever I investigated a murder. And if Rex was right and Hazel was murdered at the McMurphy, darn tootin' I was going to investigate. I just didn't need to run off my guests in the meantime.

Liz met me for lunch at the Mustang Lounge. I slid into my seat and took the menu that was handed to me. Liz did the same.

"Thanks for meeting me," Liz said.

"I'm always ready to have lunch with a friend," I said and ordered an iced tea and ham-and-cheese sandwich. "I know you're wanting information on Hazel."

"You know I don't just invite you to lunch when I want information," Liz said. Liz wore her curly hair up in a high bun, a light-gray camp shirt, and a pair of shorts.

"I know," I said. "Has Rex given a statement yet?"

"He's set an official statement to go out at four p.m.," Liz said and sipped her iced tea. "I'd love to hear your take on what happened."

I went over how the night unfolded, but I skirted around the idea of murder. I'd leave that up to Rex and his statement. "Anyway, the poor thing was dead by the time we rushed down the back stairs."

"Do you think she was dead before she fell?" Liz asked as the waiter arrived with our lunches.

"Are you talking about Hazel Green?" the waiter asked.

"Yes," I said.

"I heard she slipped on the roof tiles while doing parkour," the waiter said. "The mayor is holding an emergency council meeting today to outlaw any roof-walking on the island."

"That's probably a good idea," I said. "As long as roof decks are still allowed. I'm not the only place with a roof deck."

"You may need to get down to the council chambers, then, and make sure it's not all roofs," the waiter said and walked off.

"Great." I bit into my sandwich.

"I'm covering the emergency council meeting at one this afternoon," Liz said. "I'll put a bug in Millie Temple's ear. She'll make sure they allow for rooftop decks."

Millie Temple made it her hobby to speak at every city council meeting. She fancied herself the "voice of the people." My only hope was that she wasn't on Christine's side of things, or she might refuse to mention it.

"You're into all the gossip," I said. "Do you know if Millie is siding with Christine?"

"She is," Liz said. "But don't worry, she's also in tight with the Snyders, and they have a rooftop deck at their hotel. She'll make sure it's okay to have one."

"Oh, good," I said and sat back in my chair. "When do you think this thing with Christine will blow over?"

Liz grinned at me. "Oh, Christine will never let it go. But I think over time, people will forget they've taken sides, and everything will calm down."

"But Carol beat her at the quilting exhibit," I pointed out.

"Oh, Christine is working up a fine tizzy about that, too. She came to Granddad and demanded he investigate fraud at the county fair."

"What did Angus say?" I asked.

"He laughed at her and said she needed to up her game if she wanted to stay at the top of the categories at the fair."

"Oh, boy," I said.

"Yeah, she claimed he was siding with you and Carol and that the press was known to be biased and swore she was going to start her own newspaper."

"What did Angus say to that?"

"He told her to go ahead, he'd love to have the competition." Liz smiled as she took a bite of her sandwich. "She turned on her heel and stormed off."

I laughed at the thought, then sobered. "Did Christine know Hazel?"

"Of course," Liz said. "Hazel was raised on the island."

"She saw Hazel and me talking the other morning."

Liz pursed her lips. "You think Christine might have had something to do with Hazel's death?"

"I certainly hope not. I'd hate to think she'd start murdering anyone I talk to."

"Oh, you think Hazel was murdered?"

I felt the heat of a blush rush up my cheeks, so I tried to keep a poker face. "I have no idea. I was just thinking about all the trouble and put the two things together."

"Was Christine at the McMurphy?"

"Not that I know of," I said. "But I was in my apartment, and the lobby was closed to anyone who didn't have a key."

"I thought you had cameras everywhere." Liz leaned her elbows on the table and cradled her chin in her hands. "Have you checked to see if anyone was coming or going during that time?"

"I gave the camera downloads to Rex." I sat back thoughtfully. "He'll have more information at the press statement."

"Yeah, I figured he would," Liz said and studied me. "But you'll give me an exclusive should anything come up. Right?"

"Don't I always?"

"You do," she said. "That's why I'm buying lunch."

"Now, now," I said. "I can pay for my own lunch."

"Too late. I already gave the bartender my card and told him to charge it to me."

"Fine."

"See? That's what friends do. Besides, I can expense it." She leaned in close. "I can run another story about how you and Carol are the new reigning queens of the fair. That would work Christine up for sure."

"Oh, no. Let's try to get this thing to die down," I said. "A death at the McMurphy is bad enough. I don't need to stir up half the town. They might come for me with pitchforks and torches."

"Oh, honey, you're no monster." She patted my hand. "But I'll leave it alone. One thing's for certain, things have become much more interesting since you've been on the island."

"It's a legacy I'm not sure I like."

Dark Chocolate Coffee Fudge

Ingredients

1 14-ounce can sweetened condensed milk
2 tablespoons finely ground freeze-dried
   coffee
Pinch salt
3 cups chopped dark baking chocolate or
   dark chocolate chips

Directions

Pour sweetened condensed milk into medium-sized, microwaveable glass bowl. Add freeze-dried coffee and salt. Stir. Let set for 20 minutes to allow coffee to dissolve. Stir again. Then add chopped chocolate and microwave in 30-second intervals, stirring in between until chocolate just melts. Grease an 8x8x2-inch pan and line with parchment paper. Pour fudge into pan and cool. Cut into squares to make 48. Enjoy!

Chapter 8

"Can you tell me why you think Hazel was murdered?" I asked Rex over a glass of wine later that night. "I know why I think so. Douglas and I were all over the deck and the roof, looking for what might have caused her fall. Everything is secure. I didn't think I needed to put up 'no standing on the rails' signs."

"I'm pretty sure she wasn't standing on the rails. There was some evidence of a struggle when I got up there," he said and leaned back against my couch. Mella wrapped herself into a ball in his lap while Mal lay in a pet bed at my feet.

"Really? Because I didn't see anything," I said.

"Shane documented any evidence." Rex petted Mella softly. "And the coroner agreed there were marks on Hazel that appeared to be from a struggle."

"It had to be someone big enough to push Hazel over the railing," I surmised. "We built it to code so that wouldn't be an easy task." I sipped my wine.

"I called it a homicide in today's press meeting," he said, "and cleared the hotel of any wrongdoing."

"Did the camera recordings tell you anything? I'd hate to think the murderer spent the night in the hotel."

"We're still looking through the footage. You have a lot of cameras."

"For good reason," I said. "Wait, you don't actually think the murderer was staying at the hotel, do you? That would really scare away guests. As it is, I had half of them check out this morning. I don't think they wanted to stay someplace where people fall off the roof to their deaths."

"I can't say if it was a guest or not until the evidence all comes in—especially the videotapes."

"Hopefully the press briefing will help reassure the guests that it's okay to go back up on the deck." I took another sip. "We were just getting some good business going with it for weddings and anniversaries and such."

"I'm sure it will be fine."

I let the silence surround us in a warm cocoon for a moment. "Any idea who might have wanted Hazel dead?"

"I'm chasing a lead," he said, "but it's too soon to tell." He studied me with his killer blue eyes ringed in black lashes. "I suppose you're going to investigate this."

"It happened at the McMurphy," I pointed out. "And I'm losing business because of it."

"You know I can't condone you getting involved."

I studied him, not saying a word.

He blew out a long breath. "Just be safe and let

me know the minute you have any information of interest. I have no idea why people talk to you and not me. We even offer money on the tip hotline should anyone have credible evidence."

I smiled and leaned over to kiss his cheek. "I think they just like me better. Or maybe they like Mal."

Mal stood up at the sound of her name, then jumped up in my lap. Annoyed at the close proximity of the pup, Mella leapt off Rex's lap, landing on light feet, and walked off toward her favorite closet and the box on the top shelf. I scooted closer to Rex and laid my head on his broad shoulder. "You have to admit, we make a good team."

He put his arm around me. "Yes, we do."

The next morning, I finished stocking the shelves with fudge and left Madison in charge. I took off my chef's coat and hat and left them hanging in the hallway, then hooked Mal up to her harness and leash. "Frances, I'm going to take Mal for a walk. I'll be back soon. I have my phone if you need anything."

"Okay," Frances said as she studied her computer screen. I was glad she was in charge of accounting and not me. Frances had a better eye for detail.

Mal and I stepped out into the cool sunshine of the morning. There was a touch of fall in the air, and I didn't regret having put on a light jacket before stepping outside. Mal ran to her favorite potty spot as I noticed Mr. Beecher coming down the alley.

"Good morning," I called and waved.

He smiled and called back. "Good morning!" Mr. Beecher was an elderly man who was slightly portly and always wore a suit coat and vest. With his bald head and white beard, he reminded me of the snowman narrator from *Rudolph the Red-Nosed Reindeer*. He always walked through the alley in the morning and in the evening. "Glad to see they got things cleaned up." He eyed the spot where Hazel had landed. I'd asked Douglas to rake over the area and put down fresh dirt along the back of the McMurphy. "Terrible tragedy," Mr. Beecher said.

"I know," I said and glanced up. "We checked the rails, and everything was secure."

"I hear it might have been foul play." He reached into his pocket and pulled out a doggie treat for Mal.

"Yes, Liz did a nice write-up of it in the paper. I have no idea who could have wanted Hazel dead. Do you?"

"Well, now, I didn't know the gal very well, but I do know she stirred up quite a commotion at the city council meeting when they heard the petition about no parkour on the city rooftops."

"I hadn't thought about that," I said. "Isabel Frank asked us to sign the petition, and both Frances and I did because we were worried about young kids. I never worried about Hazel."

"You should look into the council meeting minutes," he advised. "The arguments got quite heated."

"Thank you, I will," I said.

"Anytime," Mr. Beecher said, then tipped his

hat at me and walked down the alley. As Mal and I resumed our walk in the opposite direction, we happened by the administration building for Mackinac, which was only a few blocks away. I went inside.

"Allie, what brings you here?" Becky Walters said when we entered the city administration department. "Is that your doggie?"

"Hi, Becky. Yes, this is Mal, which is short for Marshmallow. Say hi, Mal." Mal sat and raised a paw.

"Oh, isn't she just the sweetest!" Becky came around the desk and petted Mal. "What brings you by?"

"I was wondering if I could look at the minutes for the last few city council meetings," I said.

"Oh, we don't have minutes anymore. We usually just record the meetings and have them transcribed." She straightened and went back around her desk. "Would you like to read the transcripts?"

"If I could, that would be great."

"It might take a couple of hours." She looked dubious. "Your puppy will get bored."

"I'll take her home and come back," I said.

"Is there something in particular you're looking for? I can set it up for you," she said. "We have all these records, and people rarely take advantage of them. Liz does, of course, when she wants to write a story."

"I just wanted to review the meeting where they discussed the petition to keep people off the rooftops," I said.

"Oh, right. Poor Hazel." Becky shook her head. "We all thought she was amazing, jumping from rooftop to rooftop like that. Then to die doing it. Horrible."

"I see you haven't read today's paper," I said.

"No, why?"

"The police think Hazel was murdered." I picked up Mal.

"Murdered? Why?"

"I have no idea," I said.

"But I bet you'll figure it out," Becky said with a nod. "We all know you're good at deducing things."

"Thanks," I said. "I'll come back in about an hour and take a look at those transcripts."

"If you wait a minute, I can make you a copy and email it to you," she said. "Let me take down your email address. Then you can read them at your leisure."

"Thanks!" I gave her my email address, and then Mal and I said good-bye and stepped out into the bright sunlight. "Well, Mal, this was a successful walk."

Ruff!

"Hey, Allie," Carol called to me. She and Irene both wore bright tracksuits with stripes running down the sides as they power-walked my way.

"So I was right about Hazel being murdered!" Carol said. "We have to start a murder board."

"I think you should keep that at your place," I said. "Rex gets grumpy when he sees a murder board up at my place."

"Fine, but you have to come over in the evenings and help us work out who did it," Carol said.

"Oh, could we get the book club gals back together?" Irene asked. "That was a lot of fun when we helped out before."

"Do you have any idea who would have wanted Hazel dead?" I asked.

"Isabel Frank and Hazel were fighting," Carol said.

"But Hazel was a known flirt," Irene added. "I wouldn't be surprised if some angry wife or girl-friend pushed her off the roof of the McMurphy."

"Did you have the chance to review the footage of the hallways and doors at the hotel?" Carol asked. She turned to Irene. "Allie has a state-of-the-art security system. If anyone besides Hazel was on the rooftop, they would have had to come down and walk through the McMurphy, and they would have been caught on tape."

"I gave those videotapes to Rex for his investiga-tion," I said.

"But surely your system has backups," Carol said. "You should check with the company and see if they can get you copies. Oh, then you can come over tonight, and we can go through them to-gether."

"I've got plans for tonight," I said.

"Then tomorrow night," Irene said. "We'll get the book club together to help."

"Sure," I said and tried not to shake my head. "Why not. I'll bring fudge."

"I'll make tea and coffee," Carol said.

"I'll bring the booze," Irene said. "Nothing like a highball to get your brain working."

"I've got to go," I said and glanced at my phone. "I've got another fudge demonstration coming up."

"We'll see you tomorrow night at my place, then," Carol said. "Tell Frances to come. She's part of the book club, too, you know." The two ladies took off power-walking.

"Sure," I said. "I'll be sure to let her know."

"Oh, and seven o'clock sharp!" Carol called over her shoulder. "Be there or be square."

I was going to be there—because I was growing more and more worried about how someone might have killed Hazel on my rooftop and thrown her over the side of the hotel.

Chapter 9

Later that afternoon, after my last demonstration for the day, I got a ping on my cell phone that I could stop by and pick up my Best in Show ribbon. They were taking down the fair exhibits. I leashed up Mal and took her out with me. Main Street was crazy-busy as people gathered to watch the fair dissolve.

The exhibit and judging tents had already been taken down and were being packed up as we walked to the registration area. I stopped when I saw Christine talking to the exhibit coordinator.

Then I shrugged to myself. I didn't have a beef with Christine; if she wanted to make a scene, it would be on her.

"Come on, Mal," I said and walked right up to the table. "Allie McMurphy, I'm here for the candy-contest ribbons."

"That's right, you have a purple ribbon," Cathy said as she looked up my name in her deck of index cards.

"And Best in Show," I added. Mal jumped up, put her front paws on the edge of the table, and studied the coordinator as she looked through her paperwork.

"Which should have been mine," Christine said with her nose in the air. "I'll have you know that I'm asking for them to review the way they hire judges. I don't want ones who take bribes or are swayed by a pretty face."

"Thank you, I think," I said. "But I didn't bribe anyone. It's silly to keep saying it, as it just makes you sound like a poor loser."

"Well, I never!" Christine straightened. "You are going to regret you said that."

I sighed as Christine walked off.

"Don't pay her any attention," Cathy said. "She'll find something else to complain about soon enough." She handed me my ribbon.

"What happened to the fudge?" I asked. "You didn't just throw it away, did you?"

"No, we display it that day and then auction it off for 4-H that night," she said. "The Best in Show usually gets the highest bid."

"That's wonderful," I said. "Did you raise a good amount of money?"

"We did," she said. "It's going to the new fair-ground renovations and then the 4-H groups in the county."

"Great, thanks for letting me know."

"Oh, but your fudge wasn't the highest bid," she said.

"No?" I was perplexed. "Why not?"

"Christine bought her own caramels and paid a

handsome price for them to ensure they were the highest bid of the night."

"Huh, well, good for her for donating to such a wonderful cause," I said and stepped back.

"She thought maybe Liz would report on the high bid."

"Did she?" I asked.

"It was on the back page of the paper," Cathy said with a nod. "The front-page story was Hazel's fall from the top of the McMurphy."

"Oh, no," I said. "That means I took the attention away from Christine again."

"Yes, that's how she sees it," Cathy said. "Christine even said she wouldn't be surprised if you'd pushed Hazel yourself just to get on the front page."

"Well, now, that's the silliest thing I've ever heard," I said.

"Don't worry," Cathy said. "Christine is all bark and no bite. I'm sure things will settle down soon enough."

"Was it a successful fair?" I asked.

"It was an interesting one," she said. "As you know, we usually use the fairgrounds near Newberry, so this was a much-smaller-than-usual fair."

"I was happy everyone agreed to have it here while the fairgrounds were renovated, even if it did cut down on the size of the fair," I said. "Will it be here next year, as well?"

"It depends on how long it takes them to get the fairgrounds renovated," she said. "But we may move it to another place next year even if the grounds aren't ready. There was quite a bit of competition to get the fair on the island, and the committee is concerned about the small size of the park."

"I totally understand," I said as she handed me my ribbons. "It was still wonderful."

"The good news is that the carnival staff were all local this year. The committee made a conscious effort to support local small businesses."

"I didn't realize there were local carnival businesses. It must be a tough thing for this small area."

"Oh, they winter here and do a lot of local festivals, but from what I understand, they also have a summer circuit they make every year. They're doing a good business."

"Well, that's good. It's something to keep in mind when I'm on festival committees."

"Start local," she advised.

"I always try to," I said.

Mal barked her agreement, and we walked out of the red-and-white-striped tent.

"Congratulations on the Best in Show ribbon," Dorothy Hazelett said as she passed us by with a folding table in her hands.

"Thanks," I replied. "Do you need any help with that?"

"Oh, no, thanks," she said. "I'm loading up a trailer. These are all going back to the city storage barn until we need them for the next festival."

"I'm glad you didn't let Christine Keller keep you from congratulating me," I said.

"Oh, don't worry, honey, she's all grump but no bite. Things will settle down soon, and she'll be on to other things to get riled up about."

"I certainly hope so." I waved good-bye, and Mal and I strolled down the street. People stopped me to congratulate me on my win and admire the ribbon. I started to feel better about the whole thing and thought that perhaps Frances was right. This thing with Christine would all blow over.

But then I noticed the sign in the Old Tyme Photoshop window: "#TeamChristine." I sighed. "Well, Mal, if things were easy all the time, we wouldn't appreciate when they are, right?"

She looked at me with her black eyes shining. "Right," I replied to myself and hurried into the front door of the McMurphy.

Madison was in the fudge shop serving two customers. Frances was working at the reception desk. I took off Mal's harness and leash, and she went scampering off to get Frances's attention. "I picked up my ribbons," I said.

"You should stick them in the window," Frances said. "It's great publicity."

"The Old Tyme Photoshop has a 'Team Christine' sign out front." I hung up Mal's leash and halter on the hook in the back hallway.

"Well, that's just silly," Frances said.

"Yes, but how many more will appear if I put my ribbon in the front window?" I asked.

"You can't let her dictate how you publicize that you have the best fudge," Frances said.

"True." I pursed my lips and tapped my chin. "Okay, I'll put them in the fudge-shop front window, and I'll run a sale on the winning fudge flavor. That will get people to try it."

"Great idea," Frances said.

I grabbed my chef's coat off the hook and put it on, then went into the warm fudge shop. The customers had left, so I went behind the counter and put the ribbons in the front window.

"Oh, is that the Best in Show ribbon?" Madison asked.

"The very one," I replied. "I'm going to have a sale starting tomorrow on the winning flavor. We'll make two batches just in case we run out."

"Sounds like a plan," Madison said. "I'm going to head out."

"Okay, be careful." I inventoried my ingredients to ensure I had enough for an extra batch or two of the deep chocolate mint fudge.

There was a knock on my window, and I looked up to see a smiling man waving, pointing to my ribbon, and giving me a thumbs-up. It was Harry Winston. I smiled and waved back, then left the fudge shop to have a chat.

Harry was a newbie on the island. He ran a posh bed-and-breakfast, and we'd become fast friends. It didn't hurt that he was as handsome as a movie star and seemed to be as rich as Midas.

"Hi, Harry," I said as I pulled the door open and stepped out, conscious not to leave it open too long so Mella couldn't get out. My cat had a secret outdoor life, but I preferred she left from the back door and not into the busy street.

"Congratulations on your big win," he said and gave me a hug and a kiss on the cheek.

"Thanks." I hugged him back. "How's business?"

"It's going great," he said. "Although I'm sure we could swap stories about some of the guests. But I was warned that was part of the hospitality industry."

"At least I can trust that you won't have a hashtag TeamChristine sign in your window," I said and pointed at the sign with my thumb.

"What's that all about?"

"I sort of stepped in it when I beat Christine Keller out of Best in Show for the candy category. It seems she's won it twenty years in a row. She's done nothing but complain ever since that I must have cheated."

"Oh, I doubt that you needed to cheat," Harry said. "Besides, how do you cheat at a county fair?"

"Exactly," I said with a wave of my hand. "All the judges were from out of the county, so it's not like we were best buddies. I promise I didn't slip them any money with the fudge."

Harry laughed, a deep and rich sound. "I'm trying to imagine how you would go about bribing a candy judge."

"It's ridiculous, but Christine is trying to get the locals all riled up about it and take sides."

He nodded. "Hashtag Team Christine."

"Exactly." I shook my head.

"Does she even know what a hashtag means?" he asked.

I shrugged. "Maybe? The seniors here are pretty tech-savvy."

"Hey, I'm sorry to hear about that poor woman falling off your roof," he said. "That must really screw with your insurance."

"They did a full investigation, and I wasn't at fault. In fact, the police suspect it was foul play."

"That's terrible," he said. "Do they think she was pushed?"

"For all I know, she could have been dead before she fell," I said. "Rex is keeping the details quiet while he investigates."

"Are you going to investigate, too? I mean, it happened on your property."

"I'm going to look into it enough to ensure it doesn't happen again," I said.

"I don't blame you. If I were you, I'd do the same thing," Harry said. "Say, listen, I have to run. Let's get coffee or an adult beverage soon, okay?"

"Okay." I smiled and gave him a little wave as he walked off. He certainly wore his jeans well. I wasn't going to sigh. I had a boyfriend. Turning to go back in, I ran into Jenna Swan. "Oops, sorry," I said as I put my hands out to put some distance between us. "I didn't see you."

"That's okay," she said. "I think we were both distracted."

"I have a boyfriend, but a girl can always look," I said.

"I have a boyfriend, too," Jenna said, "but that doesn't mean I'm dead."

We both laughed at ourselves.

"I heard you are on the Fall Festival Committee," I said. Jenna ran a small gift shop on Market Street.

"Yes, I thought it was time for some new, younger input." She gently guided me closer to the McMurphy and out of the way of a group of fudgies.

"I agree," I said. "I volunteered to be on the committee, too."

"Great! Then we can stick together and have a bigger say in what's going on."

"Sounds good to me," I said.

"The first meeting is this week. I'll see you there."

"Bye," I said and pulled the door to the hotel open as she moved down the sidewalk. I'd begun volunteering for more committees to get to know more of the locals and disavow them of the notion that I was a fudgie.

"Frances, did we lose any more reservations?" I asked as Mal rushed toward me. I picked up my pup and gave her a squeeze. She licked me on the cheek. I noticed Mella was lounging in the sun patch from the front window.

"Only a few," Frances said. "But I was able to fill the vacancies with people from our waiting list, so we're good. Hopefully no one else will cancel."

"Oh, thank goodness," I said. "Harry stopped by, and he was wondering if our insurance would take a hit from Hazel's death."

"There's some concern from them, and they are sending out a rep this week to take a look and ensure it wasn't caused by neglect or a maintenance issue."

"It's a new deck," I said. "And the police have determined it was foul play."

"I know," Frances replied. "The insurance company knows it, too. It's just routine."

"Okay." I put Mal down. "Keep me posted."

"Will do," Frances said.

"Madison's gone home, and I'm going upstairs. Ring me if you need help with the fudge shop."

"I've got it," Frances said. "But I'll ring if we get a big crowd."

The crowds tended to start drifting back to the mainland after 4 p.m. It was now five, and I wanted to take a quick shower and then go to the office to reconcile my inventory.

Mal followed me upstairs. I tried not to worry about insurance increases. The budget was tight with all the repairs and updates. My insurance was already sky-high, as I believed they rated me and the McMurphy as a high risk anyway. Not that I blamed them.

Chapter 10

"I'm glad you came," Carol said as she opened her door. "I wasn't sure if you would show."

"Oh, no. I want to investigate this one, as it's tied to the McMurphy." I wiped my feet on her welcome mat, stepped inside, and took my shoes off. I added them to the pile of shoes already in the foyer.

"The gang's all here," Carol informed me. "Let's get you a nice beverage while they are chatting."

"Frances is here?" I asked as I followed her into the kitchen.

"Yes, she got here a few minutes early and helped me set up the murder board." Carol snagged a teacup and offered me a box of different kinds of tea. I choose a rooibos, and she placed the tea bag in the cup and poured hot water over it.

"Wait, you've already set up a murder board?" I took the cup from her and followed her into the living room.

"Well, for Hazel's board, we only have her picture so far," Carol said.

"For Hazel's board?" I was confused. Did she have more than one?

"We have a board for Mike, too," she said. "Some of us wonder if the two murders are connected. We might have a serial killer on our hands."

"Mackinac Island is a little small for all the serial killers that seem to come up," I mused. "Hello, ladies."

"Oh, Allie, I'm glad you decided to conduct an investigation and let us tag along," said Judith Schmidt.

"We wondered what it would take for you to start a new investigation," said Laura Morgan.

"It's exciting," Irma Gooseman added and sipped her tea.

In Carol's cozy living room, there was a couch filled with book club ladies; two side chairs, where Frances and Carol sat; and a cushioned stool, where I sat. Carol had two easels set up with a foam board on each. One had Mike's picture and a question mark pinned to it, the other had Hazel and Isabel's pictures.

"I'm just here to keep an eye on everyone," Frances said.

"Let's get started," Carol said. "First, there's Mike Sanders. What we know is that he was killed in the fair's haunted house. Also, he's a local, usually out on the road with the carnival during the summer. Do we know anything else about Mike?"

"If he's local, that means he has family on the island," I mused. "Do we know if he went to school here?"

"I haven't found any relatives," Carol said and bit her bottom lip in thought. "But that's a good angle. We need to check the school rosters to see if he attended."

"I can do that," Judith said. "I know the high school secretary."

"Great!" Carol said.

"Wait, there wasn't any next of kin?" I asked. "That seems odd."

"No next of kin that we know of," Carol said. "But he worked with Paul Patterson. Paul must know who, if anyone, is Mike's next of kin."

"I'll go talk to Paul," I said. "What else do we know about Mike?"

"He rented a small apartment in Harrisonville," Carol said. "There was nothing else of note. As far as we know, he didn't belong to a church parish or club."

"How old was Mike?" Frances asked, her eyebrows drawn together as if perplexed.

"He was twenty-seven," I said and looked at the ladies. "It was in his obituary in the *Town Crier*."

"Wait, did they release his body for burial already?" Carol asked.

"As far as I know, he's still at the morgue," I said. "But I can ask Shane."

"Such a pity." Irma shook her head. "To lose your life so young."

"Do we know if he had any hobbies?" I asked.

"No, but Paul may know that, too," Carol said. "These are all great questions." She stood and picked up a tray of cookies from the coffee table and passed it around to ensure everyone had a cookie or two.

I picked up a butter cookie and took a bite. "Oh, these are scrumptious," I said.

"Thanks, I made them this afternoon," Carol said and held the tray out to offer Frances her choice.

"I don't know where you find the time," I said.

"I'm not running two businesses and solving crimes," Carol said.

"Except right now, with the murder board," Judith said with a nod.

"I wonder if the two murders are connected," Laura mused over her Earl Grey tea.

"I doubt it," Carol said. "Hazel was in her mid-thirties and didn't run in the same circles as the carnies."

"Still, it seems strange that we have two murders so close together," Frances said.

"Yes, before Allie arrived, we hadn't recorded a single murder. Ever since, it seems there's one every other month." Irma pursed her lips. "It's an odd phenomenon."

"I'm certainly not murdering anyone," I said and put my teacup down hard in its saucer.

"Oh, no, dear," Judith said. "We know you haven't. It's just that it's a new experience for us, and we don't know whether the two murders are connected or not. What has your experience been?"

I sat and thought back over the last twenty-four months. "They are usually connected."

"Then we need to find out where Hazel and Mike's lives intersected if we're going to figure out who killed them," Carol said.

"Let's just say they aren't related for now," I said. "Let's go to Hazel. What I know is that Jenn and I saw Hazel arguing with Isabel the day we found

Mike's body. We believe they were talking about Hazel's new parkour hobby."

"Why did you assume that?" Barbara Vissor asked.

"Because the next morning, Isabel went around asking for signatures on a petition to ban all rooftop parkour," I said. "Frances and I signed it that day."

"That's right," Laura said. "The very next town meeting, Isabel turned in her petition, and she and Hazel got into it right in front of everyone."

"I've got the transcripts to that meeting," I said. "I'll go through them and see if Isabel made any threats to Hazel."

"If the killer threw Hazel off the roof, then whoever it was must have come in and out of the McMurphy, right?" Carol asked.

"Rex has the footage from that night, and as far as we know, no one was seen coming or going to the desktop roof," Frances said.

"That means whoever killed Hazel must have gotten on and off the roof a different way," I said.

"Do you have any cameras on your roof deck?" Betty Olway asked and snagged a chocolate-chip cookie from the tray that Carol had put back on the coffee table.

"I didn't think I needed any," I said. "But we have an order in for the security company to come out and install one now."

"Do we know where Isabel was when Hazel left the rooftop?" Judith asked.

"Wow, I guess 'left the rooftop' is the best way to describe it, since we aren't sure whether if she was living or dead when she fell," Carol said.

"Have they done an autopsy yet?" Judith asked and sipped her tea.

"Rex hasn't said." I adjusted myself in the seat, trying to find a comfortable spot. "I can find out from Jenn."

"Why isn't Jenn here?" Betty asked.

"That girl should not be running around after killers," Frances said. "She's pregnant and needs to think about the baby."

"Oh, right," Laura said. "But she's married to the CSI, and we were hoping we could get information out of her."

"It's probably best if we don't involve her," I advised. "She would want to be part of the action."

"I guess you are right," Judith said with a soft sigh.

"That's why I didn't invite her to come tonight," Carol said proudly. "I can't be responsible for putting her in harm's way."

"We aren't in harm's way, are we?" Irma asked.

"Certainly not," Judith said. "But then, you won't see any of us go chasing after a killer. We just want to figure out who did it. We are smart that way."

I tried not to take that personally, since I had a habit of chasing after killers. "I'll see what I can find out about the cause of death," I said. "What I'm pretty sure of is there weren't any bullet holes in her. Because from where she landed, it looked like the fall itself killed her."

"And it could have been the fall itself." Frances stood. "It's getting late, ladies. We have some assignments. Allie will talk to Paul about Mike. Judith will check the school rosters, and the rest of us will see if we can figure out how Hazel and Mike might be connected. What say we reconvene in a couple of days and share the information we've gathered?"

"Sounds like a good plan," Barbara said.

"Allie, why don't we leave together. It's dark, and I don't want to walk alone," Frances said.

"Do you need any help cleaning up?" I asked Carol.

"No, no, you two go on," Carol answered.

"Well, Irma and I should get going, too," Barbara said. "Come on, Laura, Judith, let's all go together."

"We'll stay and help clean up," Betty said. "Right, Mary?"

"Yes, of course," Mary replied.

"Stay safe, everyone," Carol said and closed the door behind us.

Frances and I waved good-bye to the other ladies and headed out in the opposite direction. "What are we going to do about Carol and her murder boards?" Frances asked. "Are you really going to involve her and the book club in a murder investigation?"

"I've learned that if you don't involve them, then they go off on their own and do things you can't control," I said. "Besides, it seems harmless to let them ask their questions and look through old school records."

"At least you're keeping Jenn out of this one," Frances said.

"She's been extremely busy with the late-summer weddings and bookings for next year," I said. "Plus, she and Shane are still working on their house, and she's thinking about making their second bedroom a nursery."

"Like a normal newly pregnant woman should," Frances said.

"Has she asked you about what colors are best for a baby's room yet?" I asked. "I told her I like green or yellow for a genderless theme."

"Babies like strong contrasts, like black and white," Frances said. "But I don't see why a bedroom can't be both pink and blue."

"A pink-and-blue nursery?" I pondered the idea. "Like what? Stripes?"

"Yes, one light and one dark color," Frances said. "Still gender neutral."

"I like it. I know Jenn wants to raise her baby to discover what he or she likes and not base things on gender norms."

"I like the idea of a girl getting a baseball mitt and a boy with a baby doll," Frances said. "As they grow older, they will pick what toys they like best. In the meantime, it's good to expose them to a wide variety of activities and social-emotional skills."

I laughed. "You really sound like a teacher."

"I was one for over thirty years," she said.

We stepped out to cross an empty street, the streetlight illuminating our path. "Were you really worried about walking home by yourself?" I asked.

"No," Frances said. "I just thought we'd done enough sleuthing for one night. But if you didn't leave then, they would have stayed another two hours speculating about all manner of things."

"Right," I said and nodded. "I'll walk you home anyway."

"You should call Rex," Frances said.

"Why?" I asked.

"Have him come pick you up from my place and walk you home," she said.

"I'm fine to walk home by myself," I said. "I'm a big girl."

"That's what I'm afraid of," Frances said with a teasing glint in her eye. "That you're a big girl and will suddenly think of something that must be looked into immediately, then *poof*, you'll be in trouble, and we won't know where you are."

"It's fine," I said. "Rex has my cell phone on his find-a-friend app. He can find me no matter where I am."

"That's both amazing and terrifying," Frances said. "Amazing, because you do tend to get yourself into a few scrapes and it's good that we can find you, but terrifying that he basically knows where you are at any moment of the day."

"He doesn't check it all the time," I said. "Really, he's not keeping tabs on me."

Frances shook her head. "I love Douglas, but I've not given him access to my phone," she said. "No one needs that kind of power."

"I'm sure Rex has too many other things to do than check on where I am every moment of the day."

Just as I said that, I heard the sound of a bike coming up behind us. I turned to see Rex out of uniform. "Hello, ladies," he said. He got off his bike and started walking with us. "Out for an evening stroll?"

"How'd you know?" I asked.

"I checked where your cell phone was," he said.

"See?" Frances said.

"See what?" he asked.

"She said it was both good and bad for you to have my cell phone on your find-a-friend app," I said.

"Oh, for Pete's sake, it's not like I'm stalking you. I got off shift and stopped by the McMurphy to see if you wanted to go get a drink. When you weren't there, I pinged your phone. That's it. Innocent."

"I believe you're innocent," I reassured him. "I'm actually glad you found us so that neither of us has to walk home alone in the dark."

"Yes, I suppose there is a benefit to you being able to find her phone," Frances said with a nod. "Now I won't have to worry."

"See," I said. "It's not a bad thing."

"Especially with Allie's habit of getting kidnapped." Rex walked his bike with us.

"Maybe I should be able to find your phone, too," Frances said. "In case you wander off."

"Okay, now you're just teasing me," I said. "I'm not going to wander off."

"One never knows," Frances said as we arrived at the small gate in front of her house. "You two have a good night."

"Good night," we replied in unison and waited for her to get safely inside before we walked toward the McMurphy.

"Did you have fun with the book club?" Rex asked.

"How did you know I was at a book club meeting?"

He shrugged. "Small town."

I gave him the side-eye. "Are you checking up on me?"

"Are we back on that again?" He gestured while

walking his bike. "I'm not stalking you. It's a small town. Everybody knows everything and tells everything."

"Except who killed Hazel and Mike," I mused.

"Right."

"How's the investigation going?"

He shook his head. "Not as well as I'd like."

"Does Isabel have an alibi for that night?" I asked.

"What makes you think she needs one?" He drew his eyebrows together in a concerned expression.

"She and Hazel got into a big fight at the city council meeting," I said. "Apparently over Hazel's parkour training."

"Yes, I heard about that," he said.

"They record those meetings, if you need to look into it," I said.

"I know." He parked his bike as we reached the back of the McMurphy. He glanced up, but it was too dark to see anything past my lighted window. "Hazel took quite a fall."

"I'd like to think she was already dead when she went over," I said. "I can't imagine experiencing that fall."

"Fishing for clues?" he asked as I unlocked the back door and invited him into the McMurphy lobby.

"Why ever would you say that?" I said in my best imitation of a Southern drawl and batted my eyes at him.

He laughed.

"Come with me as I do a quick check of the McMurphy," I asked.

"Sure," he said, "but only if you agree to have dinner with me."

"Haven't you eaten?" I asked as I looked at my phone. "It's nearly ten o'clock."

"I'm on a cop's schedule," he said with a shrug.

"I can offer you a drink," I said as I checked that the fudge shop was locked and turned down the lights in the lobby. I hid a yawn behind my hand. "I'm a little tired."

"I know you get up real early," he said. "Maybe tomorrow? Say, around eight?"

"Now, that sounds good," I said. "I'll cook."

"It's my day off," he said. "How about I cook?"

"Are you going to make steak salad?"

He shook his head and smiled. "If that's what you want, but I am capable of cooking other dishes."

"Then surprise me." I started to climb the stairs.

"Now, that I can do."

Chapter 11

The next morning, I met Jenn in the office. "How's fudge making going?" she asked.

"It's a pretty normal day." I sat down at my desk. "That said, I'm running a sale on the prize-winning flavor, and it's selling like hotcakes."

"Awesome! I told you that you should show off your winnings." Jenn rubbed her belly absently. It was still flat as far as I could tell, but she glowed like a pregnant woman.

"How's the event planning going?"

"Oh, we are totally booked for fall weddings," she said. "It's going to be so pretty with the trees all turning colors."

"I hope it stays warm enough," I said.

"We have the deck heaters," she said, "and if it rains, I have a backup venue."

"That's great. Where is the backup?"

"Julie's Dance Studio," she said proudly. "It's above the gift shop and is one huge, wide-open room. We can have a lot of fun decorating it."

"Oh, I didn't think about a dance studio."

"It's downtown and has great views of the lake," she said.

"Cool." I opened my email and skimmed through it. "How's Shane doing on the investigation into Hazel's fall?"

"He's working hard on both Hazel and Mike's murders," she said. "It takes a lot of time to do the investigation right."

"I bet," I said. "There's a lot of minutiae that goes into it. Is the lab backed up?"

"The lab is always backed up," she said. "It's hard on Shane. He wishes it was as easy as the crime scene shows on television."

"Yeah, I always thought it was fun to watch them run lab tests and come up with a quick answer. No one on TV ever has to worry about leaving a murder unsolved."

"True." She rested her chin in her hand. "Are you investigating the murders?"

I glanced up. "You can't. You have the baby to think about. I'd be sick if anything happened to you or the baby."

"I won't . . . much," she said with a smile and turned toward me. "What do you know so far?"

"Not a whole lot," I said with a sigh. "Did Shane tell you whether Hazel was killed in the fall or if she was dead first and then pushed?"

"Shane doesn't discuss his cases," she said and scrunched her mouth to the side. "But that doesn't mean he doesn't talk in his sleep."

"He talks about his cases in his sleep?" I leaned forward, curious.

"Only if I ask him questions about it," she said, her expression smug.

"You ask him questions while he's sleeping, and he answers you?"

"Every time," she said. "Do you want to know how Hazel died?"

"How?"

"She was strangled." Jenn nodded. "Her hyoid bone was fractured—and not from the fall. Plus, there were bruises on her neck and arms."

"Oh, my goodness," I said. "Then she didn't die from the fall. I didn't see any real signs of a struggle on the deck, but Rex said there was one."

"Didn't you see her body?" Jenn asked.

"I didn't really look. Rex had me cover her with a blanket right away to preserve her dignity, along with any evidence there might have been."

"Huh. Well, that makes sense." Jenn pushed back her chair. "Do you think it happened on the roof? That seems a little creepy to me."

"Gosh, I don't know, but I hope not. Still, if it didn't, then the killer would have had to have carried her to the roof and tossed her off. That doesn't seem very likely to me, especially since they didn't come through the McMurphy carrying her. That means they would have had to have been climbing over the rooftops carrying her body."

"Yes, that doesn't seem likely." Jenn tapped her fingers on the desk and made a face. "Someone getting murdered on the roof is not very good for the event-planning business."

"Unless your clients are true-crime buffs," I said. "So, yeah, that's a problem. We have had some people cancel their reservations because of Hazel's fall, but we've been lucky enough to fill the vacancies so far."

"Maybe that's why the killer tossed her off your roof," Jenn said.

"What?"

"Maybe the killer wanted to send you a message not to investigate."

I shifted in my chair. "Then it was the wrong way to send that message, because I promised Rex I would only investigate if someone or something I love is in danger."

"And they used the McMurphy."

"Yes," I said and blew out a sigh. "Can you keep me posted if you hear anything else from Shane in his sleep?"

"Sure," Jenn said with a grin. "If anything new comes up, I'll let you know."

"But only if you promise not to investigate yourself. I don't need you in harm's way."

"How about I promise to look out for myself and the baby," Jenn suggested, "and you'll let me join the book club."

"How does everyone know about the book club?" I threw up my hands. "It's supposed to be a cover story."

"The book club has been quiet for months, and now that there have been two murders, the ladies are suddenly meeting once a week again," Jenn said. "Pretty much everyone can see the connection. Besides, Laura Morgan was telling everyone who would listen that she was going to help you with the investigation."

"Of course, she was." I shook my head. "Then, sure, come to the book club. Who knows how many members we'll have next week? Half the town might show up."

"Great. I'll bring popcorn," Jenn said.

"Perfect," I muttered. "Just perfect."

"Allie!" Carol came rushing into the fudge shop after my 2 p.m. demonstration.

"Hi, Carol. I'll be right with you." I helped Madison thin out the crowd and did a quick survey of our fudge stores. We might need to make another batch or two to make it through the day.

Ever since I'd won Best in Show, sales had picked up. Or maybe it was the sale I was running. I washed and dried my hands and met Carol in the lobby, where she was helping herself to a cup of coffee.

"Hey, Allie, I've seen five more Team Christine signs go up around town," Carol said. "We need to make Team Allie and Team Carol signs. It's the only way to combat this. We need to prove that people are on our side."

"Carol, we've talked about this." I held back a sigh. "If we ignore her, it will go away."

"I disagree, but fine, then how about we put up Team Book Club signs?" Carol asked.

"Why do we need signs?" I countered.

"You have to fight fire with fire," Carol protested. "By the way, when are we getting together next to go over what everyone has learned?"

"We just started, and I need a little more time," I said.

"Right." Carol sipped her coffee. "Fine, I'll convene one in two days. Meanwhile, what clues have you figured out?"

"I told you, I need a few days," I hedged.

"You really aren't good at sharing, are you?" she commented. "Let me tell you what I found out."

"What?" I asked.

"I should make you wait until we meet in a group," she groused.

"Do you think you can keep a secret that long?"

"Harumph," she grumbled. "I can keep a secret. I know many secrets that I'll keep to my dying day."

"Most of them she'll whisper on her deathbed," Frances teased from the reception desk.

"Not you, too." Carol frowned.

"We're teasing," I said. "If you want to wait to tell us, I respect that."

"And if I want to tell you now?"

I shifted to one foot. "Then I respect that, too."

"Good, because I've got some interesting news," Carol said. She paused, then took me by the arm and pulled me over to Frances and leaned in close. "Guess who was Hazel's parkour teacher?"

"Who?" Frances played along.

"Mike," Carol said and straightened. "There's the connection."

"You think someone's killing off the parkour participants?" Frances asked.

"I'll tell you this much," Carol replied. "I wouldn't want to be involved in parkour right now."

"It's an interesting connection," I said as thoughtfully as possible. "I wonder what the motive would be? Is there a business in parkour competitions?"

"Not that I know of," Frances said. "Let me check on the Chamber of Commerce website."

"It was part of their outdoor guided tours," Carol said.

"'Their'?" I asked.

"Yes, Mike and Paul's guided backpacking tours," Carol said.

"Paul Patterson?" I asked. "The guy from the haunted mansion?"

"Yes, the two have been best friends since kindergarten," Carol said. "They owned several small businesses."

"Hmmm." I rubbed my chin. "Do you think there's a motive there?"

"I think it's more likely that Paul is our next victim," Carol replied. "Those two were thick as thieves. You never heard them argue."

"Wait, Paul teaches parkour, too?" I asked.

"I really don't know," Carol said. "But I can find out. In the meantime, we need to warn Paul that he could be the killer's next victim."

"That's probably not a bad idea," I said. "Also, I think we should tell Rex. That way the police can keep an eye out."

"But then our investigation won't have the upper hand," Carol pouted.

"Yes, but it's more likely the killer will be caught if more people than just us are on the trail, and isn't catching the killer what it's all about?" I tilted my head and looked at her inquisitively.

"I suppose you're right," Carol said. "But I do like the thrill of the hunt."

"As long as everyone is safe," Frances said.

"Sure, that, too." Carol nodded.

Only time will tell, I thought. *Only time will tell.*

Chapter 12

The next morning as I finished my 10 a.m. fudge demonstration, Frances waved me down. I put up the last of the fudge and left Madison to wait on the remaining people.

"Frances, what is it?" I asked as I wiped my hands on a hand towel and threw it over my shoulder.

"There's a couple of gentlemen here to see you," she said and pointed toward two guys standing near the coffee bar enjoying a cup of coffee.

"Who are they? Did they say?"

"The one guy in the blue button-down shirt said his name was Evan Tailor," Frances said. "He gave me his business card." She handed me the card.

"Who uses business cards anymore?" I wondered aloud and read, *Evan Tailor, Journalist.* "He's a journalist?" I said and looked at Frances. "Did he say what he wanted?"

"Just that he wanted to talk to you," Frances said, but she looked as curious as I felt.

"Maybe he's a friend of Liz's," I said and went

over to where the two men stood. They both appeared to be in their late twenties. Evan had short black hair and clear, chocolate-colored eyes. The other guy, who wore a dark T-shirt and jeans, had longer black hair and lighter brown skin. He had a cup of coffee in one hand and a camera in another. "Hello, I'm Allie McMurphy. Can I help you?"

"Yes, Allie." Evan set down his cup of coffee as his smile widened. "Nice to meet you." He shook my hand. "I'm Evan Tailor, and this is Dwayne Finch."

"How do you do?" I said and shook Dwayne's hand after he, too, put down his cup of coffee.

"If you don't mind, I'd like to take some pictures," Dwayne said and lifted his camera. "And maybe a video or two."

"What's this for?" I asked and clasped my hands. I had been working since 5 a.m. and had no idea what my hair looked like where it stuck out of my chef's hat. I knew my chef's coat was covered in sugar and chocolate.

Dwayne raised his camera and started snapping photos.

"I haven't given my okay yet," I said and held up my hand.

"Sorry," Evan said. "Dwayne gets a little ahead of himself. I'm the owner of a viral food video podcast. We average five hundred thousand hits a day. Our biggest day was when we interviewed Chef Gordon Ramsay. We had over a million hits that day. It's still one of our biggest draws. You got my card, right?" He went to pull out another card. I waved him away.

"I have your card," I said. "What's this about?"

"Well, we specialize in a surprise day-in-the-life photo event featuring well-known chefs and, in your case, candy makers. And today is your lucky day. We picked you to be on next week's show. Get her picture, Dwayne, she looks surprised. That's good stuff."

I wiped a random lock of hair out of my face and tucked it behind my ear as the camera clicked away. "What is the name of your podcast? Or show?"

"Well, it's really a video blog but also an Insta account and TikTok, and our website—Tailored Food Adventures," he said. "It's a play off my name."

"I see." I wrinkled my forehead. "And you ambush chefs for your Instagram?"

"Video podcast, and yes, when I can," he said and looked proud. "Some of the bigger ones we had to go through their agents and get all the legal stuff worked out, but in the end, they agreed to let us get candid. It's because we have so many subscribers. Like I said, we're viral. Real influencers in the space."

"And you picked the McMurphy Hotel and Fudge Shop?" It sounded ridiculous to my own ears.

"I've been following your story ever since you were in that fudge-off reality show. That was real gripping stuff, how you found a killer. I'd love to hear more about that."

"I'm still not certain . . ."

"Oh, my gosh!" I turned to see Jenn's face light up as she headed our way. "Is this really Evan Tailor?"

"That's me." He beamed.

"I'm a huge fan," Jenn said, her face slightly flushed. She looked gorgeous in a flowered day dress and flats. She still didn't have much of a baby bump, so they probably didn't notice she was pregnant. She shook his hand while Dwayne snapped pictures. "Allie, this is Evan Tailor."

"Yes, he told me," I said and tilted my head. "Do you two know each other?"

"Oh, no," Jenn said, slightly flustered. "I mean, I know of him, he doesn't know me. I'm Jenn Carpenter, by the way. Are you here to ambush Allie?"

"Yes," Evan said and looked from Jenn to me as if to say, *See?*

"Oh, Allie, this is a big deal," Jenn said. "Evan's show has been known to really make careers. Has she shown you the fudge shop yet?"

"I haven't—"

"Well"—Jenn put her arm through Evan's as Dwayne snapped away—"you've come at the right time. Allie just won Best in Show at the county fair and dislodged a twenty-year champion."

"Is that so?" Evan looked back at me as Jenn led him toward the fudge shop. I followed behind, curious as to what this meant.

"Yes, she made deep chocolate mint fudge," Jenn said and opened the door to the fudge shop, where a flustered Madison smoothed her hair. "Madison, this is—"

"Evan Tailor." Madison held out her hand. "I'm a huge fan."

"Thanks," Evan said and shook her hand. "And you are . . . ?"

"Oh, Madison. I'm Allie's summer intern. I'm off to culinary school in a few weeks, when the season is over."

"Madison helps me make the fudge and do the public demonstrations," I said.

Dwayne made the rounds snapping pictures.

"Nice to meet you, Madison," Evan said. "I hope you two ladies will help me convince Allie to sit down and give me an interview for the show."

"Oh, my, you just have to," Madison said, her eyes as big as saucers.

"Allie, this can really make your career," Jenn said.

"I like the career I have," I replied. "I don't need a bigger one."

"We can make you a household name," Evan said. "We've launched some of the best new brands."

"Emma Smith started on Evan's show," Jenn said. "Now she has a whole line of cookware in every department store and is branching out into dishes and lifestyle lines."

"Wow," I said. "I've never thought about branding beyond fudge."

"Well, now you can," Evan said and gave me a million-watt smile. "I'd love to taste this prize-winning fudge."

"Sure," Madison said and quickly cut a small slice from the last batch we'd made. "It's grand champion fudge. We just finished our fudge demonstration. I'm sorry you missed it."

"Wow," Evan said as his savored the fudge. "This is wonderful. I don't think I've ever tasted anything like it."

"We didn't miss the demonstration," Dwayne said proudly. "We filmed it."

"I especially like the story you tell of how your

grandfather made fudge," Evan said. "It's going to be great for our accounts."

"You were filming the demonstration?" I asked. I mean, they could have given me a heads-up. I would have at least worn a clean chef's jacket.

"The videos are great. They specialize in secret filming," Jenn said. "I've got them on two apps plus on my desktop."

"Wow," I said, not at all sure it was a "wow."

"What we'd like to do now is have you give us a tour of the McMurphy," Evan said.

"You should tell them how you solve crimes," Jenn said.

"What? 'Crimes' with an 's'? You've solved more than one murder?" Evan asked and rubbed his hands together. "This is too good to be true."

"Well, I'm not a detective or anything," I hedged.

"Don't let her be humble," Jenn said. "She's solved several murders since she took over the McMurphy and is working on one right now."

"I wouldn't say that—" I was giving Jenn *The Look* with a shake of my head.

"I heard that a woman died falling from a rooftop on the island," Dwayne said.

"She fell right off the top of the McMurphy," Jenn said and squeezed my arm in excitement. "That's why Allie is investigating."

"I—" I started to speak when Rex walked into the McMurphy.

"And there's Officer Rex Manning," Jenn said. "He's Allie's boyfriend and the lead investigator on the murders."

Evan and Dwayne rushed to introduce them-

selves to Rex. He sent me a look, and I shrugged.
If anyone was good at getting rid of the press, it
was Rex. I pulled my phone out of my pocket and
texted Liz.

Hey, Liz, I typed. *You have competition on the island.*

What? she texted back.

It seems a guy named Evan Tailor is here.

THE Evan Tailor? she texted back. *Keep him there,
I'm coming right over.*

I'm not sure that's a good idea, I typed. But it was
too late. She was already off her phone. At least
Jenn had joined them around Rex, and I could
catch my breath. I took off my chef's hat and
jacket and draped them across my arm. My T-shirt
and black pants were clean.

Rex gave me another look, and I shrugged. I
was just glad the attention was off me. I stepped
out of the fudge shop and tried to sneak around
the back of the small crowd, but I wasn't fast
enough.

"Allie," Rex called my name and pushed through
Jenn and company. He took my elbow. "I'd like to
have a word with you."

"Certainly," I said and walked with him over to
the far corner of the lobby by the coffee bar. A
quick glance told me Jenn was keeping the podcast crew busy. "What's up?"

"I was going to ask you that," Rex said. He waved
a business card in front of my face. "Who are these
guys?"

"I'm not sure," I said. "But apparently Jenn
thinks they are a big deal and it will be career making if I let them interview me."

Just then the front door opened and the bells

jangled as Liz strode in. She didn't even pause to look my way as she headed straight toward Evan and introduced herself.

"He said you were investigating the latest murder." Rex put his hands on the utility belt that rested on his hip. "What's he talking about?"

"It's just the book club," I said. "Jenn gave them the impression I was trying to solve the murder before you."

"I see," he said.

"I do have a clue," I said and turned my back on the group. "Carol told me that Mike, the haunted house guy, was Hazel's parkour instructor."

"Okay," he said as if asking me to go on.

"Well, he and Paul were best friends and owned a tour group together, as well as the carnival attraction," I said. "It's a connection between the two murders."

Rex narrowed his eyes. "I've already talked to Paul. He has an alibi."

"I'm not saying he is the killer," I said and sighed. "It just makes a connection between the two murders. We think—"

"'We'?"

"Carol and I," I said and tried not to give him the stink eye for being so obtuse. "We think Paul might be in danger."

"Because?"

"Because he's tied to both murdered people," I said.

"Allie"—he blew out a breath—"I'm not trying to frustrate you. I just need you to be clear with your thinking."

"You don't think Paul's in danger?"

"I don't think he's in danger," Rex said. "And so

far I've not gotten any motive to tie the two murders together."

"There's a second murder?" Evan asked as he approached. He nudged Dwayne to start filming us.

"I'm not going to talk to the press at this time," Rex said. He put his hat on and gave me a quick kiss before he walked out of the McMurphy.

"I've asked Evan if I could interview him for the paper," Liz said and put her arm through mine. "He agreed."

"Just being on the island will be great publicity," Jenn said.

"Excuse me." A well-dressed woman and two couples walked over to us. "Are you Evan Tailor?"

"Yes, I am," he said with a smile.

"I'm a huge fan," she said. "We all are."

I slipped away while she introduced herself and her friends, then I hurried up the stairs. If I was going to be ambush-interviewed, I at least wanted to wear a clean chef's coat and hat, and for goodness' sake, I needed to put on some lipstick.

I was cleaned up and hiding in the office going over the bills when Jenn came in. "I can't believe you're hiding up here while Evan Tailor is in the McMurphy. He came here to interview you for his podcast. What a huge honor."

"Has he left?" I asked.

"Frances got him and his cameraman rooms on the second floor," Jenn said. "I told them you'd take them on a tour right after lunch."

I glanced at my phone. "When exactly is 'after lunch'?"

"Why, after we meet them downstairs and take them to lunch, of course," Jenn said. "I was thinking the Viking Club."

There weren't many fancy restaurants on the island, but the Viking Club and the yacht club were two options. Mackinac was a hiking and biking island full of family fun but limited on highbrow culinary options.

"Wouldn't it be better for them to try some of the café food instead?" I asked. "To get a real feel for the island?"

Jenn pursed her lips and tapped her chin. "I hadn't thought of that. You know what? You're right. We can go to the Nag's Head instead."

"Why don't you go without me," I suggested as I studied the inventory. "I've got some work to do if they want to take up some of my afternoon time."

"They want to get to know you," Jenn said, "so you have to come."

I looked up from the computer. "Are you sure this is a big deal? I mean, it's a podcast."

"A viral video podcast," Jenn said. "They got Chef Gordon Ramsay—think of how big that makes them."

"I bet they had to go through his agent and set up a time with him," I grumbled.

"Oh, I'm certain of it," Jenn said brightly. "But you don't have an agent. Well, I could be your agent. I do give you some of your best ideas. And, as your new agent, I say you should get up off that chair and go out to lunch with two very nice gentlemen who want to know all about you."

"Sounds like a blind date," I grumbled but stood.

"We are going to have so much fun!" Jenn's face lit up as she took my arm in hers. "This might be your best day ever."

I hung up a clean chef's jacket and hat on the hooks beside the back door and went with Jenn to meet Evan and Dwayne for lunch. As we walked out the door, I heard my name called.

"Yoo-hoo, Allie!" It was Carol and Irma power-walking through the crowd toward us.

"Hi, Carol," I said. "Jenn, why don't you guys go on without me. I'll meet you there in a moment."

"Oh, no," Jenn said and grabbed my arm. "You aren't getting out of this that easy."

"What do these fine ladies want to talk about?" Evan asked and motioned for Dwayne to start taking video.

"It's nothing, really," I said. "Probably just about our book club."

"Oh, you mean the 'murder club'?" Jenn said with a wink.

"Are you telling me you get together with a book club to solve murders? That sounds so interesting. Tell me more," Evan said.

"Allie," Carol said as she came up to me full-speed. "I've come across another new clue."

"A clue?" I asked.

"Who are these two handsome gentlemen?" Irma asked.

I made introductions all around. "They are filming for their podcast."

"Oh, I follow their Instagram," Irma said. "They are quite famous."

"They are, indeed," Carol said. "What do you want to know about Allie? We have all the scoop."

"Carol!"

"What?" Carol said in a false-surprised tone. "We know you as well as anyone on the island."

"We were heading to the Nag's Head to grab lunch," I said. "We can talk later. I'm sure you two ladies have to finish your power walk."

"We sure do," Irma said. "But for Evan Tailor, we can stop now and talk while you eat lunch."

I tried hard not to roll my eyes. What was it with everyone and this guy? I guess I really wasn't into pop culture as much as everyone else.

"That sounds great," Evan said. "The more the merrier." He put his arm around Carol and started walking. "Now, you were saying something about a new clue? Is that to the recent murders?"

I blew out a long breath and followed behind. It was going to be an interesting day.

Chapter 13

"Do you still have cameras following you?" Rex asked as I opened my back door and let him into the kitchen.

"They went to their rooms for the night," I said. I noted that he was uncharacteristically out of uniform, wearing a tight black T-shirt and a pair of well-worn jeans.

"How do you feel about all of this?" He had a look of concern. "I know you are a private person."

I handed him a glass of wine and walked to the couch to sit down. "I'm not certain, really. But Jenn said it would be good for business, and so far, she has been right about everything."

"Except now they are caught up in your investigation." He sat down next to me, his warm presence comforting.

"I thought you didn't like me investigating."

He sipped his wine and studied me. "What I don't like is you not being safe. I can't keep you safe if you keep trying to do my job. Can you imagine me rushing into your kitchen to make fudge with no training?"

I laughed. "You would make a fine mess of it at first, I'm sure."

"Oh, I'd probably hurt myself." His eyes twinkled at me.

"They promised not to get in the way," I said. "I told them I have work to do and that my hobby of following clues is sort of sporadic. They said they have to edit and write and such, so they won't be following me every boring minute of my day."

He frowned. "They said you were boring?"

"Oh, no, I added that." I sipped the cabernet. It was warm on my tongue. "I tried to tell them to follow you, because you are actively investigating. I'm just poking around, but Jenn convinced them otherwise."

"I heard Carol had another clue to share," Rex said. "Another connection between Mike and Hazel?"

"You know, I was thinking about that." I shifted to look into his eyes. "Both Hazel and Mike had ties to Mackinac, but that doesn't mean anything. The island population is so small, we all have ties to each other."

"Thank you for that," he said.

"Did you have a chance to review the video of the town council meeting where Isabel and Hazel got into it?"

"I did," he said. "It was pretty heated."

"I've been skimming the transcript," I said. "Kurt Ford was as vocal as Isabel about it. I can't figure out why?"

"Kurt owns the Lavender Hotel on the other

end of Main Street," Rex said. "I can see why he was worried about people jumping around roof-tops becoming a thing."

"Well, it certainly has upped my insurance," I said. "Even though her death isn't listed as acci-dental, because of the rooftop deck the carrier thinks I'm a higher risk."

"Was that Carol's next clue?" Rex asked.

"What?"

"Is Kurt our newest suspect?"

I was quiet for a full moment. "Kurt was seen ar-guing with Hazel the morning before she was mur-dered. But we have no proof he was anywhere near the McMurphy at the time of her death."

"You have no proof anyone was with Hazel at the time of her death," Rex pointed out. "Whoever was up there was aware of your camera systems."

"Do you think it was premeditated?"

"It's hard to say," he said with a shrug. "I've got no motive for either death."

I sat back. "I'm sorry. I haven't a clue about mo-tive, either, beyond Isabel and Kurt's anger about the rooftop parkour. Have you gotten any further on Mike's death?"

"No." He grimaced. "I'm still waiting on lab re-sults. There were some smudged fingerprints on the body, but with no murder weapon and no mo-tive, all I can do is keep investigating."

"I saw they took down the carnival," I said. "Word has it the haunted house went back into storage for the rest of the year. They usually bring it out for fall festivals in the Lower Peninsula, but with Mike's death, Carol said Paul just shut it down for the rest of the season."

"That's probably for the best," Rex said.

"Carol said Paul stores it in a barn on his parents' property along with other outdoor gear for their businesses. I'm surprised they don't store it in the Lower, where storage might be cheaper."

"There's nothing cheaper than your own barn," Rex pointed out.

"Maybe we're looking at this all wrong," I muttered.

"What do you mean?" he asked.

"Nothing," I said. He gave me a look, and I shrugged. "How about we talk about something else besides murder? I'd hate to think our relationship revolved around other people's deaths."

"You have a point," he agreed and put his arm around me. "How about we talk about you and me?"

I leaned in to kiss him. "That's a great idea."

The next morning, I got a text from Harry asking me to get a coffee with him. I agreed. It was after my 10 a.m. fudge demonstration. Evan and Dwayne had gotten up at 5 a.m. to film me opening up and making fudge for the day. They both looked exhausted and had headed for the coffee bar.

"I'm off to meet a friend for coffee," I said. "I don't think you need to film that."

The two agreed, and I went up to my apartment, quickly changed, and put Mal on her leash. Harry wouldn't mind my pup coming along, and I felt better bringing her, since I felt as if I'd been neglecting her of late. Mella rushed out the door with us to make her daily outdoor rounds, and I closed and locked my apartment, taking in the late summer warmth and sunshine.

"Good morning, Allie," Mr. Beecher said as he walked down the alleyway. "Going for a walk?"

"Hi, Mr. Beecher," I said as Mal leapt up and did a ballerina twirl for her treat. The old man pulled a small, bone-shaped treat from his pocket and gave it to her. "How are you doing?"

"I'm well," he said and leaned against his cane. "I do smell fall in the air."

"It comes pretty early on Mackinac," I agreed. "But it's my favorite time of year, so I'm excited for it."

"How's the investigation going?"

I shrugged. "No motive, no murder weapons."

"Mike was always running around dreaming up new business ideas," Mr. Beecher said. "He didn't have much time to make enemies."

"Did you know Mike well?" I asked.

"I watched the boy grow up," Mr. Beecher said. "I think he and Paul were in love. They met in first grade and had been inseparable ever since."

"Well, that's an interesting thought," I said. "If that's the case, I've neglected telling Paul how sorry I am that he lost Mike. I thought maybe Paul would be in danger of being the next murder victim, but Rex said the police have him covered."

"It never hurts to go visit a person who's just lost their best friend," Mr. Beecher advised.

"Thanks for the reminder," I said. "Come on, Mal, we're late for our coffee date."

"Have fun." Mr. Beecher continued his walk down the alley.

Mal and I met Harry at the Coffee Bean. He had a nice outside table waiting for us. At the sight of us, he stood and came around for a hug. "I'm glad you had time to meet me today," he said.

"Of course," I said. "It's always good to visit with a friend."

"And I figured you'd bring Mal with you." He pulled a dog treat out of his pocket. Mal sat and held out her paw for a shake. He gave it a quick shake and handed her the treat. "I had them bring out a bowl of water for her, too." He pointed to the dainty porcelain bowl near the base of the table. "I'd have ordered you a coffee, but I didn't know what you wanted. What will you have?" He pulled out my chair, and I sat.

"A latte is fine," I said.

"Great, be right back."

I watched him walk away. He was dressed in jeans and a pullover and was just as handsome on the backside as the front. I sighed a little and leaned my right elbow on the table. "Well, Mal, what a great guy."

She sat up and put her paw on my thigh as if to agree.

He came back five minutes later with a paper cup filled with a warm latte. "Helen said to tell you hi."

Helen ran the Coffee Bean. "Thanks," I said and took a sip. "It's delicious as always."

"I hear you have a camera crew following you around," Harry said with a warm twinkle in his eyes.

"It was the strangest thing," I replied. "They just showed up yesterday, and Jenn and Liz went crazy over them. They seem to be some viral podcasters or something."

"I've heard of Evan Tailor," he said. "His podcast is doing quite well. They consider him an influencer."

"Would you let him follow you around?"

He sat back in his chair. "I would, yes. I think any publicity is good publicity."

"Speaking of publicity, how's your bed-and-breakfast doing?"

"Quite well," he said and sipped his coffee. "Thanks to your advice."

"Oh, please, I didn't tell you that much. You are a natural businessman. I'm sure you could sell tea to a tea farmer."

He grinned, and my heart did a little pitter-pat. "I do have a talent for getting what I want."

"I can see that."

He leaned forward with his elbows on the table and spoke low. "What I want is a date with my favorite fudge maker."

I swallowed hard and felt the heat of a blush rush over my cheeks. "A date?"

"Yes, a real, dressed-up, romantic dinner kind of date. What do you say?"

"Harry, you know I like you—"

"Then do it," he pushed. "Let me take you out for an evening cruise on the straits. I'll have nice wine and a catered dinner."

"Sounds fantastic." I tried not to sigh. "But I'm dating Rex right now."

He nodded. "Then you two are exclusive?"

I paused. Had we ever talked about being exclusive? Not really, and Rex did still have one ex-wife on the island.

"You paused," Harry said, and his grin widened. "I'll take that as a no."

"I'm exclusive," I said quickly before things got too awkward. "I'm just a one-guy-at-a-time kind of woman. I'm sorry. But you make the offer very tempting."

"I hope this doesn't mean you won't still get coffee with me or be my friend." He reached out and took my hand in his. "I'm patient. I can wait while you work through this thing with Rex."

I studied him out of the corner of my eye. "You are patient," I said. "And very, very tempting." He rubbed his thumb along my hand, giving me goose bumps. "But Rex and I have a history."

"I heard you were dating someone else when Rex came into your line of sight. I don't see what you have in common with him. He's been married twice. He's a cop. On the other hand, neither of us have been married before. We both run inns. And we're both considered outsiders on the island."

"My family has been here for over one hundred years," I protested.

"But you didn't grow up here, go to school here," he said. "I know you're doing your best to be involved. I've kept track of how many committees you're on, and I know why. In fact, I've volunteered for a few committees myself." He studied me. "I think we have much more in common."

"We did both survive our first winters on the island, didn't we?"

"We did." He pulled my hand up and kissed my fingers. "I also wouldn't ever tell you to stop investigating. I know you do it for the people you love."

"Rex is trying to keep me safe."

"Right," Harry said. "But I would be able to keep you safe and still let you do what you love."

I had to admit, his offer was very tempting. He was right. He ticked all my boxes as far as having things in common and not riding me about the investigations.

"How's that going, by the way?"

"How's what going?" I asked and gently pulled my hand back to grab my coffee and take a sip.

"The investigation," he said with a soft smile.

"It's not going very well," I said. "So far, no motive and no murder weapon, and whoever killed Hazel did a Houdini act on my roof. We have no proof anyone else was on that roof with her at all."

"I can help you with that," he said.

"Really? How?" I leaned in closer to him. Mal jumped up on my lap, and I sat back to pull her close.

"I have an idea of how it might have happened, and I'd love to be able to demonstrate it to you, if you're game."

"Oh, brilliant," I said, my excitement rising. "I'm game."

"It was around ten p.m. when it happened, right?"

"Yes," I said and petted Mal's soft curls.

"Then I promise if you meet me on your rooftop deck tonight at ten, I'll show you."

"That sounds like a proposition," I teased.

"Only if you want it to be." His grin widened. "But seriously, I've been thinking about it, and I might have an answer."

"Then I need to meet you there."

Chapter 14

So far none of the clues we had made any sense. There was a connection, but it was only passing. The book club ladies wanted to meet, but I put them off a day so I could find out what Harry thought he knew about Hazel's death.

The podcast crew spent the rest of the day taking shots around the island and interviewing people. I knew they were champing at the bit to get to a book club meeting and seeing how the ladies helped investigate.

Frankly, I wasn't looking forward to putting those two groups together.

I stared out at the lake from my rooftop deck, hugging a sweater close because the wind had a chill to it that still smelled of fall.

"Allie, I'm glad you could meet me here."

I turned and saw Harry hopping down from the roof of the Old Tyme Photo Shop next door.

"That's a four-foot gap," I said and went over to where he'd jumped. I glanced down at the gap between the McMurphy and the shop. "Was it hard to get here? I mean, Hazel seemed to make it look easy, but unless the killer was into parkour, I don't see how they got here."

"Getting to the roof of the photo place was easy," he said. They have a fire escape, and I simply went through the alley, up the escape, and across the roof to here."

"Yes, but Hazel was killed before she fell, so either the killer murdered her and dragged her across the rooftops to throw her off . . ."

"Or they fought on your rooftop and she died here," he said, sending a shiver down my spine.

"You said you thought you knew how it was done?"

"You didn't have any video of Hazel coming up to your roof, right?" he asked.

"Right," I said. "We all assume she was practicing parkour and the deck was merely a stop on her route."

"I think the killer was lying in wait for her," he said.

"On my roof? How could he or she have known Hazel's path? She kept changing it looking for the easiest one."

"She could have found her route," he posed. "And told a few enthusiasts. This is a small town. Maybe word of the route got back to the killer and he or she planned the attack."

"But how would they have known Hazel was on the roofs at that time? I mean she didn't seem to have a routine."

"The answer is quite simple. The killer was across the street when they saw her start her climb. I timed it. It took me less than a minute to hustle over to the alley, grab hold of the fire escape, pull myself up, and be standing on the photo shop roof."

"Still, the killer had to have impeccable timing to get up here and catch her as she passed by." I was skeptical.

"Unless they told her to meet them on the roof," Harry said.

"Why? Why meet someone on the roof?" I asked. "Unless the killer is a parkour student and was traveling with Hazel at the time of her death."

"There's something I think you should see," Harry said and climbed up on my attic roof. He held out his hand. "Trust me?"

"I trust you," I said and gave him my hand. He pulled me up, and we scrambled over the roof.

"I need you to jump across." He took a leap and cleared the gap with ease, encouraging me to jump across to the photo shop's roof. I was scared, but I figured as long as I didn't look down, I'd be fine. "I've got you." He held out his hand, and I took a leap of faith.

I landed, but I lost my footing and stumbled against his warm, hard body.

He held me against him for a moment. "I've got you."

I swallowed hard and ignored the pounding of my heart. "Thanks," I said and stepped away from him. I tried not to look at him or appear like that was awkward at all. "What did you want me to see?"

He took a flashlight out of his back pocket and turned it on. "I bet the police didn't consider all the rooftops as possible crime scenes." He passed the light over the back roof of the photo shop.

"Is that blood?" I asked and bent down to take a better look. "There are loose tiles up here, too." I glanced at him. "This is where they struggled."

"I think so," he said. "Now, I know you said that you and Rex went right out to the alley."

"Rex went out. I called nine-one-one first."

"Between the two of you, you had a good view of the alley, and even though the cameras didn't catch anyone, you were sure to have seen anyone climbing down the fire escape I came up on."

I stood. "That's true."

"I did some checking." He made his way across the roof. "This roof also connects to the next and the next until you reach the side street. On the far side is a balcony. The killer could have hidden there and climbed down once the police left."

"Maybe," I said. "But if they pushed Hazel off the back of the McMurphy, they could have gone across the roofs the other way and down the back of Doud's."

"Then they could have easily left on either side."

"Yes," I said and pulled out my phone.

"Are you calling Rex?"

"Yep. He and Shane need to come down here and check out the rooftop."

"Smart," Harry said. "I told you I'd help you figure out how they got away."

"You did," I agreed and punched in Rex's number.

"Manning," he answered.

"Are you still working?" I asked.

"Hi, Allie," he said. "Yes, I'm chasing down a lead."

"Well, I have another one for you. I'm on top of

the Old Tyme Photo Shop, and there are signs of a struggle and blood up here."

"That's not Hazel's blood," Rex said. "She didn't have any obvious wounds."

"Then it's the killer's blood," I concluded and looked up at Harry. "That's even better, right? It means the killer hurt themselves in the struggle. Then we are looking for someone with a fresh wound. Or maybe Hazel got some DNA under her fingernails."

"Are you on the roof now?"

"Yes," I said. "But I'm safe. Harry is with me."

He was silent for a heartbeat. "Harry is helping you investigate now?"

"At least the podcast team isn't with me," I said.

"I'm on my way," he said. "I'll bring Shane to see if we can get any DNA from the roof." Then ended the call.

"He's coming and bringing Shane," I said. "I think we should wait here until they arrive."

"Sounds good." Harry sat down beside me on the roof, and we watched the stars pop out over the straits. "Are you glad I suggested you meet me up here?"

"Yes," I said. He was close. His gaze was warm, and I was dating Rex. "I bet the podcast team will be here the minute Rex and Shane get here."

"Why?"

"Because they are coming back from the pub and just saw Rex on his bike." I pointed out the two who followed Rex down the street.

It didn't take long before Rex appeared, climbing up from the fire escape the way Harry had gotten up here. We both stood.

"Where's the crime scene?" Rex was all cop.

Harry pointed the flashlight to the torn and missing shingles and the patch of blood. "There was a struggle here."

"There's no one living above the Old Tyme Photo Shop," I said. "Marcy's moved back in with her mom."

"Which is why no one heard anything," Rex said and squatted down, running the light from his flashlight over the area.

"Did you find a clue?"

I turned at the sound of Evan's voice. He and Dwayne peered over the roofline from the fire escape.

"Don't come up here," Rex warned. "This is an active crime scene."

"Okay, cool," Evan said. He looked at Dwayne. "I bet we can get a better view from the McMurphy's deck." The two disappeared.

"Great," Rex muttered.

"I'll keep them away," I said and turned to leap back across.

"Wait, what are you doing?" Rex stood.

"I'm leaping across," I said. "It's easy, and probably how the killer got on top of the McMurphy."

Rex leaned over to eye the four-foot gap. "They had to be strong to drag a dead woman across that."

"Maybe she wasn't dead yet," I suggested. "Maybe she was trying to get away when they trapped her on the deck, strangled her, and threw her off."

"How do you know she was strangled?" Rex narrowed his eyes.

"I have my sources," I said.

He ran his hand over his face.

"I'll help her down the fire escape," Harry said. "We'll wait at the McMurphy."

"I can make the leap," I said. "You taught me that."

"For my sanity, I'd like you to use the fire escape," Rex said.

"Fine." I sighed. "Come on, Harry. We can have a nice glass of wine while we watch them work."

Rex gave me the side-eye. We scrambled down the fire escape while two other police officers came up the fire escape carrying floodlights.

"Allie, I hear you found a crime scene," Shane said as he parked his bike and grabbed his crime scene kit.

"It looks like it might be," I said. "I hope it helps the investigation."

"At this point, anything would help the investigation," Shane said. "Harry." He nodded.

"Shane," Harry acknowledged as he took my elbow. "I do like a nice glass of wine."

"I have a chardonnay in the fridge," I said. "We might as well enjoy ourselves while we watch them work."

"I agree entirely."

Chapter 15

"I heard you figured out how Hazel's killer got away without being seen," Frances said, sipping her coffee and reading the news on her computer screen.

"We found the crime scene last night," I replied and took off my chef's hat. I'd just finished the first demonstration of the morning.

"'We'?" Frances looked up from her computer.

"Harry Winston and I," I said.

"What were you doing with Harry?" Frances lifted her right eyebrow and studied me over the top of her reading glasses.

"He had an idea of how the killer got away, and so we met to test whether his idea would have worked or not," I said. "That's how we found the crime scene on the roof next door."

"I'm surprised Rex and Shane didn't find it when they processed the decking," Frances said with a frown. "It doesn't seem like them to miss an obvious detail like that."

"I think we were all distracted and believed the killer came and went inside the McMurphy. I mean, how could they have gotten across the rooftop with a body? The killer has to be strong."

"It could have just been adrenaline," Frances said.

"Whoever killed her could have just left her on the photo shop's roof, and it would have been days before someone found her," I said and drummed my fingers on my chin. "Instead, they made sure we found her right away by throwing her off my roof. Why would they do that?"

"I suspect it was meant as a warning or a way to get your attention," Frances said.

"You think her death was meant to send me a message?" I asked.

"Most likely, yes," Frances said as she picked up a cookie and went back to her computer screen. "Whoever it was knew where all your cameras are pointed."

"That means it's probably someone local," I said. "They had to have looked around the McMurphy, and I've not seen any tourists lurking in places they shouldn't go."

"Speaking of lurking in places they shouldn't go," Frances said and looked me in the eye. "Are you not dating Rex anymore, or are you interested in dating both him and Harry?"

"What? I'm not dating anyone but Rex," I said.

"There are rumors floating around that you and Harry were seen taking a bottle of wine up to the rooftop deck."

"To watch Shane and Rex work the crime scene," I said. "Really, it was innocent, and Rex was there."

"You're playing with fire when it comes to Harry," Frances said. "Rex might get the idea that you're moving away from him."

"I'm not moving away from Rex," I said. "I can have male friends."

"Okay." Frances turned her attention back to her cookie. "Don't say I didn't warn you."

I shook my head and went upstairs to change into a sundress and sweater. Rex was a confident man. There was no way he'd be upset about Harry helping me with the crime scene last night. Or would he?

The question niggled at the back of my mind as I left for the book club meeting at Carol's house. Over the last year, my love life had been as crazy as the murders on the island.

"Allie, come in, come in," Carol said, opening the door. "The ladies are all here, and we want to hear all about the crime scene."

"Forget the crime scene," Irma said as I stepped inside and took a seat on an armchair. "We want to hear about Harry Winston."

The other ladies giggled.

"There's nothing to hear," I said. "We're just friends."

"Sure," Laura said.

"Now, now," Carol said and brought me a cup of warm tea. "Men and women can be friends. We are all old enough to know that."

"Tell me, what have you ladies discovered since the last time we met?" I changed the subject as quickly as I could.

"Well, I've been digging into who was in school with Mike and Paul," Carol said as she sat across from me. "There were ten boys in their class at school. Most of them are still on the island and working."

"Did any of them have a problem with Mike?" I asked.

"That's the thing," Ida said. "We haven't found anyone who might have had a reason to hurt Mike."

"Well, that was a dead end," Carol said, sipping her tea.

"What about his parents?" I asked. "How are they doing?"

"His father died four years ago," Carol said, "and Mike's mother is in a memory care home."

"Oh, no," I said. "I didn't realize his parents were so old. I mean, Mike was just in his thirties, right?"

"Yes, dear," Irma said, "but his parents had him late in life. So they are significantly older. Well, not as old as Carol and I, but older."

"Hey!" I protested for Carol's sake.

"Personally, I don't mind being older," Carol said. "I'm fit as a fiddle and living my best life."

"I agree," Mary said.

"What about Hazel's parents?" I asked. "Are they still around? Did she have any brothers or sisters?"

"Hazel has a sister, Gemma," Carol said. "Their parents have retired to Florida but come up during the summers for a little while."

"Is Gemma around? Maybe I can talk to her," I said. "You know, see if she has any idea who did it."

"Gemma teaches at the school in the winter and works at the Grand Hotel during the summer," Irma said.

"I'll go swing by her house and see if she knows anything that can help us," I said and stood.

"I'll go with you," Carol offered.

"It's probably best if I go alone," I said. "Besides, you and the ladies can continue to study the murder board and let me know if you have any running theories."

"Laura thinks Hazel was murdered by a jealous lover," Betty said and sipped her tea.

I sat back down. "Really? Was Hazel married?"

"Oh, no," Carol said, "but she was such a pretty girl. We all suspected there was someone she was interested in, but she never said. Laura suspects it's because the man she wanted was already married."

"You think the mystery man is the murderer?" I asked.

"Well, they do say to look at the spouse or boyfriend when a woman gets murdered," Laura said with a nod.

"But there's no proof that Hazel was stepping out with anyone," Irma said. "Which only means it would be easier for them to get away with murder."

"I'll check into it, but seriously if the seniors don't know who she was dating, the chances of me finding out are pretty slim. I'll do what I can to look into her whole life. Secrets have a way of coming to the surface after a murder."

"Speaking of one's whole life . . ." Betty took a sip of her tea. "How are things going with Rex?"

I stood. "Good night, ladies, it was great to see you."

Carol chuckled. "I'll walk you out."

I grabbed my gear. "How's your husband, Barry, doing?"

"Oh, he's off on another adventure," Carol replied. "He got us a fancy, new-fangled alarm system so he can check on things from his phone."

"But he has to be somewhere with a phone signal, right? I mean, he can't be out in the wilderness."

"He's on a fishing trip in Canada," she said. "It was only fair to let him go when we cut short his last trip."

"You're very understanding," I said and opened the door.

"I'm very retired," she said. "Sometimes the key to a happy marriage is a little separation."

"Have a good night," I said, stepping outside. The chill in the air had deepened, letting me know that the warm days of summer were limited. On the island, things cooled off quickly, and I was glad to be wearing a sweater as I stepped out into the night.

I liked a nice walk in the cool quiet of early night. Some kids were still out playing flashlight tag, and it made me smile. I remembered the late summer evenings I'd spent on the island with my grandparents. My heart tugged a bit at the realization that I missed them.

"Hey, Allie," It was Harry, and I waited for him to catch up with me. "What brings you out this time of night?"

"Hi, Harry," I said. "I just left the book club meeting."

"Ah, how's the investigation going?" He stepped in time with my stride.

"It's puzzling," I said. "We haven't been able to determine a real motive for either murder, and the only connection between the two is that Mike taught Hazel parkour. That alone isn't enough reason for murder."

"Serial killers kill without motive," he pointed out.

"Oh, now you're into true crime, as well?" I looked up at him.

"I'm really interested in anything that interests you." His smile was warm.

"You know I'm still dating Rex, right?"

"You tell me every opportunity you get," he said and put his hands in his back pockets. "But that doesn't mean I'm going to stop trying. I like you, Allie. I think we'd make a great couple."

I stopped short and studied him in the streetlight. "That is a very tempting thing for you to say. I like you, too, but Rex and I have kind of had this thing for a year or so, and I want to see where it goes."

He shrugged. "I respect that—really, I do. But it doesn't mean I'm going to stop letting you know how I feel. I'm an honest kind of guy."

"A girl likes an honest man," I said. "Hey, you're an athletic, outdoorsy kind of guy."

"Thank you," he replied.

"Did you ever take any guided adventure tours on the island?"

"I did one once when I was first looking into buying property on the island," he said. "It was fun."

"What tour did you take? Was it the one Mike and Paul were running?"

"You mean the dead guy and his friend?" Harry asked and drew his eyebrows together in thought. "I think it was. Why?"

"Because the book club thinks Hazel's death is connected to Mike's because Mike taught parkour along with offering the adventure tours and running the haunted house."

"And you think Paul might be the next victim?" Harry asked thoughtfully.

"Yes, but Rex says it's a stretch. And maybe it is. I don't think the guys have so much competition that a competitor would have taken Mike out."

"No, there's only three companies that do the tours. I carry all three brochures in my bed-and-breakfast. In fact, I've been meaning to take the other two tours just so I can advise my guests on which one is best for their fitness levels."

"I don't carry brochures for activities at the McMurphy," I said thoughtfully. "I always figured that since I was just a few blocks away from the tourism bureau, it was kind of redundant."

"It wouldn't hurt you to get to know more of the business owners," Harry said. "Do you belong to the Chamber of Commerce?"

"I do," I said. "But I don't do much with them. I'm more involved in things like the festival committee and the street decorations and such."

"There's a coffee tomorrow morning," he said. "Why don't you come to it and just chat up our wilderness tour guides?"

"Do they go to the coffees?"

"Every time I've been, they have been there," he said. "They're always trying to get us hospitality folks to push their guided tours."

"Well, then I guess I need to go," I said.

"Cool, I'll see you there, then?"

We arrived at the back stairs to the McMurphy

that led up to my apartment. "What time is the coffee?"

"It's at ten in the town hall," he said.

"Oh, that's why I don't go. I usually do a demonstration at ten." I bit my lip. "But I can move it to eleven a.m. this once."

"Great. Have a good one, Allie. See you tomorrow," he said with a wink, then whistled as he walked on down the alley toward his bed-and-breakfast.

After he was out of sight, I turned and went in the opposite direction. It was time to talk to Gemma.

Chapter 16

I stopped by Doud's to purchase something to take to Gemma's place. After all, she had just lost her sister. My choice was a frozen lasagna, some French bread, and a bottle of red wine. A quick search on my phone showed me that Gemma lived in a bungalow about a half mile east of me and two blocks up from Main Street.

The walk was easy in the cool darkness, the street lit by streetlights with moths flying around them. I walked up and knocked on the door.

"Yes?" came a suspicious voice from inside.

"Hello, I'm Allie McMurphy. I was wondering if I could offer my condolences to Gemma." I glanced at my watch and realized it was after 9 p.m. and I probably should have called first.

The curtain to the front window moved, and then the door was opened. "Who are you?" It was a woman, probably in her late fifties, with smooth brown hair and wide brown eyes.

"I'm Allie McMurphy. I own and run the McMurphy Hotel and Fudge Shop. Is Gemma available?"

"Are you a friend of Gemma's?" she asked.

"I knew Hazel," I said. "I thought I'd bring over some food and see how Gemma is doing."

"I see," she said and glanced around. "Okay, come in." As I entered, she closed the door behind me and locked it. "I'm Michelle, Gemma's mom. Please come in and have a seat. I'll go get Gemma. She's been a bit torn up about her sister."

"Oh, yes, I imagine so," I said and sat down. Michelle had said she was Gemma's mom. Did Hazel have a stepmom?

Michelle stepped back into the living room. "Gemma will be right out. Can I get you anything? Coffee or tea?"

"Tea would be nice, thanks."

A moment later, a young woman around my age walked into the living room. I stood to greet her. She was tall and thin like Hazel, but a bit less athletic-looking. She wrapped a bathrobe around her and tied the sash tight. "Hello?" She looked at me through swollen eyes.

"Hi, Gemma, I'm Allie. Allie McMurphy. I run the—"

"Yes, I know who you are," she said and sighed. "Please sit."

"I brought you some food," I said and put the grocery bag on the coffee table. "It's frozen lasagna, and garlic bread, so you can put it in the freezer for another day when you don't feel like cooking. Oh, and there's a bottle of wine as well."

"Thank you," she said and sat on the edge of the couch. She tucked her hands into the sleeves of her fluffy robe. "I haven't been hungry."

"I totally understand," I said.

"You knew Hazel?"

"I did." I leaned forward in my chair. "She was very kind to me."

"It was your roof she fell off of, wasn't it?" Gemma whispered.

"The police are pretty sure she was tossed off of it," I said as kindly as I could. "Do you know anyone who would want to hurt your sister?"

"Half-sister," Michelle said as she walked out with a tray with teacups, a teapot, a pitcher of milk, and a container of sugar. She set the tray on the coffee table. "Hazel was my husband's daughter. She stayed with us every other weekend after we got married. Then we had Gemma two years later." She poured tea into a cup, added a splash of milk and a spoonful of sugar, stirred it, and handed it to Gemma. "Our visits with Hazel got fewer and further between after that. I think her mother leaned on her a lot."

"What happened to Hazel's mom?" I asked.

"Cancer." Michelle handed me a cup of tea. Gemma's hands shook, and her cup rattled on its saucer.

"After all she went through for her mother," Gemma whispered. "Then to die so young. She never had a chance."

"Oh, honey, she was living her best life the last few years," Michelle said and gave her daughter a squeeze. She turned to me. "Oh, do help yourself to milk and sugar if you want."

"I like it plain, thank you," I said.

"Are these groceries?" Michelle asked as she spied the bag.

"A frozen meal you can reheat whenever you need to eat but don't feel like cooking," I said.

"How thoughtful," Michelle said. "Let me just

put them in the freezer." She took the bag and left the room.

"Gemma," I said and leaned in close. "I'm so sorry for your loss. Do you know any reason someone would want to harm your sister?"

"Nope," she said with a sigh and sat back. She hadn't taken even a sip of the tea. It was like she held it but didn't realize it was even there.

"You two must have been very close."

"We were," she said. "Even though we had different mothers, Hazel always made sure she was the best big sister she could be. I idolized Hazel. She was so strong and did whatever she wanted, and yet at the same time she was thoughtful and went out of her way to help people. Did you know she would go for two weeks every year to help rescue puppies and take them to loving homes?"

"No," I said. "I didn't know. What other kinds of things did Hazel like to do?"

"She was very outgoing and tended bar at the Nag's Head sometimes. She was really into the parks and hiking and stuff. It didn't surprise me at all when she took up parkour."

"Did Hazel have a boyfriend or anyone close to her?

"She did," Gemma said and wrapped her hands around her teacup, letting the saucer rest on her knees. "She was a very private person when it came to who she dated, but she always hung around with Mike Sanders."

"Her parkour teacher?"

"I think he was much more than her teacher," Gemma said. "There was such a look of love in her eyes when they were together. And he was always so attentive."

"And they were lovers," I said softly.

"If they weren't, they sure wished they were," Gemma said. "She was devastated by Mike's death. She didn't even want to get up and leave the house when she found out. I'm the one who talked her into at least practicing her parkour. She used to say it took all her concentration and helped her to forget about things that were upsetting."

"So, she went out and was practicing?" I asked.

"Yes," Gemma said and looked at me with devastated eyes. "I'm responsible for her death."

"No," I said and reached out to touch her cold hand.

"Yes," she said. "If I hadn't encouraged her to get back to her practice, she wouldn't have been on your roof that night, and she would still be alive."

"No, none of that was your fault," I reiterated. "Some monster did that, not you. I was just wondering if I could help figure out who that monster is."

"You have a pretty good track record for finding monsters," Michelle said. She sat down next to Gemma. "I won't speak ill of the dead, but Hazel was not making any friends with that rooftop parkour. I begged her to stop, but she wouldn't listen to reason."

"I don't think she died because of parkour," I said and sent Gemma a pointed look. "There had to be another reason. What else was going on in her life?"

"Besides losing the love of her life?" Gemma asked. "Nothing. Before Mike died, she spent a lot of time with him. Afterward, she just did parkour alone."

"Did she ever hang out with Paul?" I asked. "I heard he and Mike were close."

"Oh, yes, they did a lot together. Hazel accepted Paul as part of Mike's package. You know, like accepting a new little sister." Gemma gave her mother the side-eye.

"I'm afraid Paul may be in danger," I said. "But Rex says he has the police checking up on him regularly, and Paul told Rex he's fine."

"What about that Ralf character?" Michelle asked. "I read in the paper he was working there the day Mike was killed.

"Ralf? The ticket taker?" I asked. "I think he was a part-time hire. I don't think he traveled with Mike and Paul on the fair circuit."

"Oh, no, he hung around with Mike and Paul," Michelle said. "I always thought it was weird that Hazel hung around with three men. She deserved better than to be another one of the gang."

"Mom," Gemma chided. "She never felt slighted no matter who joined them—even me." She looked at me. "Hazel was always saying, 'The more the merrier'."

"Then Ralf could be in danger, too," I mused and put down my teacup and saucer. "I'll let Rex know. But that also means you need to be careful as well," I said to Gemma. "Is there anyone else who hung around with Mike and Hazel?"

"It's a small island, and Hazel loved doing things with everyone," Gemma said. "But mostly it was Mike and his entourage."

"Listen, I read the city council transcripts, and it got quite heated about the parkour issue. Did anyone say anything to Hazel afterward?" I asked.

"Not that I know of," Michelle said.

"Wait," Gemma stood. "Hold on." She disappeared down the hall and came back shortly with a envelope in her hand. "This came the morning Hazel was killed. I was keeping it to give to her when she got home. It was in the mailbox, but it doesn't have a stamp on it."

I looked at the envelope and saw Hazel's name was printed on it, neatly from a printer. "Do you have a plastic baggie?"

"Sure, why?" Michelle asked.

"This might be evidence, and we really shouldn't touch it," I said.

"Oh, no," Gemma said and dropped the letter.

"It's okay," I said as Michelle went into the kitchen, presumably to get a baggie. "You didn't know. The lab will know to rule out your fingerprints."

"Here's a bag," Michelle said and gave me a quart-sized plastic bag. I carefully picked up the letter and slid it into the bag.

"I'll go drop this off at the police station," I said. "Thank you for all your help. If you think of anything else, please don't hesitate to call the police, or myself if you are nervous to speak to Rex. I'm so sorry for your loss."

"Thank you," Gemma said.

"Thank you for the food," Michelle said as she walked me to the door. "Help them find who did this to our girl, okay?"

"I'm no professional," I said, "but I promise to do all I can to help."

"Thank you," she said.

I stepped out into the cool, dark night and studied the envelope in the lamplight. It was hard to tell what, if anything, was inside. I sighed, put the baggie in my pocket, and stepped off the stoop to head back to the McMurphy. It was nearly ten, and Rex had texted me twice.

I walked quickly through the quiet streets, sometimes passing a group of fudgies going to or returning from the bars on Main Street.

I loved this time of night, with the sound of the waves off the lake and in the distance the gentle *clip-clop* of horse taxis still on duty. I rarely got to be out this time of night since I got up so early to make the fudge.

I was hurrying past Doud's when someone coming the other direction with a hood up nearly ran me down. "Oh, sorry," I said. "Cathy?"

"Hi, Allie," she said and lowered her hoodie. "What are you doing out this late?"

"I was going home after visiting a friend," I replied. "What are you doing?"

"I was heading home from my shift at the yacht club and realized I left my purse. I can't get on the ferry without a ticket."

"Oh, you work at the yacht club?"

"I started last month," she said. "They let me work around my work with the county fair. Now, I really must go if I'm going to get back to the dock in time for the last ferry."

"Sure, have a good night," I said and hurried down the alley toward my apartment stairs. It was better if I didn't go through the McMurphy lobby this late at night. I had just reached my steps when I saw them.

"Hey, Allie," Evan said as he and Dwayne stepped

out of the shadows. Dwayne had his trusty camera on, and the light nearly blinded me. "We heard you left the book club over an hour ago. Why weren't we invited? More importantly, where have you been?"

There was a meow from the steps above. It was Mella, still outside and seemingly asking the same question.

Chapter 17

I'd completely forgotten about the stalkers—er—podcasters. I sighed. "Turn off the camera and come on up where we can talk."

"Cute cat, by the way," Dwayne said as he and Evan followed me up the stairs. "She likes me."

"Mella likes most people," I said. "I wouldn't let her have the run of the McMurphy if she didn't like people." I unlocked my door, and Mal met us with a wagging tail as Mella slipped inside. "Why don't you two make yourself at home on the couch," I said. "I've got to take Mal out for a quick potty run."

"We'll watch from the landing," Evan said. "You have a way of disappearing on us."

"Right," I said as I put Mal's halter on her and connected her leash. "We'll be right back."

"We'll be here," Dwayne said and raised his camera as if to film.

Evan pushed it down with a shake of his head. "Only if there's action."

I sighed and took Mal down to her favorite pee

spot. "Let me know if Mella goes back out. I don't like her to stay out overnight."

"Will do," Dwayne called.

"I'm sorry not to take you for a longer walk, Mal, but—" Before I could finish, she had done her business and was pulling me back up the stairs to our visitors.

"Your dog likes us," Evan said as he patted Mal on the head and went inside.

"She loves visitors," I said. "Can I get you anything to drink?"

"Do you have any champagne?" Evan asked.

"Or craft beer?" Dwayne added.

I opened my fridge. "I have red wine, white wine, and iced tea."

"We'll have iced tea," Evan said. "It's sweet, right?"

I shook my head. "No."

"Oh, well, water, then," he said.

I pulled two bottled waters out of the fridge and handed them one each. "How's the podcast going?"

"It would be going better if you had let us go to the book club with you," Evan said and opened his bottle, then took a swig.

"I didn't think you'd want to visit a bunch of senior ladies," I said and sat down.

"Are you kidding?" Evan asked. "Your friend Jenn told us that the seniors on the island help you solve your murders. We want to be in on any conversations you have about the murder. It will be great for ratings."

"Well, we didn't really learn anything to help with the murder," I hedged. I wasn't about to tell them about my visit to Gemma. "How did you even know I was out? I mean, I'm usually in bed by now."

"So you say," Evan said. "But we happen to know a little birdie who tells us that some of your best cases are solved at night."

I was going to kill Jenn.

"Seriously, that Carol is a hoot and full of all kinds of information," Evan said. "We got some great sound bites from her."

Okay, so maybe it wasn't Jenn I should kill. I sent them a fast smile. "Carol loves to tell a good story. I'm sure she could tell you all kinds of things about anyone on the island."

"Oh, she can, and she did," Evan said. "Except she left out the part about the book club meeting tonight. That was very sneaky of her."

"Very sneaky," Dwayne said as he ran his hand over Mella's fur. "Your cat is really soft."

"Like I said, it was a boring meeting, but I do get your point." Sitting down in my chair, I folded my legs under me. "I will remember to include you next time. When are you leaving?"

"After the murder is solved," Evan said with a glint in his eye. "We can't leave before you figure out who did this."

"Murder investigations can take months or years," I said. "Your watchers or listeners will miss a lot of good content if you hang out here that long."

"We're sure you will figure this out soon," Evan said and stood. "Until then, we'll be capturing your every move. For now, just know we're keeping an eye on you."

"I guess that means I'll see you at five a.m. for fudge making," I said.

"Of course," Evan said. "We'll be there with cameras at the ready. Say good night, Dwayne."

"Good night." Dwayne gave me a little salute, picked up his camera, and followed Evan out my front door.

"Don't forget we know where you live and are keeping an eye on you for candid shots," Evan said.

"Right," I replied. Then I went and locked my door behind them. "Well, Mal, looks like we'd better solve this one quick."

Then I remembered the letter in my pocket. If I left now, I would certainly be followed by Evan and Dwayne. No, it would have to wait until morning, when I could sneak away.

Oh, shoot, I thought. I'd promised Harry I'd go to the Chamber of Commerce coffee in the morning. Maybe I could text Rex to meet me there and then slip him the evidence when Dwayne wasn't looking.

"That sounds like a good plan, doesn't it?" I asked Mal. What could possibly go wrong? I glanced at the clock and noticed it was already ten o'clock. Time to get to bed so I might look refreshed in the morning. After all, they'd be shooting my close-up.

Grand Champion Penuche Fudge

Ingredients
    1 cup brown sugar
    2 cups granulated sugar
    1 cup heavy cream (can substitute whole
       milk)
    ¼ teaspoon crème of tartar
    Pinch of salt
    3 tablespoons butter
    2 teaspoons vanilla extract

Directions
In heavy saucepan, stir together brown sugar, white sugar, heavy cream, crème of tartar, and salt. Place on stove on medium-high heat and stir constantly until mixture starts to boil. Stop stirring and let boil until it reaches softball stage (234–240 degrees F). Remove from heat and add butter and vanilla—do not stir. Let rest until candy thermometer reads 110 degrees F. Grease an 8x8x2-inch pan and line with parchment paper. When the fudge reaches 110 degrees F, beat with a wooden spoon until butter and vanilla are incorporated. Quickly pour into buttered pan as fudge may seize up quickly. Let cool and cut into 1-inch slices. Makes 48. Enjoy!

Chapter 18

"Putting the demonstration off until eleven is a great idea," Frances said to me. "There will be more people on the street."

"Oh, that's a good sound bite," Evan said. "Keep going."

It was 9 a.m., and the podcasters and I had been up for four hours. I'd made fudge, and they'd drunk a lot of coffee.

"Yes, but I do a ten o'clock demonstration so that I'll be the first. You know how many fudge shops there are on the island, and some are closer to the docks. And people usually buy fudge from the first vendor they stop at. I like to be the first stop."

"Well, it won't hurt," Frances said.

"I could do the demonstration by myself," Madison offered. "If you want to keep it at eleven. I'm pretty good at it now."

"Ooh, conflict," Evan interjected. "Will Allie give up control of her demonstration to her intern?"

I gave him the stink-eye and turned to Madison. "Thank you for offering. I know you would be excellent at it," I assured her. "But it's the best part of my day. Let's see what happens if we do it at eleven."

"Okay," Madison said. "I'll update the demo board." I had a small whiteboard in the window that listed the times of the demonstrations. It hadn't been updated in over a year, so I wasn't sure how easy it would be to clean off.

"And so Allie, like any good chef, doesn't give up control of her kitchen," Evan narrated. "Cut. Great work, ladies."

"We weren't working for you," I said. "Maybe you two should take a break."

"I'm going to the Chamber coffee," Jenn said as she popped down the stairs from the office. "It will be great to have you there with me, Allie. What made you think of it?"

I glanced to make sure the podcasters weren't listening. They were shooting Madison cleaning off the whiteboard.

"I ran into Harry yesterday, and he said it might be good for me to mingle with some of the tour guides so I can promote them in the hotel."

"Well, that makes a lot of sense," Jenn said. "The Rachit brothers are putting in a new zip line. Have you ever done one?"

"Oh, no," I said. "I like to keep my feet firmly planted on the ground."

"They are a lot of fun," Jenn said. "But baby and I are going to stay safe." She rubbed the small bulge of her belly.

"How's the morning sickness going?" I asked as I hung up my chef's coat and hat and put some lipstick on so I would look less like I'd been up since 5 a.m.

"Oh, it's all gone," she said. "I'm eating like a hungry horse these days."

"Good," I said as we headed toward the front door. "I was afraid you were losing too much weight."

"The doctor is keeping a close eye on me," Jenn said.

"Wait for us, ladies," Evan said, and he and Dwayne followed us out onto the sidewalk.

The walk to the town hall was short, and I opened the door for Jenn to go first. The scent of old polished wood and meeting room hit my nose. I waved the podcasters inside. "You two might want to talk to the Chamber president and see if it's okay to film."

"We know the drill," Evan said.

There were people inside talking and laughing. I glanced at my watch. We were only five minutes late.

"Girls, welcome!" Mayor Boatman said and waved us over. "Good to see some fresh faces at the coffee. There's coffee and donuts over there, help yourself."

"Thank you," I said.

"Oh, and Allie"—she put her hand on my forearm—"we have a festival committee meeting next week. Don't forget."

"I haven't yet," I said with a smile.

"I just like to remind all my volunteers," Mayor Boatman said. "I know how busy you girls are with your businesses and book club." She leaned in close. "I see you have a film crew following you, too."

"Yes," Evan said and Dwayne put his camera up on his shoulder. "Please, Mayor, say something to Allie. We'd love to have a clip of you two interacting. Especially if it's about the murder."

"Really?" I said and rolled my eyes. "Mayor Boatman, you don't have to do anything on camera."

"I'd love to," she said and adjusted her blazer. "I hear these podcasts are very popular." She fluffed her hair. "I'm ready, boys." Then she turned to the camera. "Allie, how's the investigation going?"

"Slow," I admitted with a sigh. "We can't seem to come up with a motive."

"I'm sure you'll stumble across the answer soon enough. You always do," the mayor said.

"Thanks for the vote of confidence," I said, unsure how to take her comment.

"Oh, that wasn't confidence," Mayor Boatman said. "That was me letting you know I'm keeping an eye on the situation. Murder isn't good for our community, and I'm afraid we're getting quite the reputation."

"Allie, you came," Harry said, rescuing me from the mayor and my film crew. He took my hand and pulled me away. "I'd like you to meet Joe Shooter. He runs an adventure tour business."

He guided me to a tall man with short brown hair wearing a plaid shirt and jeans.

"Joe, this is Allie," Harry said. "Allie, Joe."

"Nice to meet you in the flesh, Allie," Joe said and shook my hand. "We hear a lot about your adventures."

"Oh, another good sound bite," Evan said as they rushed over to film, leaving Mayor Boatman midsentence.

"'Adventures'?" I asked.

"Adventures, exploits, you know—the solving of murders and such." Joe let go of my hand. "You seem like a very brave woman."

"Not brave enough to zip-line," I said.

"You don't have to zip-line to prove your bravery," Harry said. "You go toe to toe with real killers."

"This just gets better," Evan said. "Are you getting this, Dwayne?"

"I understand you have questions about Mike and Paul's adventure tours," Joe said, ignoring the filming.

I glanced at Harry, and he nodded, encouraging me. I glanced at the film crew and back. He answered with a shrug and a go-ahead wave of his hand.

"Yes," I said. "Some people think the connection between Hazel and Mike's murders is parkour. You see, Hazel was taking lessons from Mike. Do you include parkour in your tours?"

"Oh, no, we don't do that," Joe said. "We stick to stuff normal people like, like zip-lining, hiking, and canoeing. Parkour was Mike's baby. He learned it when he and Paul were on the road with the haunted house."

"How long had he been practicing it?" I asked.

"About four years, maybe five," Joe said and sipped his coffee. "Mike took lessons in the offseasons from a guy in Mackinaw City."

"Do you know that guy's name?" I asked.

"Sure, it's Richard Witmore," Joe said. "I'll give you his number. You can call him if you're interested in learning more about parkour."

I handed Joe my phone. "If you could, please," I said.

He put the number in my contacts, and Harry handed me a cup of coffee.

"Just a splash of cream, right?" Harry asked.

"Perfect, thanks," I said and took the cup.

"I gave her the number of Mike's parkour trainer in Mackinaw City," Joe said and handed me my phone.

I put it in my pocket and wrapped two hands around my cup. "Paul and Mike were your business competitors, right?"

"Oh, yeah," Joe said. "But it wasn't a rivalry, if that's what you're thinking. We were all pals from school. I was the first to start the tours with my friend Jason Moore. But when Paul and Mike wanted to get in on the action, we were fine with that. There's a lot of business here during the season, and we were struggling to keep our tour groups down to a size we were comfortable with. If the group gets too big, you get stragglers, and people are more likely to get hurt or lost."

"Joe's group lets you rappel off the cliff by Arched Rock," Harry said. "I signed up for one of those tours next week."

"Oh, I think I'd much rather stay on top of the cliff," I said and sipped my coffee. "But, Joe, you and Paul and Mike aren't the only businesses with adventure tours."

"No, Sam Halter and Big Tom Rigley have tours as well, but they stick to fishing and water tours."

"Would they have had any reason to hurt Mike?" I asked.

"Oh, no," Joe said with a shake of his head. "We all got along really well."

"Thanks," I said and turned to Harry. "There's just no motive that I can find."

"Well, you didn't ask about the other carnies," Joe said.

"What other carnies?" I asked.

"See that big guy over there?" Joe pointed to a round, bald man who was maybe six feet tall.

"Yes," I said.

"That's Yeller the Clown," Joe said. "He runs a sideshow trailer that traveled together with Paul and Mike for years. Then something happened last year, and the two broke up. I heard they haven't spoken since."

"Sounds like I need to talk to Yeller," I said. "Thanks, Joe, nice to meet you."

"No problem," Joe said. "A friend of Harry's is a friend of mine. You really need to come out and try our adventure tours. Trust me, after one, you'll be addicted."

"Maybe sometime," I said. "When I'm not busy making fudge."

"Great job, Allie," Evan said. "This will make a great detective scene for our podcast."

"I wasn't trying to make a great scene," I said. Dwayne put his camera down. "Why don't you two go get some coffee and interview a few of the local celebrities?"

"Coffee does sound good," Dywane said.

"Fine," Evan said. "But let us know if you do any more sleuthing."

"You'll be the first ones I tell," I said with my fingers crossed behind my back.

"Come on, Allie," Harry said and put his hand on the small of my back. "Let's go talk to Yeller."

I blew out a deep breath. "Clowns are not really my thing."

"You don't like clowns?" His smile widened.

"They are a little creepy, don't you think?"

"Well, they're supposed to be—a little," Harry said. "I mean, they put on makeup and exaggerate their features: big feet, funny hair, ball nose."

"I thought they were supposed to be funny, and I just didn't get it," I said as we walked toward the man.

"Sure, some are jesters, but some are creepy on purpose," Harry said. "Hello, I'm Harry Winston. I own a bed-and-breakfast in town. This is—"

"Allie McMurphy," Yeller said. He seemed ordinary enough in his dark T-shirt and jeans. There wasn't a clown nose in sight.

"Yes," I said and bravely stuck out my hand. "Are you Yeller the Clown?"

He shook my hand, and his grin widened. "You know who I am. That's a real compliment. I'm a huge fan."

"Oh, no, I've never seen your act," I admitted quickly and withdrew my hand. "Joe told us who you were."

"Ah," he said, unfazed by my correction. "Well, now you know." He pulled a card out of his pocket and handed it to me. "Here's my card. I've got a website where you can see various photos and some video clips of my act."

"Oh, thank you. I'll check them out. Say, Joe told us that you used to travel with Mike and Paul when they took the haunted house around."

"Oh, yeah, that was rough," he said. "Hearing that someone had killed Mike. I mean, who does that?"

"That's what I'm trying to find out," I said.

"Right," he said. "Do you think I'm a killer?" His

eyebrows went up, and he pointed at his chest. "Because that would be a hoot."

"Oh, no," I said. "I don't know enough to think that. I was just wondering what happened. Why did you and the guys break up?"

"It was silly, really," Yeller said. "I mean, looking back on it and now knowing that Mike is dead. We fought over how many weeks we were going to be on the road. You see, I have a young family and Mike and Paul were bachelors, so they wanted to keep going, but I needed to be home more."

"Oh," I said. "That sounds reasonable."

"Do you think Paul will keep the haunted house?" he asked.

"I don't know." I shrugged. "I don't really know Paul that well. In fact, I haven't seen him since the day we found Mike."

"I haven't seen him either. He must be lying low," Yeller said thoughtfully.

"Where would he go to lie low?" I asked, more curious than anything.

"He has a bungalow in Harrisonville," Yeller said. "Why? Are you thinking of talking to him?"

"Mostly I was just curious," I said. "But you know what? I am worried he might be the killer's next victim."

"Why's that?" Yeller asked.

"Because he was Mike's partner, and he taught Hazel parkour," I said.

"And now both are dead," Yeller said and shook his head. "Yeah, it makes sense to suspect he'd be next."

"Rex told me they have cops going by to check on him regularly," I said.

"That's good," Harry agreed. "Let's stick to only two murders. I don't want anyone else hurt."

"Me, neither," I said.

"Listen, I see my friend Bruce," Yeller said. "So nice to meet you. You have my card. Talk soon?"

"Sure," I said and sipped my coffee.

"Are you glad you came?" Harry asked.

"Yeah, I haven't done one of these since I first got here. I need to do more."

"I'm going to go get a donut," he said. "Want anything?"

"No, the coffee is enough," I said.

He took a step, then looked back at me. "Feel free to mingle. Just watch out for Opal Sanders. She spits when she talks."

"Right, thanks," I said and grinned into my coffee. Maybe I should go out and pay Paul a visit. I wondered if any of the ladies from church ever took him food. I mean, he had just lost his best friend and partner.

"Allie." It was Suzanne McGee. Suzanne had asked me to join the Main Street Decorations Committee earlier this year. She also owned a flower shop on Market Street.

"Hi, Suzanne," I said. "I didn't know you came to these things."

"I've been a Chamber member for about five years now," she said. "But I don't always get a chance to mingle. I have been training a new florist for the summer, and she's watching the shop for me now."

"Oh, cool. I have a summer intern, too,"

"I heard your first pair of interns left you in a lurch," she said.

"They did, but for good reason." I sipped my

coffee. "Do you need any help putting out the late summer decorations?"

"I've been working up some things I thought would be pretty nice. Hanging baskets of mums and trailing greenery," she said. "We're changing out the decorations this weekend if you want to lend a hand."

"I'm always up to help out," I said. "I just don't want to find a weapon in the flowerpot again."

"Oh, I think that was a fluke," she said. "I've been doing the decorations for years and have never found anything like a gun. The worst I've ever found was some gum stuck on the bottom of the handing flowerpots."

"Yuck." I made a face. "Who does that?"

"Well, people will sometimes do weird stuff in a crowd," Suzanne said. "Thanks to you and Jenn for sending so many bridal parties and anniversary events to my shop? I love coming to the McMurphy and decorating it for events. Your rooftop deck has such a lovely view."

"I agree," I said. "I've had it closed for a few days out of respect for Hazel, but we start back with a wedding reception this weekend."

"Poor Hazel, what a terrible way to die," Suzanne said. "A fall like that. But I'm not surprised. She was getting a bit insane with her parkour."

"Did you know Hazel well?" I asked.

"She and I went to high school together," Suzanne said.

"Oh, I'm terribly sorry for your loss," I said quickly.

"We weren't that close. We've just both lived here our whole lives."

"I didn't really know Hazel." I sipped my coffee. "What was she like? Did she have a lot of friends?"

"She had a few friends." Suzanne shrugged. "But no one really close. She spent the last few years nursing her mom before the old girl died. Hazel was just saying that she had worked through most of her grief and was finally trying to find herself. Now this. Why parkour? Why rooftops? No one else was jumping around so far off the ground like that."

"I think she might have liked the fact that no one else was doing it," I said. "I'd forgotten about her mom."

"It was cancer," Suzanne said. "She fought hard and well, but ultimately she just got too tired."

"I thought you didn't know her that well," I said.

"My mom was a close friend of Hazel's mom." She shrugged. "They could never understand why Hazel and I weren't close, but she liked to jump around buildings, and I—well, I like to watch plants grow. We were just too different."

"Mackinac Island is so small. Did Hazel have any enemies?"

"Are you asking if I knew of anyone who would want Hazel dead?" Suzanne raised her right eyebrow. "No, Hazel was the most selfless person I've ever known. I don't think there's a reason why she died other than just being at the wrong place at the wrong time and slipping. She fell off your rooftop, didn't she?"

"Yes," I said. "We've had it inspected. There's no reason she should have slipped."

"Like I said, wrong place at the wrong time," Suzanne said.

If only that were true, I thought. It wasn't my place to mention the crime scene. Let Rex hold his press briefing and Liz report on it. I wondered again what the connection was between parkour and Hazel and Mike's deaths. Someone, somewhere, had to know what happened. It was just a matter of time before I figured out who that was.

Chapter 19

Scheduling the fudge-making demonstration for an hour later than usual actually had a better turnout.

"Wow," Madison said when the crowd finally thinned. "Maybe you should change your times to eleven a.m. permanently."

"After today I may consider it," I said as I washed my hands. "But it could just be a fluke."

"Then we have to test the theory," Madison decided. "Let's make it eleven for the rest of the week and see what the average crowd looks like."

"That's a good plan," I said and took off my chef's hat and coat. "I've got to take Mal for a walk. She was mad at me for going to the Chamber coffee without her."

"Have fun," Madison said. "I'll man the fort."

"Thanks." Lucky for me, the podcasters were upstairs editing their film. It gave us all a brief break.

It was sad that soon the summer season would be over and I would lose Madison to her school. It made me wonder if Hazel had ever had a chance to go to college or if she had simply spent time with her mother instead. The truth was, I didn't know much about Hazel except that she cared for her dying mom and worked for an insurance agency. Had she always worked there, or only after her mom died? Had she worked anywhere else? Maybe it was time I dug a little deeper. Frances might know something. I took down Mal's leash.

"Frances," I said as I hooked on Mal's harness first. "Were you teaching when Hazel was in school?"

"The year she graduated was my last year," Frances said. "Why?"

"Did you know about her mom?"

"Of course, the community rallied around Rose. She lived three years longer than the doctors thought. So, there was something to all the dinners we brought her and the prayers we said for her."

I snapped the leash to the harness. "Did Hazel want to go to college?"

"She always had plans to become a nurse," Frances said. "Hazel used to love to hang around the clinic and pretend she was a helper. In fact, she was a candy striper her junior and senior years of high school."

"Her mom died a few years ago?"

"Five years," Frances said. "We all thought Hazel would take the insurance money and go to college, but she didn't. She just stayed on the island. For the first year, she didn't even work. I think she was trying to figure out what she wanted to do with the rest of her life."

"And she didn't have a boyfriend?" I asked as

Mal danced around me, impatient to go for the walk.

"She was too busy once her mom got sick, and after Rose died, most of the men on the island were already married. She dated a fudgie every now and then, but nothing really stuck."

"I understand she worked for an insurance guy in St. Ignace. Did she live off the island?" I asked. "I didn't think so since she was around a lot."

"Yes, she worked in St. Ignace," Frances said. "But she still lived in her mother's family home."

"What happens to the home now?"

Ruff. I looked down to see Mal telling me I was being too slow to go.

Frances looked up from her computer. "I'm sure a relative will take it over, or maybe they will sell it and take the money. It happens sometimes when people have small families and there's no one left to inherit."

"She was so young, I bet she never thought about not having a family and such," I said, and I felt a hint of sadness. "Okay, enough melancholy," I said. "Come on, Mal, let's go for that walk."

Mal jumped up against my leg and gave a joyful bark. As if to say, *finally!*

"Have a good walk," Frances said. "Bring back some more coffee from Doud's if you can. We're running low, and I still have to make an inventory order."

Mal and I left out the back so she could go to her favorite spot. While Mal sniffed around, I wondered if anyone on St. Ignace might have had a reason to kill Hazel. If they did, then her death was most likely not connected to Mike's after all.

I felt stuck on this one.

Maybe I should let go of Hazel's death for a moment and think about Mike's. I decided that Mal and I would walk past Paul's house, and I could talk to him. He might know more than he thought. Maybe I could trigger something out of him. Mal and I took off down the alley, and when we hit the road we ran into Irene.

"Hello, Allie. Hi, Mal," she said as she power-walked toward us. "Nice day out, isn't it?"

"It sure is," I said.

"I see you aren't playing into Christine's game of 'who's side are you on'," Irene said. "I half-expected you to put up signs to counter her signs."

"I want people to know I didn't cheat, and neither did Carol," I said. "But I'm not going to make it another contest. Christine has lived on the island her whole life, and that's a battle I would lose."

"Not if you had Carol on your side," Irene said. "Carol's got more friends on the island."

"I don't want Carol to play that game, either. I believe if we just ignore her, then she will look like the poor loser she is."

"Okay," Irene said with a shrug. "But you have to know that nearly ninety percent of the businesses on Main Street have a *Team Christine* poster in the window."

"What? Ninety percent? Why? Is she paying them?"

Irene laughed. "I wouldn't put it past her. See you." She waved and power-walked away.

"Come on, Mal, let's take our walk," I said and headed down the sidewalk next to the big park. The marina was full today of people laughing and chatting. Then I remembered there was a boating event going on this weekend. On Mackinac it was a rare summer weekend that we didn't have anything going on. Boaters had already begun to arrive.

"Hi, Allie," Mrs. Peterson said as she passed us. "Out for a stroll?"

"Taking Mal on her walk," I said.

"I wondered if you were going to protest all the *Team Christine* signs," she said with a shake of her head. "She seems intent on burying you with flyers."

"I'm not trying to win a popularity contest," I said with a faint smile. "I'm sure she would beat me."

"Is it true that you paid off that judge?" she asked.

"What? No—I don't have enough money to pay off a judge," I explained. "I just finished remodeling the McMurphy twice in as many years."

"That's what I told the sewing circle," she said with a nod. "Christine comes from old money. If anyone was paying off judges, it would be her."

"Thanks for the vote of confidence," I said.

"Anytime, dear, anytime. Ta-ta!"

Mal and I went on our way past St. Anne's Church and up the street. It was the long way to Harrisonville, where Mike lived, but I didn't mind the walk. I really needed to stretch my legs, and Mal loved the longer walks.

We passed Jenn's house, and I noticed the fresh paint on the exterior. She and her husband had been working hard on their remodel with the baby on the way. Shane came walking around the corner. "Allie, what brings you out this way?"

We met him at the gate to the short picket fence that enclosed the front yard. "Mal and I are going for a longer walk," I said as I studied him. He wore coveralls that were splashed with drips of pale yellow. "Did you just finish painting? It looks great."

"Thanks," he said and pushed up his bottle-round glasses. "Jenn picked the yellow with green shutters. I think it looks great."

"It's nice and pale, almost cream," I said. "It's a really good color. How's the interior going? Jenn hasn't let me back inside. She says you want to have a housewarming and reveal next month. Will it be done already?"

"Ever since we found out Jenn was pregnant, we've been working overtime on getting the place ready for a family," he said.

"How are you doing that and working two crime scenes?"

"The county hired me an assistant," he said. "It's actually an intern, but four hands are better than two."

"Cool, anyone I've met?"

He blinked at me from behind his thick glasses. "I doubt it. They are fresh out of school and don't live on the island."

"Okay, well, maybe I'll get to meet him when you have your official housewarming."

"Her," he corrected me. "Her name is Shannon Stone."

"Wow, good for her," I said. "Is Jenn home?"

"No, she's out with some last-minute arrangements for this weekend's wedding."

"Oh, right, the Goodmans," I said. "They are getting married at Saint Anne's and have rented the yacht club for the reception."

"This one is a pretty big deal for her," he said. "They are from Chicago and part of the 'in' crowd."

"She's doing so well with her business," I said. "She's a natural."

"For sure," he said.

"Well, we must keep walking," I said, "or it's not a walk."

"Take care," he said.

Mal and I walked up the hill to Harrisonville. Paul's cottage was on our end of the small town, so it was easy to get there. He lived in a small two-story home painted brown with green shutters. The curtains were closed as if to keep out the light and anyone who might want to enter.

Mal and I went up to the door anyway. I rang the doorbell, then knocked. I could hear someone bumbling around inside. "Hello?" I called. "Paul?"

I knocked again, and the door popped open. It was dark inside and suddenly quiet. "Hello? Paul?" I called again. "It's Allie McMurphy. We met at the haunted house."

There was no sound. I stepped inside, and Mal sniffed around the old wood floors. I didn't like the silence. I got out my phone. "Paul," I called again. "Your front door was open. Are you okay? Should I call for help?"

Mal dragged me through the curtain-darkened living room toward the kitchen. Where we found a man sprawled out on the floor.

"Paul?" I rushed to him and checked. He had a pulse but was not reacting. I dialed nine-one-one.

"Nine-one-one, wha—"

I cut Charlene off. "Charlene, it's Allie McMurphy. I'm at Paul Patterson's home. He's unconscious but breathing."

"Oh, dear," she said. "I'll get help on the way. What's the address again?"

I gave her his address. "I hope they get here quick!"

"They will be as quick as possible. Do you know what happened? Is anyone else there with you?"

"I have no idea," I said. I had let go of Mal's leash, and she was sniffing through the kitchen. "Nothing seems to be out of place."

Then I noticed the kitchen door was ajar. "Wait, it looks like whoever was here left out the back door." I got up and moved through the kitchen. I pulled the curtain back to see if I could see anyone, but the yard looked empty.

"Allie?" Charlene asked.

"I don't see anyone," I said. Then I heard a noise like someone rushing out the front door. I hurried across the kitchen and reached Paul just as the front door slammed shut. Mal barked and ran to the door. I headed toward the door when Paul groaned.

I stopped and went back to attend to him. "Paul, are you okay?"

He groaned again and tried to say something. I leaned down and got closer, hoping to understand.

"What did you say?"

He mumbled something, but I couldn't tell what.

"Paul?" I shook his shoulder gently, and he moaned again. "What is it? Who did this?"

"Get," he whispered.

"Get who?" I asked. "Get what?"

He moaned and lost consciousness again. Just then, Mal barked, and there was a knock at the door. I went to the door and opened it.

"Oh, Rex, George," I said and stepped aside. "Come in. Paul is this way."

They rushed over to him.

"Thanks, Charlene," I said into my phone and pressed *End*. The new female EMT came in with a gurney and followed George.

"He's through there," I said, pointing to the small hall between the living room and the kitchen.

Rex checked Paul and then came over to us, letting the EMTs work. "Allie, what happened?"

"I don't know," I said honestly. "I stopped by to check on Paul because I was worried he'd be the next victim."

"I told you we have patrols stopping by regularly," he said with a stern look on his face. "Was anyone else in the house?"

"I didn't see anyone," I said. "I noticed the kitchen door was open, and I didn't want to touch the crime scene, so I just pulled back the curtain to look outside. Then Mal barked, and I heard footsteps and the front door slammed. I was going to see who was here, but then Paul mumbled something."

"Someone was here, then," he repeated. "You could have been seriously hurt."

"I had Mal with me, and we're okay," I said.

Rex's frown deepened. "What made you come into the house in the first place?"

"When I knocked the second time, the door popped open," I said. "I thought I'd heard someone bumbling around inside, so I stepped in and called out, expecting Paul to pop out and say something. But we found him lying there."

Mal sat next to my feet and barked as if to agree with me.

"You said Paul said something?" Rex pushed on.

"Yes, I couldn't make it out, but he said the word 'get,' I think."

"Maybe he was trying to tell you to get out," Rex said with a raised eyebrow.

I shook my head and put my hands on my hips. "I'm sure he was asking me to get help."

Just then, George and the second EMT rolled the gurney past us with Paul lying on it. "Is he going to be okay?"

"He's got a concussion," George said. "And a nice gash on his head. We need to take him to the clinic and do some X-rays. He may need to go to the mainland."

"How terrible," I said.

As they wheeled Paul out, Shane showed up with his crime scene kit on the back of his bike. "Allie," he greeted me as he walked up the porch and into the living room, kit in hand. "I thought you were out walking Mal. Aren't you a little far from my house?"

"Hi, Shane," I said. "Mal wanted a nice long walk and I thought I'd stop by and check on Paul."

"Sounds like it's a good thing you did," he said. "What have you touched?"

I walked him through what Mal and I had disturbed in the house—which wasn't much. "I've pretty much got it down to touch as little as possible. I only moved the curtain to see if I could spot anyone outside the kitchen window."

"Got it," he said and went to work.

"Let's get outside." Rex waved his hand toward the door.

Mal and I went out onto the porch, and Rex followed. "I just had a feeling that Paul would be the next victim," I said.

"I know, you told me," he said. "But I told you we had it covered."

"Apparently not," I said as the ambulance started up its sirens and rolled down the street.

"To be fair, you probably saved his life," Rex admitted. "But you could have just as probably lost your own."

"I'm careful," I countered.

"Sure, that's why you've been kidnapped and nearly killed so many times. You'd think you would learn."

"'Learn'?" I quipped. "What's to learn when I always come out alive?"

"Someday," he warned, "you won't be so lucky. It only takes one time."

"Then Mal and I will just make sure that someday never comes."

Chapter 20

I spent the rest of the afternoon at home baking and thinking about who might have wanted to hurt Paul. Later that evening, I went to visit Paul at the clinic. The podcasters followed me there, but they weren't allowed inside the clinic for privacy reasons. I only got in because the nurse on duty knew me well and had checked first with Paul before she let me in. Luckily Paul was conscious. They were keeping him overnight for observation, but he wasn't in bad enough shape to go to the mainland.

"Knock, knock," I said as I entered the curtained-off area where Paul rested in the bed. He had a big bandage on his head, and his eyes had blackened.

"Come in," he said. "I heard you were the one who saved me."

"I didn't do anything but check on you," I said. "But I brought you some homemade cookies." I lifted the plate in my hands. "They're peanut butter."

"My favorite," he said and took a cookie off the plate. I put the plate on the bedside table. "These are good. Thanks."

"I'm lucky I know the nurse and she let me bring in food. How are you feeling?" I asked.

"That seems to be the question of the day. They come in hourly to check my pupils and ensure I haven't died or anything."

"That's good," I said. "I've had a concussion and know the drill. It's annoying but really for the best."

"Why were you checking on me?" he asked as he lay back down on his tilted bed. His gaze studied me.

"I just hadn't had time to ask how you were doing with Mike's death and everything," I said. "I thought I'd walk Mal by your place and say hi."

"Right," he said and blew out a breath. "You must be investigating."

"Not investigating formally," I said. "I just want to get to the bottom of what happened to Hazel. I know she took parkour lessons from Mike, and I thought maybe you would know something. But really, I was mostly worried about you because of your connection to both victims."

"Oh, so you must be the one who had the police come by my place daily," he surmised.

"Yes, for your safety," I admitted. "They didn't bother you too much, did they?"

"No, mostly they just walked down the block and back. But fat lot of good it did me since I'm here now."

I sat down in the chair beside the bed. "Do you have any idea who attacked you?"

"Not a clue," he said. "But the doc said it was because of head trauma and I should remember in a day or two."

"I'm surprised they don't have an officer assigned to watch over you while you are in here and waiting to remember."

He waved his hand. "I said no to that business. This is Mackinac. It's not as if someone is going to get past the nurses."

"Hmm," I said. "I'd worry about that."

There was a knock at the window, and we both startled. I got up and looked out. It was Evan and Dwayne. Evan made motions asking me to open the window. I shook my head and tried to wave him away.

"Who is that?" Paul asked.

"It's a couple of podcasters who are trailing me," I said. "They do this thing where they pop in and trail a chef for a day and record their life. They were pretty upset when I ditched them and then found you. I think they are going to be camping out at my door from now on."

"Oh, wait, you aren't talking about Evan Tailor, are you?"

"Yes." I tried hard not to roll my eyes. "Do you know him?"

"I love his videos. You should have seen how it went with Gordon Ramsay." He straightened up in his bed. "What do they want?"

"They want me to open the window so they can record our visit. You see, the nurse won't let them in."

He chuckled, then groaned at the pain it caused. "I told you I was safe and didn't need a police officer. Open the window for them."

"What? No," I said. "You deserve your privacy."

"I don't mind being part of their show," he said. "Go ahead and open the window."

"I'd better ask the nurse," I said. "She might kick me out and not let me back in if I open the window."

"Open it anyway. I'm only here for twenty-four hours," he said. "Doc said I could go home once they are sure there's no concussion issues."

"I don't know . . ." I hedged.

He adjusted to sit up even straighter. "I'll tell her I opened the window and you told me not to," he said.

"Fine." Against my better judgment, I opened the window.

Dwayne stuck his camera inside, and Evan spoke. "We're outside the clinic with Allie McMurphy as she visits the victim of the latest attack from the murderer."

"We haven't connected Paul's attack to the murders," I said.

"Hi." Paul waved, and Dwayne moved the camera to take in the picture of him in his hospital bed.

"That's Paul Patterson," Evan said. "The latest victim on Mackinac Island. Paul, how are you connected to the murdered man, Mike Sanders?"

"Mike was my best friend and business partner," Paul said.

"Do you know who attacked you?" Evan asked.

"He doesn't remember due to the head wound," I said.

"Yeah, the doc said it could be days before I remember, if I remember at all. But I wanted to say, this gal here, Allie, she saved me."

"Once again, Allie McMurphy stumbled onto the scene of the attack," Evan said. "Allie, you told us earlier that you were worried for Paul. How did you know this was going to happen?"

"I didn't know," I said.

"But you went over to see Paul and found him unconscious on the floor."

"I did," I said.

"Did you see who attacked him?" Evan asked.

"No," I said. "I didn't. Mal alerted me that there was someone in the house, but they left before we could discover who it was."

"Once again, dear listeners, pup Mal helps to sniff out a perp."

"A 'perp'? Really?" I put my hands on my hips.

"That's the term," Paul said. "The perpetrator broke into my home and hit me hard on the back of the head. I have seventeen stitches. He might have killed me if it hadn't been for Allie."

"'He'?" Evan jumped on the word. "The perp was a man?"

Paul frowned and rubbed his chin. "I can't really say," he said. "I've got no memory. 'He' is just something I say when I don't know the gender. You know, like they taught us in school."

"They don't teach it that way anymore," I said. "The right term is 'they' unless you know the gender preference."

"Whatever," Paul said. "I was there when Mike was murdered."

"You were?" Evan asked as the camera zoomed in. "Did you see him get murdered? Does the killer know you were there?"

"I was shoved from behind into a jail section of the haunted house," Paul said. "They locked me in quick as can be. By the time I turned around, all I saw was a figure in a dark hoodie with a knife in their hand moving quickly toward where Mike stood."

"You told me a murderer was in the building," I said with a frown. "How did you know the person in the hoodie was going to murder Mike?"

"I didn't know," Paul said. "I figured since I was stuck in the jail display, I might as well act the part."

"You mean telling me there was a murderer loose was just a coincidence?" I asked and put my hands on my hips. "That seems a bit odd."

"Allie," Evan said. "Do you think Paul knows more than he's telling?" He pushed the microphone toward me as the camera turned.

"I don't know anything," Paul protested, then clutched his head and groaned. "It really was a co-incidence. Mike's been my best friend since preschool. Frankly, I just don't know what to do," Paul said. "But if I knew anything, I would tell the police."

"You two never argued?" Evan asked.

Paul studied the journalists in the window and chuckled nervously. "Does that matter?"

"No, no," Evan said. "I was just wondering if you and Mike ever had any disagreements. Did you know of anyone who might want to kill him? Or you?"

"No one," Paul said, as he shook his head then winced. "We've been doing the same thing for years. First the fair circuit, then the adventure groups, and finally the parkour classes. I wanted to help earn some extra money for my mom. The winters are getting harder and harder for her, so I thought I'd get her a little trailer in Florida so she could snow-bird."

"That's very sweet," I said. "Did you hear about Hazel?"

"That she fell off your roof?" Paul asked. "Yeah, I heard. I told her she needed to stop jumping rooflines, but she wouldn't listen. She said the best gossip could be heard on the rooftops."

"What does that mean, I wonder." I studied him.

He shrugged. "I never did it, parkour on rooftops, so I have no idea what she was talking about."

"But Mike was training her, right?"

"Yes, she was Mike's star pupil," he said, then snagged another cookie off the plate and turned to the podcasters. "You guys are missing out if you've never had one of these cookies."

I looked at the journalists. "I'll make you some tomorrow."

"That would be great," Dwayne said. "I'm a little peckish."

"Let's get back to Hazel," Evan said. "How good was she at parkour?"

"She could work out the swiftest way over any number of obstacles. She had amazing balance and coordination," Paul said. "She told me she'd been rock climbing since she was young and that parkour used a lot of the same skills. To balance your body and work out patterns where others may not see them."

"She was good at working out patterns. Maybe she worked out who killed Mike and the killer got her," I said, thoughtfully tapping my chin.

"If she did, she didn't tell anyone," Paul said.

"Are you sure you don't remember what happened at your house? How you got that concussion?"

"It's all a bit blurry," he said and rubbed his head, then winced again.

"It's okay," I said. "I was just curious. Maybe you'll be able to remember some parts in the next few days. Like we said, it comes back that way. Bits and pieces. I'm glad you are okay. I told Rex I was worried you would be next on the killer's list. He'd promised me to have patrols go by every hour or so. I don't know how this could have happened."

"I don't know how it happened, either," Paul said and drew his eyebrows together. "But thank you for thinking of me."

"Allie," Evan said, "do you really think it was the killer who hit Paul on the head?"

"I think there's a good chance it was the killer," I said, then reached out and squeezed Paul's hand. "I'm also concerned they will come back once they find out you survived."

"Like I said, I'll be extra careful," Paul said and patted my hand. "I'm fine, really."

"Just be sure and tell Rex when you remember what happened, okay? When I left your house, Shane had set up the crime scene grid and was working through it. If the perpetrator left any trace, he'll find it."

"Thanks," he said. "And thank you again for the cookies."

"Can we interview you when you get out of the clinic?" Evan asked.

"Sure thing," Paul said and laid back his head. "I'm pretty tired."

"I'm going to close the window now," I said and

pushed the journalists out. "Meet you guys around front." I pulled the window down and locked it. "Thanks for talking to them," I said to Paul. "You didn't have to interact with them, you know."

"I know," he said. "But I like the show."

"I should be going." I walked toward the door, then turned and faced him. "Just one thing."

"What's that?" he asked.

"Who inherits your businesses now that Mike's dead?"

He frowned at me. "I do, I guess," he said. "We had an LLC and were partners. I guess as the surviving partner, it's all mine."

"And who gets it if *you're* dead?" I asked.

"That would be my mom," Paul said. "She gave Mike and me seed money to buy the haunted house and get started in our other businesses."

"Does your mom live on the island now?" I asked. "You said you wanted her to be a snowbird."

"She loves it here," he said. "But like I said, the winters are hard on her. Harder than she'll admit. I was hoping the outcome at the fair would have convinced her to move south."

"Was your mother a participant at the fair?"

"Yes," he said. "In fact, you beat her at the candy Best in Show."

"Oh, I don't remember a Mrs. Patterson in the contest," I said.

"Oh, no, my mom remarried when I was a very little boy," Paul said. "I just never took her new name. My dad died of a heart attack in his thirties."

"Who's your mom?" I asked, curiosity pulling at me.

"You know her," he said. "She's Christine Keller,

and boy, would she be mad if she knew I was enjoying your cookies." He snagged another and took a bite.

"Christine is your mom?" I felt stunned. How did I not know this?

"The one and only," he said. "Thanks for the cookies."

"You're welcome," I said. "Get well soon."

"Oh, I'm sure I will," he said.

I turned and left the curtained room quickly before I ran into Christine. That would be an encounter I wouldn't want to have. Especially not with the podcasters hanging around.

No-Bake Fudge Bites

Ingredients
   1 cup chopped dates
   1 cup oatmeal
   1 cup shredded coconut (unsweetened is
      best)
   ½ cup nut butter (almond, peanut,
      cashew, your choice)
   ¼ cup honey
   ½ teaspoon cinnamon
   1 teaspoon vanilla
   1 cup dark chocolate chips
   Powdered sugar, coconut, cocoa, or your
      choice of toppings to roll them in.

Directions
   In food processor, combine dates, oatmeal,
and coconut. Process until finely chopped.
Add nut butter, honey, cinnamon, and vanilla. Pulse until well combined. Finally add
chocolate chips and pulse lightly until incorporated. Roll into 1-inch balls. If you wish to
coat them with a topping or several, place
topping into shallow bowl. Roll balls until
coated, place on parchment paper, and refrigerate until set. Makes approximately 28.
Enjoy!

Chapter 21

The next morning, I concentrated on fudge making and my demonstrations. It was Saturday, and the hotel was full of guests due to the Goodman wedding. Jenn was hopping busy, and for the first time I was glad the reception wasn't at the McMurphy.

Unfortunately, my podcaster friends shadowed my every move. Dwayne wasn't even trying to take any more video as they were more interested in how I was going to solve the case—if I was going to solve the case.

Frankly, I ignored them as best I could. I was hoping they would become bored and leave to do some investigating on their own.

Which wasn't a bad idea.

I called Carol while Madison waited on a few customers who wandered in.

"Hello?" Carol said.

"Hi Carol, it's Allie."

"Oh, hi, Allie. How's Paul? Any further breaks

in the case? Do you think his attack was linked to the murders?"

"Listen, Carol, I don't really have time to talk," I said. "I was wondering if you could get the book club together this evening."

"Oh, of course," she said. "We would all love to hear your new theories."

"I don't want to meet for me," I said. "I was hoping you and the ladies could go over your theories with Evan and Dwayne. Maybe give them some interviews for their podcast?"

"Those lovely young men? Of course, we'd love to," Carol said. "What say we meet at seven at my house? I'll have the murder board set up."

"That's great!" I glanced over at the two men as they lounged near the coffee bar doing something on their phones.

"Will you be there?" Carol asked. "Or is this just the book club?"

"I'm hoping just the book club," I said. "I need a break. They are following my every move."

"Well, I don't blame them, seeing as how you slipped away to talk to Paul and then discovered he'd been attacked. I can only imagine how exciting that would have been for their video."

"Don't you start, too," I said and held back my sigh. "Can I tell them to meet the book club at seven?"

"Yes, dear," Carol said. "We'll all be ready for our close-ups."

"Thank you," I said and hit *End* on my phone.

"Trying to ditch your entourage?" Madison asked with a smile.

"Oh. My. Goodness. They are making me crazy," I said. "I need to solve these murders fast, or I just might go nuts."

"What are you going to do while they go to the book club?" she asked.

"Breathe," I said. "Maybe get some book work done in the office."

"I thought Frances handled the books," Madison said as she handed the last customer their box of fudge.

"She does," I said, "but there are still things I need to oversee, like inventory and signing paychecks."

"Oh," she said, her eyes growing wide. "Yes, signing paychecks is important."

"I'm going to go out and tell Evan about the book club tonight," I said and glanced at my phone. "Are you good to handle the last hour by yourself?"

"Sure," Madison said with a twinkle in her eye. "I don't want to come between you and my paycheck."

I headed out of the glass-walled fudge shop, and Evan and Dwayne jumped right up the minute I entered the lobby. I took in a deep breath and blew it out. "I know I have to be boring you."

"A good photojournalist knows it takes a lot of boring hours to get the right shot," Dwayne said.

"I promise, I won't do anything but walk my dog today," I said and took off my chef's hat.

"And that's how you got us last time," Evan said.

"Well, I'll let you go on our walk with us this evening," I began. "But I wanted to let you know that the book club is meeting at seven tonight and is really eager to talk about their part of the investigation. Carol will have an updated murder board, as well."

"Are you going to be there?" Evan asked, his eyes narrowing in suspicion.

"I plan on getting some office work done tonight," I said. "You're welcome to stay here and watch me do paperwork if you prefer."

The two men looked at each other.

"The book club will talk with us about the investigation?" Evan asked.

"That's right," I said. "Carol may even have a new clue or two."

"I say we go to the book club meeting," Dwayne said. "It would be great to get some 'B' roll of the senior ladies helping to solve the murder." He glanced at me. "They might even have some dirt on Allie if we ask the right questions."

"Oh, I'm sure they'll have plenty to say," I said. "The seniors know pretty much everything that goes on around here."

"Evan?" Dwayne asked.

"Fine, but only if Allie goes," Evan said.

"I have some things to do in the office tonight," I explained again.

Evan shrugged. "Then we'll stay in and keep an eye on you."

"But the book club ladies would be great to interview," I pushed back.

"And you might decide to go after the killer," Evan said.

"The killer is probably lying low right now," I said. "After all, I nearly caught them at Paul's."

"Or the killer might still try to kill Paul. Maybe we should check in on him again tonight," Dwayne said. "Come on, Allie, you know you want to do it."

"You won't leave unless I promise to go to the book club?" I asked.

"You have to promise," Evan said. "I do believe you are a woman of her word. Aren't you?"

"Fine," I said with a sigh. "But you two can go first. I'll come after my book work is done."

"Great!" Evan agreed. "In the meantime, we'll just make sure you don't decide to go sleuthing without us."

"You know, you don't have to keep hanging around," I said and unbuttoned my chef's coat. "You have got to be starving. You haven't moved all day from the lobby."

"We had sandwiches delivered," Evan said. "Your friend Jenn really helped us out."

Great, I thought. "Okay, then I'm going to talk to Frances and go up and take a shower, change, and walk my dog. You two do what you want." I turned on my heel and tried to ignore the fact that they followed close behind.

The two men followed me everywhere I went the rest of the day. The only peace I got was when I shut the door to my apartment and even then, they stationed one on my front door and one at the back.

Mal didn't seem to mind them walking with us. I swear, she pranced along even sassier than ever. We ran into Mr. Beecher on his twice-daily walk.

"Allie, are you okay?" he asked as Mal jumped up and turned for her treat.

"Yes, why?" I asked me.

He took a small treat out of his waistcoat pocket and gave it to Mal. "You seem to be followed by a couple of young men."

"Ah, yes, let me introduce you," I said. "Mr. Beecher, this is Evan Tailor and Dwayne Finch. They are documenting my investigation. Gentlemen, this is Mr. Beecher."

"How do you do?" Mr. Beecher asked. He seemed amused at my predicament. "Has Allie been behaving herself?"

"Yes, I have," I said. "And I've been quite boring."

"Except when she sneaks off and finds men who've been attacked and barely misses discovering the murderer," Evan said. "We're sticking with her like glue today."

"You have to admit, that's one way of keeping you safe," Mr. Beecher said to me.

"Not you, too." I frowned. "I'm perfectly fine without an escort."

"I'm sure Mal here will take good care of you." Mr. Beecher gave Mal a scratch behind her ears. "Gentlemen, enjoy your walk. I understand the book club is meeting at seven."

"Yes, and these two are going," I said, waving toward the cameraman and his documentarian.

"Without you?" Mr. Beecher raised an eyebrow.

"I've got some book work to get done, but I promised I'd go straight to the book club once I finished. In the meantime, they can get some good interviews from the ladies for their podcast episode."

"I'm sure the ladies will have fun telling you all about Allie," Mr. Beecher said. "Have a good evening." He walked down the alley, and I took Mal up the street toward Market Street, then down to the water's edge and back. I was trying to get my steps in for the day, and Mal loved to sniff things out.

The men were quiet behind me, and I imagined they had to be really bored. Maybe they would give up once they saw that my life was rather ordinary.

"Oh, Allie, yoo-hoo!" I turned and saw Mayor Boatman. "Allie, I see you still have your gentlemen friends. Have you taken them to see the sights? The fort is magnificent, and Arch Rock, and well, certainly you've given them a carriage ride around the island."

"I haven't had time," I said. "But maybe *you* could show them around."

Never one to miss a cue, Mayor Boatman put her arms through theirs. "Gentlemen, you really must take in all the sights of Mackinac if you're going to tell the real story of our beautiful island."

"But we really need to stick with Allie," Evan said as politely as possible.

"Nonsense, she's just headed home, aren't you?"

"Yes," I said and tried not to get my hopes up. "I am, in fact, headed home to do some paperwork before the book club this evening."

"See, nothing for you to report. Now, gentlemen, let me show you around. I'll even spring for a nice dinner. What do you say?"

I turned and kept walking toward the McMurphy. I knew Mayor Boatman wasn't going to take no for an answer. I might have even power-walked back.

After all, a girl's got to do what a girl's got to do to get some peace in her life. Not that it lasted long. As Mal and I turned the corner toward the McMurphy, I saw Christine power-walking straight toward me, and she was loaded for bear, as Grammy Alice used to say.

What in the world had I done now?

Chapter 22

"Allie McMurphy!" Christine called my name. I was tempted to smart off and answer like Papa Liam. *That's my name, don't wear it out!* But I bit my tongue instead. Mal sat down beside me and tilted her head at the woman bearing down upon us.

"What were you doing in my son's home?" she screeched.

"I imagine he told you why I was there," I said calmly. "You're welcome, by the way."

"For what?"

"For calling the police and scaring off Paul's attacker," I said. Mal looked from me to the fuming older woman.

"I want to know what business it is of yours going to see Paul in the first place?" she said. "You and your silly investigations. For all I know, you went there to accuse him of murdering his best friend."

"What?" I asked. "No, I just had questions."

"Questions you should keep to yourself," she said. "Really bad things happen wherever you go."

"I'm the one who asked the police to check on Paul regularly." I carefully crossed my arms. "Aren't you worried that someone is killing everyone around Paul? I would think you of all people would be afraid for your son."

"Of course, I want my son to be safe," she said. "That's why I want you away from him. I won't let you bring your investigations and shenanigans into my son's life. He's all I've got now, and I won't let you take that from me, as well."

I paused for a moment and took a deep breath. "You must be incredibly worried."

"Of course, I am. That's why I'm here asking you—"

"Telling me," I corrected her.

"To stay away from my son. You've done enough harm stealing my candy Best in Show ribbon."

"I didn't steal . . . look," I said, trying to calm her down a bit. "I promise I won't see Paul again unless he asks me to. Does that help you to feel better?"

"What would make me feel better is for you to leave my home and my things alone."

"I'm sorry?" I said. "But I've never been to your home or touched your things."

"I mean this island and my activities. You have insinuated yourself too far into the senior community and even the Chamber of Commerce. You should go back to Chicago or Detroit or wherever it is you came from and leave us alone."

Now I tilted my head. "Why are you so intimidated by me?"

"I'm not intimidated. I'm . . . disgusted."

"And angry from the sounds of it," I said.

"Don't you try and tell me how I feel," she said. "Just stay away from me and mine. Or else!"

"Or else what?" I asked. Now might have been a good time to have had the video guys with me. It wasn't every day I was threatened by a local.

"Trust me, you don't want to know what my 'or else' is," she said. "Good day!" With that, she tossed her nose up in the air and stormed off down the street.

I looked at Mal. She jumped up against me as if to say that everything was going to be okay. I picked her up and hugged her. "Well, that was interesting. I hope she gets over her mad. Don't you?"

Mal licked my cheek in response, and I headed toward the McMurphy. Clearly, I wasn't going to change my life to make someone else happy. At least that wasn't a lesson I had to learn. It was too bad Christine was as old as she was and hadn't learned it yet.

Evan and Dwayne did not return to follow me. Thank goodness for a mayor who was all about promoting our beautiful island. I kept my word and had a nice, quiet dinner and enjoyed my pets before I headed to the office to work.

Even though it was Saturday night, I was alone. Rex was working overtime on the murders and Paul's assault. He texted me that he was thinking of me and wished we could get together soon. I understood. The last thing I wanted was to try to have a nice date with my boyfriend while being followed around by my entourage. Or worse, stalked by an angry Christine.

I tried to put it all out of my mind as I worked on inventory and other paperwork—until I finally looked up and saw it was nearly 9 p.m. I had promised to make an appearance at the book club, and I meant to keep that promise.

Closing up my office, I checked on my pets before heading out into the cool night.

Mackinac was pretty quiet at night, with only a few people staying on the island proper. There were kids playing in the yards and firepits going in front of the hotels with lawns so that marshmallows could be roasted.

I made my way to Carol's house, worried I was later than I'd promised and that the seniors might have said things I didn't want the general public to know about.

I reached Carol's house and knocked. The porch light was on, but it seemed quiet inside. Frowning, I knocked again and rang the doorbell. No one answered. I tried the door, and it swung open into the semi-lit living room.

"Hello? Carol?" I called. I reached for the light switch and turned on the main lights. The living room was a mess, as if someone had been looking for something. The murder board was on the floor, and it looked like someone had stomped it with their foot.

"Hello?" I was getting nervous. I checked around, but there was no one in the living area. I tried the kitchen. There were dirty cups and tea service on the counters. A cake had been cut into, which meant the ladies must have been here. I felt the teapot. It was still warm.

What in the world had happened?

I grabbed my phone and called Irma Goose-man.

"Hello?" She answered her phone.

"Hi, Irma, it's Allie McMurphy."

"Oh, hi, Allie, dear, how are you?"

"Did you come to the book club tonight?" I asked.

"Sure did," she said. "It was so much fun talking to those nice young gentlemen and being interviewed. I might even have a career in pictures. You're never too old to live a dream."

"Irma, who all came to the book club?" I asked as I looked around at the couch cushions askew and the lampshades wonky.

"Why, everyone, dear," she said.

"And did you leave early?" I asked.

"No, no, we pretty much all left at the same time," Irma said. "Carol said she had a theory she wanted to share with those two nice boys and scooted us all out."

"What time was that?" I asked and looked at my watch. It was only 9:15 p.m.

"Oh, I would say about eight thirty or nine," she said. "I got home a few moments ago and have only had time to get ready for bed. I'm sorry you missed it, dear. It was so much fun."

"I bet it was," I said. "Thanks, Irma. Oh, and everyone left then, together?"

"Everyone but the two gentlemen and Carol, of course. She lives there, you know."

"Yes, I know," I said. "Before I go, are you sure Carol didn't say she was going to take the two men somewhere?"

"Oh, no, it's after nine," Irma said. "Where would Carol take them?"

"Okay, Irma," I said. "Thanks."

"You're welcome, dear. Good night."

"Good night," I said and hit *End* on my phone. I sighed and studied the disarray around me. It wasn't like Carol to leave her door open or leave her home looking like this. Something was very wrong. I dialed Rex.

"Manning," he answered in a distracted tone.

"Rex, are you busy?"

"What's wrong, Allie?" He became more alert-sounding. "You don't call when you know I'm working unless something bad has happened. Are you safe?"

"I think I'm safe," I said, looking around. Just to be sure I stepped over to the door and put my back to the wall. That way I could run fast if someone came up and tried to hurt me. "I'm at Carol's. I was supposed to meet her and the two podcast guys here with the book club, but the door wasn't locked."

"You went in," he continued as I took a breath and tried to gather my thoughts.

"Yes, and no one is here. The place looks like it's been ransacked, though. I called Irma and she said the book club ended and everyone went home between eight thirty and nine, so I must have just missed what happened. Anyway, Carol and the podcasters are missing."

"I'm on my way," he said. "Stay on the phone with me."

"I will."

"Why didn't you call nine-one-one?"

"I wasn't exactly sure anything had happened. I mean, you know Carol, she keeps a very tidy house and would definitely not have it look such a mess with the book club ladies coming over. I figured it wasn't a nine-one-one emergency, so I called you. I'm currently near the door. Should I walk through and describe what the rest of the house looks like? I didn't check the bedrooms or the bathroom—maybe Carol is in trouble. Maybe the guys just left, and I missed them on my way here."

"Stay where you are," Rex said. "Please. We're only a few blocks away."

It seemed like forever but was less than five minutes when Rex and Charles pulled up on their bikes. I hung up the phone the minute I had them in sight.

"No sign of Carol?" Rex said as he hit the kickstand on his bike and took off his helmet.

"No sign," I said. "And no sounds from the house. Is Carol's husband out of town again?"

"Yes," Charles said. "He stopped by before he left and asked us to keep an eye on Carol."

Rex brushed by me as his intense gaze took in the door and the living room area. He disappeared deeper into the house.

"Did the door look broken in?" Charles asked me as he took notes on his notepad.

"No," I said. "I rang and knocked, but no one answered, so I thought maybe the book club was still going and they just didn't hear me."

"You let yourself in," he said.

"I let myself in," I agreed. "I called for Carol. But there was no answer, so I checked the kitchen. But I didn't see anyone."

"And so you called Rex?"

"No," I said and leaned against the house. "I called Irma Gooseman to see if she knew what had happened here."

"And did she?"

"No, she said everyone left between eight thirty and nine and everything seemed fine."

"Carol was alone then?"

"I don't know," I said and drew my eyebrows together. "I think Evan Tailor and Dwayne Finch might be with her. They've been documenting my investigation of the murders."

"But they were with Carol and not you," he said, more question than statement.

"I believe so," I said. "They were going to the book club tonight to do some interviews, and Irma confirmed they were there. She said Carol scooted everyone out so she could share some idea she had with the podcasters."

"Podcasters?" Charles looked up at me.

"Video bloggers," I said. "They have a kind of podcast/video show/blog thing. I don't get it, but it seems like plenty of people love it."

"I see," he said. "Are you sure the men are with Carol?"

"Not positive," I said. "Let me call the McMurphy front desk and see if someone can go up and check to see if they're in their rooms."

"Might not hurt," Charles said. "I'm going to have a look around the outside of the building. You might want to stay right here."

"Okay," I said and thumbed through my phone contacts to punch the number of the McMurphy. It was well after Frances and Douglas went home. I had part-timers who were scheduled to watch the front desk from 6 p.m. to midnight. After midnight, I relied on my security system and my night service, which would call me if anyone needed me.

"McMurphy Hotel and Fudge Shop," eighteen-year-old Patty Walkstall answered.

"Hi, Patty, it's Allie. Do you happen to know if Evan Tailor and Dwayne Finch are in their rooms? They would have come in between eight thirty and now."

"I didn't see them, Ms. McMurphy," Patty said. "Do you want me to ring their rooms?"

"Could you? I'm looking for them."

"Sure thing, hang on." She put me on hold, and it reminded me that I wanted to update the hold music. She popped back on. "No one's answering in either room."

"Okay, thanks," I said.

"Do you want me to contact you if they come in?" she asked.

"Yes, please," I said.

"Is everything all right?" she asked. "They might ask me, you know."

"Yes, everything is fine," I replied. "I just need to talk to them."

"Okay, sure thing."

"Thanks." I hit *End* on my phone and stared off into the dark night. What had happened? Had Carol taken them off on some wild-goose chase? Or worse, had she figured out who the killer was and they'd all gone to confront them? But if they had just left, why was the house in such disarray?

I guess I had to wait for Rex to find out.

Chapter 23

"No one's inside," Rex said as he stepped out. "I've called Shane in."

"Do you think it's a crime scene?" I asked.

"It looks like one," he said. "The back door was ajar, and there was blood near the threshold."

"Oh, that's not good," I said.

"Do you have any idea who would want to hurt Carol?"

"No," I said. "No one. Everyone loves Carol, except for maybe Christine Keller. She's a little peeved at Carol and me for bettering her at the fair this year."

"I doubt Christine took three hostages at knifepoint," Rex said. "Are you sure the podcasters are with her?"

"I called the McMurphy and had the front desk call their rooms. No one answered."

"Okay," he said with a nod, his expression thoughtful.

"I told Patty to call me if they came in." I found myself moving from side to side, restless at the thought that something might have happened to Carol.

Rex put his hand on my shoulder, and it calmed me a bit. "We'll get this figured out quickly."

"The book club was trying to solve the murders," I said and looked inside. "Did you see that someone smashed the murder boards?"

"I saw," he said. "Why don't you let Lasko walk you home?"

I glanced down the driveway to see Officer Megan Lasko pulling up on her bike. "I'm sure I'd be fine walking home by myself."

"Maybe," Rex said with a nod toward Megan. "Or maybe you'll decide you need to go find Carol on your own."

I crossed my arms. "You can't waste police officers just to babysit me. You've got possibly two murderers on the loose and now a kidnapper."

"I understand you are upset and worried about your friend," he said and held me. "I'm not patronizing you. I just don't want to have to worry about you while I'm trying to do my job."

"Then let me just take myself home," I said. "I've got my phone if anything happens or if I don't feel safe. You can track me if you want to."

"All right," he said. "Go on home, and I'll resist the urge to track you. Text when you are safely locked in your house."

I looked up at him. "Okay?"

"Okay," he repeated and let go of me. "You've been through enough scrapes, I have to figure that you know what you're doing. I just wanted to offer assistance if you weren't feeling safe. And trust me, no one would be feeling safe after the last two homes you've walked into."

I took a deep breath and blew it out slow. He was right. Safe was the last thing I was feeling right now, but I was also right. He needed all hands on deck to catch this killer before they hurt Carol or the guys. "Then I'll head home."

"Like I said, text me when you get there," he said.

"I can do that," I replied and stepped off Carol's front porch. Megan stopped me at the end of the drive.

"Are you okay?" she asked.

"I'm fine, thanks," I replied.

"Do you need someone to walk you home?"

I smiled. "No, thanks, though." I headed off into the dark away from Carol's house and wondered what the heck had happened there. Was there something she had dug up that I hadn't listened to? Was there a clue in my memory that would help me find out where she and Evan and Dwayne might have been taken?

I reached the back of the McMurphy and went in through the back door. The lobby was a few feet ahead of me, and I stepped from the hall into its warm light. "Hi, Patty."

She looked up from her phone. She was stationed behind the reception counter, her jeans-clad legs wrapped around a stool. "Oh, Ms. McMurphy." She straightened. "Is everything okay? You don't usually call or come down here this time of night."

"I'm fine," I said. "Did you happen to see Evan or Dwayne come in after I called you?"

"No, ma'am," she said. "I would have called you like you asked me to if I did."

"Okay," I said. "Thanks." Rounding the corner, I

headed up the stairs. The guys were staying on the third floor, so I stepped up and walked down to their rooms, one across the hall from the other. I knocked on Evan's first and waited, but there was no answer. Then I stepped directly across the hall to Dwayne's and knocked again. This time, Mr. Ballard stuck his head out of his room door. "Are you looking for someone?"

"Hi, Mr. Ballard," I said. "Yes, I was just looking to see if these guests were in."

"Why? Is there a leak or something?"

"Nothing's wrong with the building," I said. "Thanks, though."

"Huh," he said. "Well, then, good night."

"Good night," I said, then walked back to the stairs and went up to my apartment. Mal greeted me at the door with a bark and a slide into my legs. I bent down, picked her up, and held her close. "Have you two been good while I was out tonight?"

Ruff.

I supposed that meant yes. I glanced at Mella on top of the sofa. She opened one eye when I came in, as if to say, *Oh, you're back.*

I put Mal down. "What are we going to do, ladies? Carol seems to have been kidnapped, along with those two podcasters."

That got Mella interested, and she sat up and studied me.

"Who would have done that and why?" I asked my pets. Neither of them had an answer, and I yawned hard. It was nearly ten and my bedtime. "Oh, I forgot to text Rex." I hit his number.

"Allie, are you home safe?" he asked.

"Home safe," I said. "I checked on the podcasters, and they didn't answer their doors, so either they are not there or they are already asleep. It doesn't make sense to think they are asleep and didn't come check in on me."

"Okay, we'll take it from here," he said. "I'll keep you posted."

"Thanks," I said and went to hang up.

"Allie," he said before I could hit the *End* button.

"Yes?" I asked.

"I love you."

I was silent a moment, surprised. "What?"

"Listen, I have to go, Shane just found something," he said. "Try to get some sleep. Good night."

"Good night," I said, and he ended the call. I looked at my phone as if it were something I'd never seen before. "Did he just say that he loved me?" I asked my pets, but they were not answering. Mal was staring at the treat bowl near me, and Mella was on the kitchen counter licking her paw.

"Oh, man," I groaned. "I didn't tell him 'I love you' back. So, that sucks." I played with my phone wondering if saying, *I love you, too*, by text was appropriate. It turned out that I did love him. I had known it since the last time I'd nearly died and he'd been there. It was why, no matter how tempting Harry was, I wasn't going to leave Rex. I guess I was in it for the long haul.

That revelation—and my worry for Carol and the guys—had me lying in bed wide awake. I checked my phone every five minutes for a text from Rex telling me they'd found them, but none came. About 4 a.m., I got up and got dressed. Mal was excited to go on an early-morning walk, so I put on her halter and leash and we stepped out into the cool quiet of predawn.

Mella pushed past us to run down the stairs and out into the alley.

"What's your hurry, girl?" I asked her.

Mal and I went down, and Mal did her business while Mella walked like she was on a mission down the alley. As soon as Mal was ready, I decided to follow her. Mella had her own secret outdoor life, sometimes showing up at her original owner's door, sometime disappearing altogether.

There was nothing else to do, so we followed. Mella led us down the alley a few blocks and then up a side road. She was headed toward the woods in the state park, and she wasn't slowing down. We got to the top of the hill near the governor's mansion, when she stopped and delicately sniffed the air before turning right into the park.

"What are you up to, girl?" I muttered. Mal was happy to track her sometimes-friend and always-roommate. We picked our way through the woods. I used my cell phone as a flashlight, keeping one eye on Mella and the other on the path in front of us. We had walked for what felt like an hour before Mella stopped near a large old pine. She sat there and licked her paws. I stood still for a few moments to see if she was going to keep going, but she didn't.

The sky had started to turn pink, and my phone told me I needed to head home soon if I was going to get my fudge done on time to start the day with a full counter. Still, something made me stay. I sat down on an old stump and let go of Mal's leash.

Mal sniffed the ground closely and didn't seem

to care that Mella was within pouncing distance. Suddenly Mal started digging.

"What is it girl?" I asked and went over. I shone my light on the spot and noticed it didn't look like the rest of the forest floor. Squatting down, I brushed away a few pine needles, only to discover most of the loamy surface was actually glued down. Onto what? I kept brushing until I found square edges, one of which Mal keep digging at.

I reached over, ran my fingers underneath, and found a latch of some kind. I pressed it, and the board sprang open by about an inch. Mal sniffed the air coming in from under the board, and Mella was beside me as if to say, *Open it.* I did and shone my light into what looked like the mouth of a tunnel that actually had stairs, not a ladder. I tried to see to the bottom, but my light didn't penetrate the darkness there. I had no idea how far down the stairs went.

I studied them. They seemed very old and worn. Suddenly Mella brushed past me and moved down into the tunnel. "Mella, no!" I whispered. But it was too late—she was gone into the darkness. Mal looked at me intently. "Oh, this feels like a scene from a bad horror movie, Mal," I said. "I'm sure someone somewhere would be shouting, 'Don't go down there!'"

Mal just stared at me with her black button-shaped eyes. We both knew I was going down the stairs. "Well, let me at least text Rex what is happening," I said. I typed: *Rex, I couldn't sleep so I went for a walk. Followed Mella into the woods.* I glanced around. How could I describe where I was? I hadn't been paying close attention, but I thought we were northeast of the governor's mansion. I added that information, as if that would help. I told him about the tunnel that Mella had gone down and that I was going after her.

Then I grabbed Mal's leash, and we headed down the dark stairs. I sent my text just as I closed the cover to the tunnel. That way Rex wouldn't have time to tell me not to go.

Easy Chocolate Peanut Butter Cups

Ingredients
1 cup chocolate chips, divided (I like dark chocolate, but semisweet or milk chocolate also work here)
½ cup peanut butter
3 tablespoons powdered sugar
Pinch of salt

Directions
Line mini-muffin tins with paper (think cupcake wrapper). Then, in a glass bowl, melt chocolate chips by microwaving for 30 seconds at a time and stirring until the chocolate is smooth. Let cool slightly while you combine the peanut butter, powdered sugar, and salt. Pour 2–3 teaspoons of chocolate into bottoms of the lined tins and coat. Scoop 2 teaspoons of peanut butter mixture into the centers and top with remaining chocolate. Refrigerate until set. Makes 12.

Chapter 24

The tunnel had packed-dirt walls that smelled damp and loamy. Then it switched to hard rock that had a slightly basic smell. There was no sound as we descended. I counted the steps—fifty-seven—and we hit the bottom of the tunnel. It was cold down there, so I wrapped my sweater tighter around my body. "Hello?" I called. The sound fell into the deadened darkness.

Luckily the tunnel only went one way. Using my phone as a flashlight, Mal and I stepped gingerly down the tunnel. A glance at the ceiling showed it had been chiseled out of rock.

I'd known there were smuggler tunnels on Mackinac, but I'd assumed they were closer to the lake for easy access of storing and transporting goods.

Mal pulled me forward, her nose to the ground. The tunnel narrowed, and I stooped to avoid the ceiling. We wandered for what felt like a long time along the tunnel before we came to a branch. "Now what?" I asked Mal.

She sniffed the ground in a circle, then started down the left tunnel. I followed. So far there hadn't been any sound but that of my footsteps. I was completely turned around and had no idea where we were or how far we'd been traveling.

"Mella?" I called. There was no answer. "Hello?" Still no answer from the cold darkness. There was soot on the ceiling, so someone at some time had been down here with a torch. Which was good—that meant there was good airflow and Mal wasn't leading us to our deaths due to suffocation.

The tunnel finally came to an end, and there was Mella, licking her paws as if she always traveled through secret tunnels.

"Mella!" I picked her up. "What are you doing?" *Meow.*

Mal joined in with a bark and scratched on the side of the wall, her little stub tail wagging.

"What is it?" I shone my light to see that there was a door. It looked like it was made of wood with iron hinges and an old lock. I put Mella down and investigated the door when I heard a faint pounding. "Hello?" I called. The knocking seemed to speed up. Was someone stuck behind this door somehow?

I grabbed the handle and tugged. It budged open half an inch. "Hello? Is someone in need of help?" I called into the dark space.

I heard what could have been a muffled reply, and that was enough for me. I kicked at the lock until it broke, then yanked at the door until it opened far enough for me to slide between it and the wall.

Both my pets had gone through before I could stop them, but at least Mal stopped, turned, and barked at me. "Mal, come here," I called. "There could be something dangerous down here."

Mal padded back to me, and I picked up her leash. I wished I'd had a leash for Mella, but my kitty was long gone into the darkness.

I shone my light into another dark passage. "Hello?" I called as I walked. "Is anyone there?"

The muffled sounds grew louder the farther I moved down the tunnel. Following the sound, I came to another door. This one had a brand-new-looking lock on it.

I heard muffled sounds of "help" and maybe a groan. "It's okay," I said. "I'll get help." I glanced around and realized I had no idea how long it would take to get out of the tunnel and find someone to help. Mella looked at me expectantly as she waited by the door. Mal sat and tilted her head at the different sounds coming from behind the door.

What in the world was I going to do? I didn't have a key to unlock this lock, and I doubted kicking it would have the same effect as it did on the last lock. There were no holes in the door, so I couldn't see inside. Frowning, I stepped back and studied the entire door. The lock was new, but the hinges were old. Would it be possible to take the door off by the hinges?

It would be better if I called Rex and got some help down here, preferably with bolt cutters, but my phone had no bars.

"Looks like the hinges are our best bet," I muttered and laid my phone down so the flashlight app shone straight up onto the hinges. Studying them closely, I could see that some of the screws were already working their way out of the wooden door frame that had been placed into the chiseled-out rock.

I stuck my fingers between the hinge and the door where the screws were weaker and tugged. I pulled and pulled, but the screws only came out a few millimeters. It was going to take a lot more than that to get the door off. I studied the lock again and wished I had lock-picking skills. Maybe it was something I needed to work on should I ever get in this kind of situation again.

Then I heard footsteps coming my way. I wasn't going to take any chances and hid in the dark along the wall, hugging my cat in one hand and my pup in another.

The person was a black shadow in the darkness with a flashlight illuminating a circle of light in front of them. I slid another step back to avoid the light.

The figure stopped at the door, and I heard the lock disengage.

Mal started to growl low, then she suddenly leapt out of my hands. She attacked the person, who beat her off, then turned and ran down the hallway. Mal raced after them.

I didn't know what to do: to save Mal and expose myself or to use the time to see who was behind the locked door. The mumbling grew louder. I grabbed the lock out of the door and threw it into the darkness. Then Mella and I flattened ourselves against the wall and waited. There was no sign of Mal or the person who'd opened the door. I slid over, swung the door wide, and flashed my light inside. It was some kind of storage room filled with old wooden crates.

Mella wriggled out of my arms and raced off to

a corner. I shone my light that direction and saw two people with sacks over their heads, their hands and feet bound.

"My goodness, are you alright?" I asked as I raced to them. I pulled one sack off of the first person and discovered Evan. He had a gag between his teeth. I hurried to untie it so he could talk.

"Oh, thank goodness," Evan said. "I didn't think anyone would hear us."

I untied his hands so he could untie his feet, then I pulled the sack off the next person and saw it was Dwayne. Mella circled in his lap and laid across his legs. I untied Dwayne's gag. "You are very lucky," I said. "Mella must really like Dwayne. She led us right to you."

"Good kitty," Dwayne said. "I knew you were the best cat ever." I untied Dwayne's hands and went back to the door.

"Hey—flashlight," Dwayne said. "I can't see to untie my feet."

"Sorry." I turned toward him but kept my foot between the door and the sill. "I wanted to make sure we weren't going to get locked back in."

"Good call," Evan said as he stiffly moved toward me, then held the door open.

Dwayne got up, holding Mella against him. I swear I could hear her purring. "No, really, how did you find us? Wherever the heck we are?"

"I followed Mella," I said. "There was an entrance to a tunnel in the middle of the woods—never mind that now. Let's get out of here."

I shone my flashlight down the hall both ways, but it was empty. "This way." I turned toward the way I came in and led the men out. My heart pounded, and I was worried to death about Mal. The way back seemed to go quicker than the way down. We reached the fork in the tunnel, and I paused, not quite certain which way to go. I kicked myself for not leaving some sort of marker. After all, if Rex had tried to follow me down the tunnel, how would he have known which way to go here?

"Which way?" Evan asked.

"I'm not sure." I was honest. It was then that I heard a bark in the distance. I pushed past the men. "Mal? Come here, baby!"

I could hear her running toward me as I hurried back down the tunnel. Like magic, she leapt out of the darkness and into my arms. I held her tight, then checked her all over. "Are you hurt?"

She licked my face, and my heart melted.

"Allie, shouldn't we be getting out of here?" Evan asked. I turned to find them right behind me. "You have the only flashlight, and I don't do dark."

"Right." I hurried back to the fork in the path and put Mal down. "Which way, Mal?"

She nosed the floor and started down the one on the left. I quickly grabbed her leash and hurried to the end of the tunnel, where the steep stairs rose in front of us. "It's fifty-seven steps up," I said. "You guys go first."

"Dwayne . . ." Evan waved Dwayne up the stairs, then followed him. I picked up Mal, shone my light as far as I could up the steps, and followed swiftly behind them. I had the eeriest feeling that someone was behind me, but Mal didn't bark, and when I glanced back, there was nothing but darkness.

I heard Dwayne push on the hatch before my light reached the top of the stairs. Broad daylight shone down between the tree branches.

Mal barked with delight at the sight of sunshine, and I agreed. Evan helped me the rest of the way up and out of the tunnel, and we heard people calling my name in the distance.

"We're here," I called. "Over here."

There was the rushing sound of people hurrying through the woods. Rex reached me and held me tight. "Good Lord, you scared the justice out of me," he said. Then he pushed a step back to look me in the eye. "Don't *ever* go into a tunnel alone again!"

"I wasn't alone," I said. "I had Mal, and I was trying to find Mella. Plus, I texted you where I was."

"Are these the two men we've been looking for?" Lasko asked as she eyed the two dirt-encrusted and disheveled gentlemen.

"Yes," I said. "Mella found them. They were locked in a room down in the tunnel."

"How were you able to get through a locked door?" Rex asked. "No, never mind. All three of you look like you need a going-over by the doc and a good hot meal."

I glanced at my phone to see what time it was— 10 a.m. I was late for my demonstration, and there would be no fudge for the crowds today. I looked over at a bewildered Dwayne holding on to Mella and Evan telling Officer Brown what he knew.

Some things were worth the loss of a day's worth of fudge making.

Chapter 25

"Carol's still missing," Rex said as he handed me a tall mug of hot coffee and a package of mini donuts out of the vending machine.

My exam by the doctor had been pretty quick and simple. A few bruises that I didn't remember getting were all I had by which to remember the adventure. Mal was covered in tunnel dirt, but the doctor had looked her over, as well, and could find no obvious signs of trauma. Mella sat on the chair beside me licking her paws. She was the only one who seemed unfazed by our adventure.

Both Mal and Mella had been supplied with water and treats and were happy for all the attention.

"There wasn't time for the guys to tell me what happened," I said. "Did they tell you?"

"Yes, and I think it's best if we keep that information quiet right now," he said.

"But Carol wasn't with them," I said. "Do you know what happened to Carol?"

"We're trying to find that out." Rex sipped his

coffee and encouraged me to do the same. "What made you decide to go into the woods at five in the morning?"

"I couldn't sleep, so I decided to take Mal for a walk. Mella got out with us and headed off as if she had someplace to go, so I followed." I shrugged.

"And how did Mella know about the tunnel entrance and where the men were being held?"

I shrugged. "I wondered the same thing." I glanced at my cat. "But she won't tell me. Maybe you can get it out of her?" I blinked innocently at him.

Rex shook his head. "Are you sure you're feeling okay?"

"I'm fine, truly."

"And you don't have any idea what the person who unlocked the door looked like?" He studied me.

"It was very dark," I said. "They could have been your height, give or take a few inches. Dark clothes. They wore a hat or a hoodie, maybe a scarf. It obscured the shape of their head and hid their face."

"If they didn't know you were there, why hide their face?" he asked and snagged a donut from the package in my hand.

"Maybe they were worried the guys would recognize them," I suggested.

"But you said they had bags over their heads," he pointed out.

"Maybe the person who unlocked the door didn't know that," I suggested. "For all we know, they were trying to help the guys until Mal came out of the dark barking and biting. She chased them down the tunnel. It had to have startled them."

Rex patted Mal and let her lick the powdered

sugar off his fingers. "Who would be afraid of a little dog like Mal?"

"There are people who are afraid of dogs—and little dogs in particular," I said. "I think mostly she scared them, appearing in what was supposed to be an empty tunnel."

"Mal didn't have any marks on her," he said. "Which means they didn't fight back. This afternoon we're putting together a crew to explore the tunnels and see where they go. Maybe Carol is still down there."

"I wondered that myself," I said. "Poor thing. She's spunky, but it's hard to be trapped, especially underground."

He took my hand and squeezed it. "I know you know from firsthand experience."

"Listen, Rex, I'm sorry I didn't respond when you told me you loved me."

He straightened. "It's okay if you're not ready."

"No, no, I'm ready. I love you, too. It's just you hung up so quickly, and I didn't want to text it to you the first time, and well, I've never said that to anyone before—"

He cut me off with a deep kiss that had my heart beating quickly. Mal tried to sneak in between us, and he pulled back.

"Mal!" I said.

Rex laughed. "She's a good dog." He stood. "You can go home. Do you want me to get someone to walk you home?"

"Oh, I think we'll be fine," I said, handing him the donut package and tossing the remaining cup of coffee. I gave him a quick kiss, picked up Mella and Mal's leash, and made my way out of the clinic into the bright blue sky.

The streets were filled with tourists who'd come to the island for fudge and shopping, or maybe a carriage ride or a hike in the parks. All I could think about was the kiss and telling Rex I loved him. It was a small step, I supposed, but for me it was a big one.

I met Irma power-walking in a powder-blue sweatsuit and bright white tennis shoes. "Oh, Allie, I'm so glad I ran into you," she said as she did a U-turn and started walking beside me, her arms bent and flapping like a bird's. "How are you?" she asked. "I heard you found the two podcast guys. Did you find Carol? Where was she? Do you know who took them and why?"

"Hi, Irma," I said, and Mella purred in my arms. Mal pranced beside us as I picked up my speed to match hers. "Unfortunately, I haven't found Carol."

"But wasn't she with the two young guys? I mean, we left her with them. It would be strange for them to be kidnapped and not Carol. Unless—" Irma stopped short and covered her mouth. "Unless Carol is dead."

I placed my free hand on her arm to comfort her. "Let's not jump to conclusions," I said. "All we know is that she is missing and she wasn't with Evan and Dwayne when I found them."

Irma picked up her pace and shook her head. "None of this makes any sense. Why Carol? Why the podcast guys? I mean, if you were worried about what we knew about the murder, you would have kidnapped the entire book club, and no one else is missing."

"I'm afraid I don't have any of those answers," I said. "Maybe the guys will be able to shed some light on the situation."

"Have you talked to them? Did they tell you who did this?"

"I didn't have the chance," I said. "Rex whisked them off to the clinic and then kept them under police custody."

"Well, they are going to have to let them go sometime," Irma said. "Then the book club will really want to meet with them and grill them. There may be something they know that won't make sense to them but will make perfect sense to the rest of us."

"Maybe," I said. "At this rate, I wouldn't be surprised if they took the next ferry off the island and went back to where they came from."

"Nonsense," Irma said. "You watch, this will make them more invested than ever in our little investigation."

"I'm surprised you're exercising alone today," I said. "Don't you usually have someone with you?"

"Oh, sometimes I like to go by myself and take a new route," she said. "That, and Carol is missing and Irene just can't bring herself to take their usual route."

"I'm so sorry," I said. "I'll be sure to check in with Irene later today to make sure she's doing okay."

"Not a bad idea," Irma said.

"Are you sure you're okay to power-walk by yourself?" I asked, a little worried for her taking a new route. "I mean, you aren't taking your regular route. What if something happens? How will we find you?"

"Nothing's going to happen to this tough old bird," she said. "But just in case, I've got an emergency button I wear around my neck." She pulled out a long chain with a plastic button. "All I have to do is punch it and it calls nine-one-one and tells them my exact location." She paused. "Too bad Carol didn't wear one of these."

"Or if she had her cell phone, we might be able to ping it," I murmured.

"That might still work," Irma said. "She carried that thing religiously. Did they find it in the house?"

"I don't think so," I said.

"Then maybe Rex can use it to find her, after all," Irma said.

We approached the McMurphy. "Maybe that's not a bad idea," I said. "Listen, I've got to go make fudge and get my fur babies safely inside. We'll talk soon."

"Bye, Allie," Irma said. She picked up her pace and headed down Main Street toward Doud's.

I entered the McMurphy to find Frances staffing the reception desk as guests checked out and Madison happily making fudge in the fudge shop.

"Hi, Allie," Madison said as I put Mella on the floor and unhooked Mal's leash. "I saw you weren't here when I arrived, so I just started in on the regulars."

"Thanks, Madison," I said and stepped into the open door of the fudge shop. "You got so much done."

"And we've already had our first crowd come through," she said proudly. "Sold out of the mint dark chocolate and the chocolate walnut."

"Wow, I'd better watch out, or you might just become my competition."

She grinned and shook her head. "No, you're so creative in your flavors and recipes. I could never compete. Besides, school is starting in two weeks."

"And you will be missed," I said. "I'm going to go get cleaned up, and I'll be back down to help."

"No rush," she said.

I waved at Frances as I walked through the lobby. She was checking out Mr. and Mrs. Goodman, the parents of the bride who had just gotten married. Then I headed up the stairs to my apartment. My pets followed.

I paused at the second floor and wondered if the guys had been allowed to come back and get some rest. I decided not to knock on their doors to see if they were there. If they were, they might be either resting or packing. I didn't want to disturb them either way. I made a mental note to have Frances call me if they came down to check out. I'd love to hear their story, and I imagined so would Liz. In the meantime, I had a shower to take and fudge to make.

Later that afternoon after the 2 p.m. demonstration and while Madison was cleaning up before she left for the day, I saw Dwayne and Evan come dragging in. They looked exhausted.

"Lock up when you're done, please," I said to Madison. "Great job today." Then I hurried out of the fudge shop to find the guys falling into the wingback chairs by the elevators. "Hi, are you two doing okay?"

"What an adventure," Evan said.

"They took my camera," Dwayne groused.

I pulled off my chef's hat and unbuttoned my chef's coat. "Who took your camera?"

"The people who put us down there," Dwayne said.

"Oh," I said. "Right. Do you need anything? Coffee? Tea? Water?"

"No, thanks," Evan said. "The police kept us well hydrated."

"Can you tell me what happened?" I asked.

"We've heard that question at least twenty times today," Evan said.

"I don't think I can get a new professional camera out here for at least a week," Dwayne said. "How are we supposed to take video if we don't have equipment?"

"You could use your cell phones," I suggested.

"Right," Evan said. "Except our captors took those, too."

"Captors with an 's'? Does that mean there was more than one?" I asked.

"One with a gun and one to take away our electronics," Dwayne said.

"Did they take Carol's cell phone, too?" I asked.

"We haven't a clue," Evan said.

"They put hoods on us, and we couldn't see anything after that." Dwayne slumped farther down in his chair and put his hands in his pockets.

"Why don't you two go up to your rooms and rest," I suggested. "Let me know when you're feeling better. I can order pizza, and we can strategize our next move."

"I don't think we'll be strategizing anything," Evan said and sat up. "I think, for us, this case is over. We learned a valuable lesson."

"What's that?" I asked.

"Leave the investigating to the police," Evan said.

Chapter 26

I spent the rest of the day thinking about what I could have happened to Carol and wondering how the two men came to be tied up and locked in a room in a tunnel. On the one hand, I wasn't surprised my pets had found them—my fur babies were really good at sniffing out trouble. But on the other hand, I wondered why my pets hadn't found Carol. Who was she with? Was she alright?

I took Mal out for her evening walk and made sure Mella stayed in the apartment this time. While Mal did her business, I pulled out my cell phone and dialed Carol's number. It was a simple strategy, but as far as I could tell, no one had tried it.

The phone went straight to voice mail.

Hmm, that was a dead end. Maybe if Mal and I walked over to Carol's place, I could call again and see if I could hear the phone ringing. I mean, Rex hadn't told me they'd recovered the phone. Then I sighed. Shane would know. I hit a button on my phone, and it rang.

"Hey, Allie," Jenn answered. "How's the investigation going?"

"Not too good," I said.

"What? I heard you found Evan and Dwayne," she said.

"But not Carol," I said as I walked down the darkening street. "Irma said something about Carol always having her cell phone with her, and I was wondering if you know whether or not they'd found it."

"Oooh, are you asking me to get information from Shane?" she teased.

"You are my best contact," I quipped.

"I can ask," she said, "but I'm not sure he'll tell me."

"Well, I might have found a phone," I fibbed. "I was wondering if it would be hers or if they'd already acquired it."

"Wait, you found a phone? Do you think it was the killer's phone?"

Darn, I hadn't thought that they might want me to actually produce a phone. "Maybe?"

"Hmmm, or maybe you didn't find a phone, and you just want me to tell Shane that so he'll tell me if they have Carol's phone or not."

"You are smarter than me," I said and sighed.

"You never could tell a lie without giving yourself away." Jenn laughed. "Shane is due home in a few minutes. I'll ask him and get back to you. In the meantime, how are the guys? Are they okay?"

"They're just tired," I said. "They haven't told me anything about what happened. Dwayne was upset that they took his equipment, and I wouldn't be surprised if they give up and go home in the morning."

"He said '*they*' took his equipment?" Jenn asked. "Which means it was more than one person who kidnapped them?"

"Yes, I picked up on that, too," I said. "But all Evan said was that one person had a gun and another person tied them up. Which means we are looking at either two killers or a killer and an accomplice."

"Yes," Jenn said. "Wait, are you out walking alone?"

"Yes," I answered, "but it's fine. I'm fine. There's no one around."

"You've said that before," Jenn said. "Why don't you come over? I'm making meat loaf for dinner so there's plenty, and that way you can ask Shane yourself."

My stomach grumbled at the idea of food. I'd had no clue I was hungry. "That sounds wonderful," I answered. "You make the best meat loaf."

"It's my secret ingredient," she said. "And no, I'm not going to tell you what it is because then it wouldn't be a secret."

I laughed at the old joke. "Okay, well, Mal and I are walking past Carol's place first, then we'll head your way."

"Okay, but if you're not here in thirty minutes, I'll send out a search party."

"Sounds good," I replied. "See you soon." I hit *End* on my phone. Mal and I were a few blocks away from Carol's place. I looked carefully around and let Mal go where she wanted. But I didn't see anything, and Mal didn't leave the sidewalk.

I called Carol's phone again. It rang a few times, and Mal's head popped up. She sat for a moment and tilted her head. The phone went to voice mail, so I hung up. "What, Mal?" I asked. "Did you hear something?"

She sat for a moment longer, then got up and put her nose to the ground again.

"Mal, can we find Carol?" I asked.

Mal pulled harder on her leash toward Carol's house. I followed swiftly behind, and we soon ended up at Carol's front door. "She's not here, Mal," I said and peered into the darkened windows. I couldn't go in, as the house was sealed up as a crime scene. I tried calling Carol again, and Mal tilted her head. This time she pulled me toward Carol's back door. "It's not in there, baby," I said. "Shane and Rex did a thorough search. They've probably found it already."

I ended the call when it went to voice mail again. "Mal," I said. "Find Carol."

My pup jumped up and scratched at the back door. I had to admit, Mal's certainty that Carol was in the house had me stumped. The daylight was fading, so I texted Jenn. *Mal says Carol is in her house. I'm going in.*

Going to break the seal? Jenn texted back.

Yes, I said. *Just wanted you to know.*

You have twenty minutes before I tell someone, she texted back.

Ok. I put my phone in my pocket and jiggled the locked door. I didn't know how to pick a lock, so I stared at the door, while Mal scratched at it. Sighing, I walked around the house looking for an unlocked window. Mal followed me, sniffing the ground. There it was. The bathroom window. It was a little high and very narrow, but I could see it was cracked open a bit. I jumped up, grabbed the window ledge, and held on with my right hand as I pushed the window up with my left hand. It slid fairly easily, and I let go and dropped down to the ground.

I stared back up at it. Did I have enough upper body strength to jump up and pull myself through the window? I found myself wishing I had started that strength training program I'd planned on at the new year and then promptly forgot.

"Okay, here goes," I said, then took a few steps back to get a running start. I leapt up, grabbed the sill, and used my feet to help push me up and partway through the window. The sill hurt my stomach and I was sure I would be bruised, but I wriggled my way through until I landed arms-first in Carol's bathtub.

It took me a moment to catch my breath, and I realized I'd scraped my arms and my shin. But my joy at getting into the house outweighed the soreness. I scrambled out of the tub and turned on the bathroom light. Then I opened the door. "Hello?" My voice echoed through the house, but there was no answer. I walked toward the back door, turning on the lights as I went, until I hit the kitchen and opened the back door.

Mal came running in with her leash gathered in her mouth. As soon as she entered, she dropped the leash, put her nose to the floor, and sniffed about.

"Something had better be here," I warned Mal, "or we are both in big trouble." Mal ignored me and continued to sniff the kitchen floor. "Mal," I said, "go find Carol."

Mal stepped up her game. She moved across the floor of the kitchen, and I followed behind her as she sniffed her way to the living room area, then to the first bedroom and back out, then the second bedroom. Carol's home was one story with a basement. There wasn't much more room to go before we hit a dead end. "Come on, Mal," I muttered, mostly to myself.

She went back around to the kitchen and scratched at the basement door. "Fine," I said, "but you could have gone there first, you know." I opened the door, and she disappeared down the stairs before I could turn on the light and follow her.

Carol's basement was partially finished, with her husband's workshop in the back. Mal went straight to the workshop area. I turned on the light for that part of the basement, and she moved toward the far-left corner and put her front paws up on a wooden box. "What is it?" I asked. I saw the box was bigger than a large trunk and made completely out of wood. There was a latch and a padlock on it.

Mal barked at me as if to say, *Open it!*

Well, one thing was for sure, the police hadn't looked in this box. Not with the lock still on it. "This is nuts," I muttered. I grabbed a pair of bolt cutters off the workbench and squeezed hard. They barely bit into the metal, but I kept trying. When I had it nearly three-quarters cut through, the phone rang.

"Darn it," I muttered and answered my cell. It was Jenn.

"Where are you?"

"I'm in Carol's basement," I said. "I'm fine, just trying to cut through a padlock."

"Okay, why?" she asked.

"Because Mal said I needed to look inside this box."

"Wait, Mal talks now?"

"Stop it," I said. "You know what I mean." I grabbed a fat screwdriver, stuck it in the lock like a lever, and pushed until the lock fell open. "I've got it!"

"What's in the box?" a male voice asked.

I yelped, dropped my phone, whipped my head around, and put my hand on my heart. "Goodness, Rex, you scared the living daylights out of me."

"Oh, yes," I heard Jenn faintly through the phone. "I called to tell you that Rex might be checking on you."

"Thanks, Jenn," I said and picked up the phone. "I'm hanging up now."

Rex leaned against the door frame in full uniform, his arms crossed and his blue gaze staring me down. Mal sat beside him, watching me as if to say, *She did it!*

"How'd you know I was here?" I asked. I currently knelt on the hard cement floor of the basement and looked up at him. The screwdriver was still in my hand.

"The neighborhood watch called to tell me someone was in the house, turning on all the lights," Rex said. "I called Jenn as I was heading over on the off chance she knew where you were."

"I'm glad you didn't come in, guns blazing," I said.

"Oh, I had my gun out," he said, his tone serious. "I had no idea if someone else had followed you inside and was holding you captive. I cleared the house."

"Oh," I said and put my hand to my throat. "Thank you?"

"So answer the question," he said. "What's in the box?"

"I don't know, but I'm going to find out," I said, and I lifted the top of the box. Mal jumped up and looked inside.

It wasn't really a box, but a passage into a dark someplace. "I need a flashlight," I said. I stood and grabbed a flashlight off the workbench. Mal jumped into the box and was gone down in the darkness. "Mal!"

Rex was beside me with the flashlight off his belt in his hand. "It goes down about eight feet," he said.

I looked and saw a narrow set of stairs. "Oh, thank goodness there are stairs," I said. "I thought Mal had just leapt into the darkness. There's no way she could climb down a ladder."

Rex climbed into the box and headed down the stairs. I followed.

"Mal," I called my voice muffled by the dirt above and around us.

"This looks old," Rex said as he hit the bottom of the steps and looked at the ceiling and the walls of what appeared to be a tunnel.

"This must be an old smugglers' tunnel," I said. "Like the one that ran under the McMurphy. I had no idea Carol had a tunnel entrance in her home."

"It makes sense. Her house was built in the 1800s," Rex said.

"Clearly Carol's husband knew it was here," I said. "That padlock was not ancient. Do you think this is connected to the tunnel where I found Evan and Dwayne?"

"I don't know," Rex said. "I have a team coming in tomorrow to go down and map out these tunnels."

"Well, I'm not waiting until tomorrow to get Mal back," I said.

"Hmm," he said. "I figured." He checked his cell phone. "No reception down here."

"Who needs cell service when I have a big, strong cop with a gun?" I fluttered my lashes at him, and he rolled his eyes.

"The smart thing to do is to go back up, make a call to the station, and get some backup," Rex said.

"Go ahead, go back up," I said with a shrug. "I'm going to go look for my dog."

Rex held my arm for a moment. "Just give me two seconds."

"Fine."

"Thanks." He hurried up the stairs and made his phone call.

I flashed the light from my phone into the tunnel. It was short, maybe five feet high, and it was narrow, as well. It was pretty clear that whoever had dug it wasn't a miner and didn't intend to smuggle large boxes. "Mal," I called into the darkness. "Here, girl!"

I heard a faint bark and headed toward the sound, more worried about my dog than whether or not Rex was behind me.

Chapter 27

"Allie, wait!"

I paused at the sound of Rex's voice. "Sorry, I heard Mal and just reacted."

He caught up to me. We both had to stoop to fit. Rex shone his flashlight ahead of us. "These must have been old smugglers' tunnels. They were running liquor through here during Prohibition."

"Seems like they could have made them bigger," I groused as we moved forward. "The tunnel where I found the guys was much larger."

"It had rooms," he said. "So it makes sense they didn't want to have to stoop to get through them."

We moved through the tunnel. It was not straight and seemed to be dug around bigger rocks.

"Mal!" I called. "Here, girl!"

We heard her bark in the distance.

"I told her to find Carol," I said and held on to the back of Rex's shirt as we navigated a perilously narrow opening. "Do you think this is connected to the tunnel where I found Evan and Dwayne?"

"I doubt it," Rex said. "There are only a few smugglers' tunnels on the island."

"But there are caves on the island," I pointed out.

"Yes," he said.

"Someone could have dug into and around the cave systems," I pointed out.

"Mal! Here, girl!" Rex called.

The answering bark was closer. I pushed Rex to go faster. We came to an opening that was even narrower. "How far away from Carol's house are we?" I asked.

"Not as far as you think," he said. "This has been twisting and turning."

"It's too bad we don't have cell service," I said. "I was calling Carol's cell, and I think Mal heard something a few blocks from Carol's house."

"Even if you were calling her phone," Rex said. "I doubt it was ringing down here."

He made a valid point. I tried not to sigh as we climbed through the narrow passage and saw that it opened into a larger cave. It felt good to be able to stand up straight. Our flashlights flicked around the cave. When I heard a bark that sounded very close, I moved to the left. There was a boulder, and behind the boulder was Mal. She sat with her paw on something.

"Rex," I called. "It's Mal. She found something."

He approached as I bent down and picked up my dog.

"Mal, are you okay?" I asked. "What did you find?"

"There's no way," Rex muttered as he grabbed a glove, reached down, and picked up the article.

"What is it?" I rocked Mal more to comfort me than to comfort her. Her stub tail wagged hard.

"It's a cell phone," he said and studied it with his flashlight.

"Do you think it's Carol's?" I asked. "I told Mal to find Carol."

Rex scratched his head. "It would be strange if it were," he answered, then got out an evidence baggie and slipped the phone inside.

"But you're collecting it as if it were," I pointed out.

"Just to be on the safe side," Rex said. "I doubt we'll be able to identify the phone until we can unlock it and get into the contacts."

"How are you going to unlock it?"

"Well, if it is Carol's phone," Rex replied, "then it's likely her husband, Barry, knows the code and can help us out."

"But we're going to check out the cave, right?" I flashed my light around. "I mean, if it is Carol's phone, she might be down here somewhere."

"Agreed," he said. "We can do a quick search of this cave, but then we need to go back. I've got a team—"

"Coming out tomorrow to search and map the tunnels and caves," I finished his sentence.

"Yes." His tone was serious. "They are professional spelunkers, and it will be much safer for everyone if we let the pros do their job."

"Fine," I said. "Carol!" I called her name and swung away from him with my light. He was right. I really didn't know anything about caves, except how to follow my pets through them and hope I didn't get stuck somewhere.

We searched the small cave up and down. There were two tunnels that exited the cave, plus the tunnel through which we'd come. Lucky for me, Rex had marked our entrance, or I might have gotten completely turned around. The last thing I was going to do was to put Mal down and have her run off again.

Spotting no further signs of life in the cave, we returned to the stairs. I noticed on the way back up that they were actually carved into the soft limestone. When I emerged from the tunnel, the bright light of the basement blinded me for a moment, and Mal barked and wagged her tail. Someone took my elbow and helped me out of the box. When my eyes got used to the light, I saw it was Megan Lasko. "Thanks," I said.

Rex climbed out behind me.

Charles was also there, along with another officer who looked very young and very new. Charles looked down the stairs and into the darkness. "Do you think this is the way the kidnappers took Carol?"

"No," Rex and I said at the same time.

"There was a lock on the box when I first saw it," I said.

"They could have come back and locked the box," Charles said.

"They wouldn't have had time," Rex replied and brushed a bit of the dust off his uniform. "If the timeline holds up between when the book club left and when Allie arrived."

After seeing his uniform, I looked down at my own clothes. How on earth had I gotten so dirty?

Jenn and Shane came into the basement work-shop area. "I had to see it for myself," Jenn said and pushed her way over to see the stairs. "Wow, and this was inside this box the entire time?"

"Carol had to have known about it," I said. "It would have come up when they bought the house. And that was a relatively new lock." I pointed to the padlock I had tried to cut and ultimately pried open.

"Wait, Shane, do we have tunnels in *our* base-ment?" Jenn asked.

"No," he replied. "It was not in óur survey, and trust me, no one is going to come popping up from our basement."

"But it happened at the McMurphy," I pointed out. "I had it walled off, of course."

"See," Jenn said. "Are you sure?"

"Positive," Shane said and raised an eyebrow in my direction.

Okay, so the last thing I wanted was to upset my pregnant best friend. "I'm sure Shane would know if you did," I assured her.

"Okay." Jenn stepped back and crossed her arms. "I know you would not keep this from me when we are prepping for a baby to come into our house."

"The smugglers' tunnels are rare," Rex said. "I'd heard of them as a kid, but I hadn't actually seen any of them until Allie came along."

"This is the third one I've seen," I said. "The first was two years ago, and then the second and third in the span of a day."

"Okay," Jenn said. "So, they are rare. What about Carol? Was she down there?"

"Mal found a cell phone," I said.

"Is it Carol's?" Jenn asked, looking at Rex.

"Shane will know better than I," Rex said. "Carol's husband, Barry, comes back to the island tomorrow. If he helps us unlock the phone, then it's most likely Carol's."

"And if he can't help you unlock it?" I asked as I held Mal tight.

"Then we are back at square one, still looking for Carol," Rex said. "We'll be mapping the tunnels, so we'll have more information later this week."

"I suppose we missed dinner," I said to Jenn.

"Oh, honey, it's nearly eight p.m. Are you hungry? Do you need to eat?" Jenn said. "I can get you some leftovers."

"No, thanks," I said. "I'll go home and eat something there. I need to get to bed in less than an hour if I want to actually make the fudge tomorrow. And part of that time is shower time."

"You are kind of dusty," Jenn said. "You should see your hair."

"Great," I muttered. I turned on my heel. "Rex, do you need me for anything else?"

"No," he said. "But I'd like to walk you home, if that's okay."

"Works for me." I gave Jenn a hug and waved good-bye to Shane, who was already trying to pull prints off the phone we'd found.

Rex walked me out of Carol's house. I didn't let Mal down so she couldn't Scooby-Doo her way home. I didn't want my fur baby to disappear down another rabbit hole.

"You know," I said, "I could call Carol's phone. If Shane saw that it rang, then we would know for sure it was hers."

"I'm sure you've done enough," Res said as he walked beside me. I noticed how tired he looked.

"This hasn't been an easy investigation for you, has it?" I asked.

"No," he said. "This one doesn't make any sense, at least yet. I'm sure Carol discovered something. She didn't tell you?"

"No." I sighed. "I've been so busy and frazzled with the podcasters following me around."

"I know how you get when someone gets in your space," he said.

"I'm sorry I'm so weird," I said and bumped against him.

"It's what I love best about you," he said.

"Your acceptance of me is what I love best about you," I said and bumped against him again. He put his arm around me as we walked. The streets were as silent as the caves and tunnels; the fudgies had gone home for the night, and those who stayed on the island were either in their rooms watching television or sitting around firepits enjoying the cool quiet of a night at a state park.

Mal stayed in my arms, comfortable, as we approached the McMurphy. I realized I hadn't checked in with Frances. But a quick glance at my phone told me it was well after nine, and there was no time to call her and Douglas.

We reached the McMurphy, and Rex walked me up the back stairs to my apartment. "I hope you get a nice, hot shower and something to eat," Rex said.

"Thanks." I unlocked my apartment and put Mal down to pick up her leash and go inside. "Are you going to get dinner?"

"Don't worry about me," he said and leaned his shoulder against my door frame. "I'll grab something. Right now, I need to get back to Carol's and ensure we have someone covering the basement opening."

"I understand," I said and leaned into him. "Thank you for going down there with me. I really am not sure how Mal knew about the tunnel or Carol's phone, but I do hope it helps us to find her."

"I think it will," Rex said and kissed my forehead, then my mouth. "If it turns out to be Carol's phone."

"I can totally call it," I said. "I'm sorry I didn't think of that before."

"It's okay," he said and held me tight. "It's been a long day. You need to shower and ensure you eat. I'll take it from here."

"Good night," I said and gave him a quick kiss.

"Good night," he replied and waited for me to close and lock my door before going down my stairs. I looked at both my fur babies. "I bet you guys are hungry."

Mal barked, and Mella jumped up on the counter. I fed them and checked that they had clean water before I headed to the shower.

If Carol was down in the tunnels, then it was just a matter of time before Rex and his crew found her. What I needed to do was go to bed so I'd have a clear mind in the morning. That way I could work harder on the problem of who'd taken Carol and why. What I *was* sure of was that it had something to do with the murders. If I could just learn what Carol found out, maybe I could figure out who took her and why.

But none of that would happen if I didn't get some food and some rest.

Tomorrow would be a better day. I just needed to be ready for it.

Triple-Chocolate Cookies

Ingredients
 1 stick cold butter ($\frac{1}{2}$ cup)
 1 cup brown sugar
 1 large egg, cold
 $1\frac{1}{4}$ cup flour
 $\frac{3}{4}$ cup baking cocoa
 $\frac{1}{2}$ teaspoon baking soda
 $\frac{1}{4}$ teaspoon salt
 1 cup dark chocolate chunks
 1 cup semisweet chocolate chips

Directions
   Heat oven to 350 degrees F. In a chilled bowl, cream butter and sugar. Add egg and mix. Slowly stir in flour, baking cocoa, baking soda, and salt. Combine until smooth. Fold in chocolate chunks and chocolate chips. Scoop small ice-cream scoops onto parchment-lined cookie sheets. Bake for 12-14 minutes until set. Remove from oven and let cool to firm up before removing from cookie sheet. (The cookies should be thick. If they spread too much, chill the remaining dough for 30 minutes and try again.) Makes a dozen large, thick cookies. Or a dozen and a half smaller cookies. Enjoy!

Chapter 28

"I understand you had quite the adventure," Frances said.

"Yes, yesterday was full of surprises. Did you and Douglas know there were smugglers' tunnels under some of the houses?" I asked, leaning against the reception desk where Frances worked.

It was Monday. The fudge shop had finally emptied out, and I'd just finished cleaning up after my first demonstration. I'd given Madison the day off since she had been working so hard lately and I knew in just a few weeks I'd be back on my own when she went back to college.

"Oh, yes, everyone on the island knows there are tunnels," Frances said. "We explored some of them as kids."

"I knew about the tunnel in the McMurphy basement, but I had no idea they also had openings in some of the other basements here."

"Only one or two houses have entrances," Frances said. "The owners keep it quiet so strangers don't pop up unexpectedly. Plus, you know, quite a few of the houses are kept in the family, and it's a small town. People don't want too many people to know they're connected to smuggling."

"Carol had an opening in her basement. Mal found it."

"Hmm, that seems about right," Frances said. "The Tunisians lived in that home for over sixty years. They might have even forgotten about it. Do you think the kidnappers knew about it?"

"There was a fairly new padlock on it," I said. "But we don't think the kidnappers took them out that way. Unless one person took them down and another locked it up . . ."

"Or they could have come up that way and locked it behind them," Frances suggested. "The fact that they are using the tunnels means that whoever took Carol knows the island well."

"Then they are most likely locals," I suggested.

"But you didn't find Carol in the tunnels," Frances said. "Maybe she wasn't down there. Maybe whoever took them took her somewhere else."

"Mal found a cell phone in the tunnel," I said. "It might be Carol's. She might have dropped it on purpose to tell us something."

"You couldn't tell last night if it was hers?" Frances asked.

"No, the phone was locked. Rex says that Barry is coming home today, and he'll help them unlock it."

"Why don't you just call Carol and see if it rings?" Frances asked.

"That's what I said last night." I straightened. "But Rex wanted it done by the book or some such nonsense."

"Sounds like he didn't want you to find out what was on the phone," Frances suggested.

I made a face. "Now, that makes the most sense of all."

"Listen, you have a lot on your plate right now." Frances looked away from her computer and studied me. "Why don't you take the afternoon off? I can cover the fudge shop and the front desk. We don't get a lot of check-ins on Mondays."

"I still have the two o'clock demonstration," I said. "I need to stay on schedule at least through the season."

"Okay," she said. "Go get yourself some lunch and take a nice nap or something. I know you're not sleeping well."

I rubbed my hand over my face. "It shows, huh?"

"Exhaustion and hot sugar are not a great mix," she said. "Your grandfather taught me that."

"True," I said. "Thanks." I headed up the stairs, and Mal followed me. We ran into Jenn as she left the office.

"Hey, Allie," she said. "Did you get some dinner last night? I have leftover meat loaf if you want it."

"I'm good," I said. "Thank you, though. Say, how long was Shane over at Carol's last night?"

"A good while," Jenn said. "He walked me home when you left with Rex and then went back. I think he came in around two this morning. I believe they went back through the house to see if there was anything else they might have missed. Like an open bathroom window." She winked at me. "He went in late to work this morning."

"Do you know whether or not the phone was Carol's?"

She shrugged. "Sorry, we didn't talk about the case this morning. You know everything I know."

"Right," I said. "What are you working on this week?"

"We have the Siebinskis' family reunion this weekend."

"Oh, that's right. They bought out the entire hotel," I said. "You had planned on using the rooftop deck for the day. Are you still planning to do that?"

"No." She shook her head. "The family has asked me to find new accommodations. Which was pretty tough last-minute, let me tell you."

"But you are a fabulous event planner, and you found a place, didn't you?"

"Yes, I was able to reserve one of the parks for Saturday, along with a canopy in case it rains." She had pride in her voice.

"Wonderful." I smiled, then got serious. "Do you think our deck will be out of commission for long? I mean, yes, it's only been about a week, but I put a lot of money into it, and you do use it to party-plan."

"I know," she said and tilted her head my direction. "It will be okay. I think once the killer or killers are caught, things will go back to normal. It's just in the news right now."

"Okay," I said and sighed. "At least they didn't change hotels."

"Most likely because they can't," Jenn said. "All the hotels are sold out for the season. We have a waiting list, too."

"Well, that's something," I said. "I'm going to wash up and take Mal for a walk."

She stopped me. "I think you need to take a nap. You have dark circles under your eyes."

"Well, I love you, too," I said, trying not to take her and Frances's advice the wrong way.

"Just looking out for you, girl," she said.

"Okay. Come on, Mal. I think we need to take a nap."

Ruff!

It's amazing what a little extra sleep can do to lift your spirits and clear your mind. I took two hours and then got up, ate a sandwich, and went downstairs for my 2 p.m. demonstration. It was pretty successful as far as Monday afternoons usually went during the season. I was happy to see the fudge was flying off the shelves.

The fudge shop didn't bring in as much revenue as the McMurphy did, but it was a large part of the tradition of my hotel and worth all the work, as far as I was concerned.

That said, maybe I should close the shop on Tuesday and give myself and Madison some extra rest.

"Frances," I said, catching her attention. "I'm done for the day, if you could watch the shop until five and then close it down."

"Sure," she said. "Are you taking the rest of the day off?"

"Yes," I said and took off my chef's hat. "I've decided you and Jenn are right. I need to take some quality 'me' time. I'm going to close the shop tomorrow, too. Tuesdays are our lightest days even during the season."

"Good," she said. "You haven't taken any real days off since you started the shop."

"True. Mostly I miss days when I'm in trouble or when someone I love is in trouble."

She looked at me over the top of her glasses. "I know you want to make your Papa Liam proud and make the McMurphy a success, but if you don't take time off regularly, well, you're going to really burn out. I have even taken vacation since you've been here."

"Most of that was for your honeymoon," I couldn't help but point out. "But you're right."

"I know," she said. "Now, take some real time off. I don't want to go up and find you working in the office. Everything can wait forty-eight hours."

I shrugged my shoulders and rolled my neck. "I'm going to go up and shower and maybe take Mal for a walk."

"Just a gentle walk by the lake." She wagged her finger at me. "You need time off from the case, too."

"But Carol—"

"Is in good hands with Rex and his crew," Frances said. "Now, scoot." She waved me toward the stairs as the bells rang and a couple came in looking at fudge. "Go!"

I went upstairs, determined to really rest. Maybe read a book or work on a new recipe. I was just getting into my apartment when my cell phone rang. I didn't recognize the number, so I let it go to voice mail. If it was important, they'd leave a message.

I showered, washed and dried my hair, and put it up in a bun. Then I put on a fun sundress and checked my phone. Whoever called had left a message. My phone service always translated my messages into text, so I could read the beginning of the message. *Allie*, it said. *It's Carol. You probably aren't answering because you don't know this number. I got the phone out of my captor's pocket.*

I picked up the phone and put the message on speaker. It really was Carol. I knew a couple of things from listening to the message. One: Carol was alive. Two: Carol wasn't in the tunnel because she was able to call out. And three: She sounded more jazzed than scared. It was like the whole kidnapping was a lark and she was enjoying every moment of it.

And so, Allie, Carol's message said, *I don't know where I am. I'm in a small room with only one small window, and it's dark. Fortunately, I remembered your phone number, and this phone lights up when you turn it on. I'm using it as a flashlight, but all I see is four walls and some shelves. Okay, got to go. Someone's coming!*

And just like that, the message was over.

I knew I had to take this straight to Rex. "Come on, Mal," I said, then grabbed her halter and leashed her up. "Let's go see if Rex can find Carol."

Ruff!

We went out the back, down the stairs, and through the alley toward the police station on Market Street.

"Allie McMurphy!"

I glanced over my shoulder to see Yeller the Clown in all his glory. "Oh, hello. Yeller, is it?" I stopped, and Mal hid behind me at the sight of a grown man wearing a red-ball nose, colorful make-up, and shoes ten times the normal size. I didn't blame her. Mal was little. Those shoes might get her.

"Yes, that's right," he said and honked a horn. "I'm flattered you remembered."

"You're kind of hard to forget," I said and flashed him a brave smile.

"Oh, yes, especially in costume." He laughed. Then he glanced around and pulled me over to the side. "I'm glad I ran into you. I wanted you to know that I heard about your friend Carol. Whoever did Mike in might have taken her, as well."

"Yes, they just might have," I agreed.

"Look, I've been thinking about that day at the fair," he said, his tone low for my ears only. "I stopped by the haunted house that morning to see Mike. He was busy running around like a chicken with its head cut off. He said he had just figured out that someone had been embezzling from the LLC that he and Paul owned all the businesses under. I asked if he knew who it was, but he only said he was close to figuring it out."

Bingo! I thought. "Did you tell Rex this?"

"Naw, for some reason, he and the rest of the officers avoid me."

"It might be the costume." I flicked his big white ruffled collar with the multicolored dots on it.

He laughed heartily. "Oh, right, as if cops are afraid of a grown man in a clown costume. I entertain at fairs and kids' parties, for goodness' sake."

"Well, you have to admit, seeing a grown man in a clown costume is kind of . . . surprising."

"That's what makes things funny," he said and did a little dance. "The surprise."

"Well, thanks for the information," I said and patted his shoulder. "If you remember anything else from that day, please let me know. I'll talk to you later."

"Thanks, Allie," he said. "I'm off to see a kid about a pony." He honked his horn and walked crazily down the street.

I looked at Mal, and she looked back at me. We both kind of shrugged, then continued toward the administration building where the police station was. Someone had been embezzling from Mike and Paul's business. Why didn't Paul report this? Did he not know? Was Mike killed before he could tell Paul? It'd been a few weeks. Would Paul have even looked over the books by now if that was Mike's job? Maybe I should go pay him a visit and see. But right now, we had to get a phone number to Rex so that he could find Carol.

Chapter 29

"The number seems to be assigned to a burner phone," Rex said. "And it will be difficult to trace."

"But we know she's not underground, or she wouldn't have been able to send the texts," I pointed out. "We also know that she's alive—and she's probably tormenting her captors, if I know Carol. She has spunk."

"It did sound like she was enjoying the whole ordeal," Rex said. "How are Dwayne and Evan? Have you heard any more from them?"

"The last I knew, Dwayne wanted to leave, but Evan wanted to stay. Which means they were both trying to figure out how to get new filming equipment. I think they took the ferry into Mackinaw City around lunchtime. They should be back anytime." A quick glance at my phone told me it was nearly 5 p.m. Mal and I had been hanging around Rex's office for a while. "Oh, and Yeller the Clown told me he spoke to Mike the morning that Mike was murdered."

"Why didn't he come in and let us know?" Rex asked and leaned back in his chair.

"He said he tried to tell you, but you were avoiding him."

"Right," Rex said. "I'm not a fan of clowns, but then, few people are. Did he say what they talked about?"

"He said Mike was upset when he saw him. Something about the books not being right." I bent and picked Mal up so she could snuggle into my shoulder.

"Hmm, it might be a motive," he said. "Thanks for the tip. We'll look into the business records."

"You haven't already?"

"We need to have probable cause," he pointed out. "Up until now, there hadn't been any."

"I see," I said.

"What are you doing for dinner?" he asked.

"I didn't have any plans," I replied and leaned toward him from my seat across his desk.

"Why don't I take you out? I'm off in a couple of hours. Shall I come by your place around seven?"

"Don't you need to look further into where Carol might be—you know, ping a cell tower or something?"

"I've got people working on that," he said and leaned toward me. "In the meantime, I'd like to spend some time with the prettiest girl on Mackinac Island, and possibly the world."

"Mal only eats kibble at home," I quipped and batted my lashes at him.

Rex chuckled. "If I have to bring Mal to get to you, then let's bring Mal."

"What about Mella?"

"Cats, dogs, any animal you want, as long as you are there, too."

I leaned over and kissed him. "I'll be ready."

"Great." He straightened. "I'm going to let you go, as I have some work to finish up between now and then. So, seven o'clock, right?"

"Right." I stood. "I won't make you take my fur babies this time." I winked, and Mal and I walked out of his office.

The light outside was bright, and the day was warm. The wind on the lake stirred the waves just enough to make a low, soothing roar.

"Mal," I said and put her down so she could walk on her leash. "Let's go pay Paul a visit. Surely by now he's seen the books in the business and would be concerned about the embezzlement."

We walked up the hill toward Paul's place in Harrisonville. In the daylight, it was a whole lot nicer-looking. As I approached the door, I remembered that Christine was Paul's mother. I paused before I started knocking. What would I say if Christine were here?

I knocked anyway.

I could hear someone on the other side of the door, and then it opened. Paul stood there looking a bit worse for wear. He wore a T-shirt and jeans and had his head bandaged. "Allie, what brings you here?"

"Hi, Paul," I said. "I'm just checking to see how you're doing after your ordeal. How's your head?"

"Better," he said. "Come on in. You, too, little dog." He waved us both in and closed the door behind us. "Go ahead and have a seat. Can I get you something to drink?"

"No," I said with a shake of my head. "Mal and I are good, thanks. Like I said, I was just checking on you. How are you doing?"

"Sit, sit," he said and pushed us toward his couch.

I sat on the edge of the seat, and Mal jumped up in my lap.

"I was just on the computer," he said. "Doing a little business." He motioned toward the laptop on his end table and took a seat in the blue recliner.

"I didn't mean to interrupt you," I said. "We were just out on a walk and ran into Yeller the Clown. He was asking about you, so I thought I'd stop in and catch up."

"Oh, you weren't interrupting," he said. "I'm not much of a business guy. I was just looking at the accounts and trying to figure out where the numbers were, but I think I'm going to have to take everything to an accountant."

"Did the numbers seem off?"

"Why do you ask?"

"It's something Yeller said to me today," I said. "He said he ran into Mike the morning he was killed. Mike had said he'd noticed a discrepancy in your books and was looking into why the money didn't add up. Did Mike mention that to you? Is that what you were looking for?"

"Huh," Paul said and rubbed his chin. "I don't remember Mike talking about it. But now that you say that, yes, the numbers do seem a little off." He shrugged. "It's why I'm going to take the books to an accountant. I'm sure they need to be audited before the money all goes over to me."

"Did Mike have an heir?"

"You asked me that before," Paul said. "Like I

told you, on his death, the entire business goes to me. You see, we were too busy to have spouses and families and such."

"What about parents or siblings? Did Mike have any next of kin?"

"Like I said, I was his only next of kin," Paul said. "Mom was my next of kin, but if she died, then it would have all gone to Mike."

"Right, I'd forgotten Mike didn't have any living family," I mused. "There's been a lot going on. Anyway, I'm sure you're glad your mother is still alive."

"Yeah." He nodded. "Mom's going to take over part of the business now and keep the books like Mike did, while I go out and do the fairs and carnivals."

"It's great that you want to go into business with your mom," I said. "My mother and I aren't that close."

"Yeah, my mom is highly involved in my life. I accept that."

"Did they ever figure out who attacked you or why?" I leaned back against the couch. "Was it a home invasion? A robbery?"

"No, nothing was missing, as far as I could tell. If it was whoever got Mike, then they botched their attempt at killing me. The police certainly have no clue," he said and shrugged. "You were the only person around who might have seen something. To be honest, my memory is a little blurry on all that still."

"Maybe we should be looking into whoever does your books or has access to your accounts. They could have been embezzling, like Mike suspected, and when you got the files, they might have come into your home looking for the evidence."

"Yes, I don't think they realized I was home," he said. "But they didn't get my laptop. All the files are still here." He patted the computer.

"You might want to beef up the security in your place," I suggested. "They may come back to do a more thorough search, since I seem to have interrupted them the first time."

"Smart," he said. "I'll order one of those smart security systems that will alert me if anyone enters the house."

"That's a great idea. I work with a great company if you want a referral." I glanced at my phone. "Oh, I've got to go. I have a date in an hour and want to get ready. Thanks for being so gracious and letting us in on last-minute notice." I stood. "Is there anything I can get for you? Groceries? Headache medicine? Some fudge maybe?"

"No thanks." Paul rose. "My mom would be furious if I let you help me after I refused to let her help me."

"Ah, got it," I said. "Mal and I will be on our way. Good luck with the books. If you need me to recommend an accountant, let me know. My hotel manager, Frances Devaney, is great with accounts, and she also knows everyone on the island. She wouldn't steer you wrong."

"Thanks, Allie," he said and walked me out. "Good night."

"Good night." I waved to him as Mal and I walked off the porch and headed toward the street. The walk home was quiet, and Mal hurried as if to say, *Let's go get some dinner.* I agreed. I stopped just before we hit Main Street and texted Rex. *How should I dress for our date?*

I watched the dots dance on the screen letting me know he was typing in his answer. Finally, his response popped up. *Let's go to dinner and dancing at the yacht club.*

Sounds fun! I texted back and hurried toward the McMurphy. If I was going on a fancy date, I needed to find something appropriate to wear. That was going to be hard, considering I lived in black slacks or sundresses.

Chapter 30

I twirled in front of the mirror as I video-chatted with Jenn on the phone. "I think this dress will do," I said. "What do you think?" The dress was a blue, rough silk, vintage 1950s style with a scooped neck, short sleeves, and a poufed-out skirt.

"You look amazing," Jenn reassured me. "You are going to have so much fun."

"We usually just get dinner or have a picnic," I said. "But after I told Rex I was taking tomorrow off, he asked me out on a real dinner and dancing date."

"Well, you should take time off more often, if that's what he's going to do," Jenn said.

"How's my hair?" I asked nervously. I'd tamed my wavy hair into a French twist and put on real makeup with black cat's eyeliner and a red lipstick.

"Perfect," she said. "Now, don't be nervous. It's just a fun dress-up date."

"Yes," I said with a nod, then took a deep breath and blew it out slow. "Of course." There was a knock at my back door. "Oh, I've got to run. I think that's Rex."

"Have fun, and call me when it's over," she said. "I want to hear all about it."

"Okay," I said as the knock came again. I ended the call and hurried to the door. Mal was already there sniffing at the door. I did a quick look through the peephole and frowned, then opened the door.

"Wow," Harry said when he saw me. "You look gorgeous. What's the occasion?" he asked and bent to scratch behind Mal's ears.

"Rex is taking me to the yacht club for dinner and dancing," I said.

Harry stood and gave me an appreciative look. "Maybe I should be the one taking you out for dinner and dancing."

"Harry—"

He raised his hands. "I know, I know, you're dating Rex. But if I could persuade you, you should be dating me."

I put my hands on my hips and tried not to roll my eyes. Harry was handsome and smart and rich and also a hotel owner, but I'd told Rex I loved him, and I meant it. "What brings you by?"

"Oh, right, yeah," he said and leaned against the door so that we stood practically nose to chin. "I was wondering if you wanted to go do some more rooftop sleuthing. I've been thinking about Hazel and why she was killed."

"Really?" I tilted my head. "Why do you think she was killed?"

"With all that rooftop jumping, I think she might have overheard something she shouldn't have."

"Oooh, that's an interesting idea," I said. "Do you think she overheard Mike's killer telling someone they did it?"

"Or she overheard enough conversation that she figured it out herself and was trying to get to your place to tell Rex."

I thought about that. "Why wouldn't she just use her cell phone?"

"Because she didn't have it," Rex answered as he stepped up onto the landing of my back door. The little landing was very crowded with both men standing there. "Winston." Rex acknowledged him with a nod.

"Manning," Harry greeted him back. Neither of them seemed particularly friendly toward the other. I shook my head. Mal jumped up onto Rex, trying to get him to give her an ear scratch.

"Were you trying to steal my date for the night?" Rex asked, obviously trying hard to make a joke of it.

"Just had a question and stopped by on my way home," Harry said. "Talk soon, Allie?"

"Sure," I said.

"Good night," he said and headed down the stairs to the alley. Rex and I watched in silence as Harry whistled his way down the alley until he disappeared.

"Are you ready?" Rex asked.

"Let me get my purse," I said and went inside. Rex followed and closed the door before my pets could run out.

"Are you bringing Mal and Mella?" he asked.

"Oh, no, not to dinner and dancing," I said. "They are both fed, and their water bowls are clean and full. They'll be okay until we get back."

"Good," Rex said. "Then, shall we?" He opened the door and held out the crook of his arm.

"Be good, babies," I called, and we walked out and closed the door. I locked it and headed down the stairs behind Rex.

"You look beautiful, by the way," he said as I took the last step into the alley. His blue gaze was warm and appreciative.

"Thanks," I said. "Jenn helped."

"I thought Jenn was home with Shane."

"She was," I assured him. "We were video-chatting."

"Oh, right," he said and held out his arm again. I put my hand through it, and we walked in comfortable silence to the yacht club.

The yacht club was a converted mansion across from the marina. The night air was cool, and the sounds of music and laughter floated out the open windows of the club. We walked across the porch, and Rex held the door open for me.

Inside was filled with light and warmth and white linens and sharply dressed waitstaff.

"Reservations for two," Rex said to the woman behind the reception desk.

"Got it," she said. "Right this way."

We followed her to the back of the dining area to a table with a clear view of the live music and yet secluded by a wall on the side from the rest of the room. She waved her hand, and a waiter appeared and pulled out my chair. I sat down and he tucked me in as Rex took a seat across from me with his back toward the wall.

"Ramsey will be your waiter tonight," she said. "Enjoy your evening." Then she turned and left, gliding between the tables with a practiced ease.

"What can I get you to drink?" Ramsey asked.

"I'd like a bottle of champagne," Rex said. He looked at me. "Does that work for you?"

"Yes, sounds wonderful," I said.

"Good, sir, and was there a particular vintage you were looking for?" Ramsey asked.

"I'm not a connoisseur," Rex said plainly. "I'm not going to pretend that I am. Can we have a nice mid-market vintage? Something very good, but don't waste your best stuff on me."

Ramsey tilted his head. "Very good, sir," he said with a tone of real respect and walked away. A busser appeared. "Still water or sparkling?"

"Sparkling," Rex replied, and I nodded.

"Good." The busser filled our glasses from a fresh bottle of sparkling water, then he moved away toward other tables.

"Everything is so lovely," I said. I looked at Rex. He wore a dark navy suit, a pale blue dress shirt, and a blue ombre tie and pocket square. "You look very nice."

He reached across the table and took my hand in his. "So do you."

"This is really romantic," I said, waving my free hand toward the piano man singing slow songs.

"I wanted it to be," he said. "I've been thinking—"

"Here are your menus," Ramsey interrupted. "Is this a special night, by chance?"

"Oh, I–" I started.

"Yes," Rex said at the same time. He glanced at me and took my hand. "Yes, it's a special night."

"Then might I suggest our chef's menu this evening?"

I glanced at the menu in front of me. "Is that the special?"

"It's four courses that the chef prepares himself for special diners," Ramsey said.

"We'll have that," Rex said.

"Wonderful choice," Ramsey said and took the menus back.

I leaned forward. "Isn't this going to be a little expensive?" I knew that neither Rex nor I had trust funds, and our jobs didn't exactly pay a mountain of money.

He squeezed my hand. "Don't worry about it."

"Okay," I said and took a deep breath. "I accept that you are going all-out to help me celebrate taking a day off."

"Which brings me back to what I've been thinking about—"

"The champagne is coming," I said as I watched Ramsey approach with a champagne bottle on ice and two champagne flutes.

Rex pulled back and let Ramsey act out his show of opening the bottle with a pop and a flourish as he poured us both glasses of champagne.

"Thank you," Rex said as a way to get rid of the waiter.

"Is it a special night?" an older gentleman with white hair and a well-starched white shirt leaned over and asked. His gaze went to the champagne, then to me, then back to Rex.

"Every night with Rex is a celebration," I answered him before Rex could. I could see Rex was getting a little put off by all the interruptions. I raised my glass. "To quiet celebrations."

"To you," he said as he raised his.

"To us," I said. We clinked glasses, and I took a sip. It was lovely, bubbly, tangy, and sweet all at the same time. It made me wonder if I could concoct a champagne fudge.

Rex stood and held out his hand. "Dance?"

"Sure." I rose, and we stepped out onto the dance floor and came together in a slow, soft shuffle. "What were you trying to say before all the interruptions?" I rested my cheek on his chest and listened to his heartbeat. It picked up.

"I've been thinking about us," he said softly, the tone rumbling in his chest. "I was wondering . . ."

I looked up at him. "What?"

"I was wondering if you would marry me," he said. "I know, I'm not down on one knee, and this isn't exactly a planned event. But I just thought that since we love each other, we should start talking about a future together."

I stopped moving. Also, the spit in my mouth dried up, and I just blinked at him.

"Oh," he said and took a step back. "Too soon. Too soon." He took my hand and drew me back to the table, where Ramsey flitted about bringing out the fancy appetizers. As I sat back down, I couldn't think of a thing to say. Not a single thing.

The silence was awkward and deafening, and Ramsey went about explaining the dish as if nothing was going on. When he finally left, Rex leaned in. "I'm sorry. I botched that."

"No." I shook my head.

"No," he repeated. "No, you don't want to get married, or no, you don't want to marry me."

He kept saying that word out loud, the word

seemed to stun me to pieces. I don't know why it did. It wasn't like I didn't think about it.

"No, don't be sorry," I finally got out.

He took my cold fingers into his hand. "Look, I heard Harry Winston has been pressing you hard, and if you're not sure about us . . ."

"How is the appetizer?" Ramsey asked. The man had a real talent for getting in the way, and for a brief moment I thought Rex was going to stand up and punch him.

"We haven't tasted it yet," Rex said the words slowly as if Ramsey were an idiot.

"Ah, well, I'll be back shortly to bring out the next course," the waiter muttered and quickly disappeared.

"I'm sorry." I managed to get the words out. "First I botched telling you I love you, and now I'm botching this."

He squeezed my hand. "I didn't do it right."

"Wait." I pulled my hand away. "Are you asking me this just because Harry's been joking around about wanting to marry me?"

"Allie, he's not joking."

"Fine, joking or not joking," I said. "You didn't answer the question. Are you telling me you love me and asking me to marry you because you don't want me to date Harry?"

"No," he said. "No, I said I love you because I do love you. I'm asking you to marry me because I want to spend the rest of my life with you."

"Are you sure? Are you really sure you don't just want to beat Harry to the punch?"

"Allie."

"Don't 'Allie' me," I said and put my napkin on the table. "I think I need some fresh air and time to think." I stood, and he stood with me. I took a step, and he reached out as if to stop me. I glared at him.

Ramsey rushed over. "Are you leaving? But you haven't tried the mushrooms yet, and the duck is superb."

"Put it in a doggie bag," I said, and I left. The outside air felt better, and I tried to calm down as I walked. First of all, what the heck was up with the last-minute romantic dinner proposal? Then, for him to say he needed me to choose him over Harry, as if I hadn't already over and over. Ugh! I was too mad to even call Jenn, my hands were shaking so hard. I crossed the lawn at the foot of the fort and marched up the alley behind Doud's and the McMurphy.

"Whoa, Allie, are you alright?" Paul approached me from the other direction and stopped me before I got to the McMurphy.

"No, I am not alright." I crossed my arms in front of me.

"Is there anything I can do?" he asked.

"Unfortunately, no," I said.

He touched my arm. "Are you sure?"

"Yes, I just need to get home," I said. "Wait, what are you doing back here?"

"I was taking a shortcut to Doud's."

"But aren't they closed this time of night?" I asked and glanced at my phone. "They close at eight."

"Oh, man." He sounded disappointed. "I needed some eggs. I guess I'll need to get them in the morning."

"Well, you've got a bit of a walk home," I said and took a step forward, but he didn't move.

"You've brought Mal by a couple of times, so you know it's not that far," he said and grabbed my arm.

"What are you doing?" I asked. Then someone behind me threw a dark sack over my head. "What?" I started to fight, but then I felt a needle stick and the next thing I knew, I was waking up in some place that was cold and dark. My hands and feet were tied with what felt like plastic zip ties, and the dark sack was still over my head. I was lying on the ground—I could tell because I could scratch the dirt. Which meant it was a dirt floor. As I rolled to sit up, my skirt bunched around me, probably exposing more than I wanted. "Hello? Is anyone here?"

I listened for breathing, but I could only detect my own. I used my teeth and wiggled my head until I could pull the sack off my head. It didn't matter much because it was still too dark to see anything. I took a deep breath and recognized the rocky scent of tunnel. "Hello? Anyone?"

Frowning, I tried to remember what exactly had happened. I was mad at Rex, and I walked home. I ran into Paul in the alley. He'd grabbed my arm, and someone else had pulled the sack over my head. Who? And most importantly, why?

Easy Fudge

(no sweetened condensed milk)

Ingredients
   ½ cup butter
   8 ounces cream cheese
   1 teaspoon vanilla
   Pinch of salt
   ½ cup, plus one tablespoon sifted cocoa
   6 cups of sifted powdered sugar

Directions
   Butter an 8x8x2-inch baking pan and line with parchment paper. In a microwaveable bowl, place the butter and cream cheese. Microwave in 30-second intervals, stirring in between until butter and cream cheese are melted and smooth. Add vanilla, salt, and cocoa. Then add powdered sugar 1 cup at a time until you get a smooth, thick batter. Scoop it out into the pan and pat until level. Cut into pieces and refrigerate until set. Pull the pieces apart and serve. Makes 32. Enjoy!

Chapter 31

How was it that I always seemed to get kidnapped? For goodness' sake, you'd think I would figure out a way not to by now. But I hadn't been paying attention, and Paul didn't seem like a killer. I mean, if he was the killer, then who had attacked him? And clearly, there were two people involved: Paul and whoever put the sack over my head. Why kidnap me? I didn't have a clue who'd taken Carol or killed Mike and Hazel.

I blew out a long breath and tried to tamp down the panic. Rex had a crew out mapping the tunnels today, so I was sure someone would find me. In the meantime, though, I was getting cold, and my hands were tightly bound behind my back. I had to think.

I started taking inventory of myself. As far as I could tell, I wasn't hurt. Even my head didn't hurt, so whatever they'd used to knock me out was chemical, not physical.

That was a clue. Who would have access to something that could knock people out?

A doctor. A nurse. A veterinarian. Maybe a dentist. Then there were assistants who would also have access to whatever drug they used.

I realized my feet were bare. They'd taken my shoes. What to do next? I needed to try to stand, so I bent my knees and rolled so that I was kneeling, then I pushed up with my hands and wobbled, and fell. But I kept trying until I could stand. It was so dark I had no idea where to go, and my feet were still tied together, so walking was impossible. I hopped a couple of times and hoped I didn't go face-first into a wall. If I could just get my hands free . . .

Then I remembered I'd read that the locking mechanism on zip ties was the weakest area. I wriggled until I could feel the bump in the tie, then I wiggled some more until it was between my thumbs. Then I raised my arms as high as I could, bent at the elbows, and thrust down and apart. My wrists hurt, but I felt a little give in the zip tie. I tried it again, and this time the zip tie broke.

I rubbed my sore wrists, certain they were bruised, and bits were damp so I'd probably bled a little. It was simply pitch black, so there was no way to tell. I wondered if I could do the same with my ankles. I was pretty sure I needed to sit down.

I squatted and then plopped to the ground. It shook my tailbone and up my spine, but darn it, I needed out of these restraints. I found the knob on the zip tie and maneuvered it around to between my ankles, then I pulled my knees up and apart and flung my feet down in a fast move. It didn't work. I tried again. Still nothing. Finally on the third try, the zip tie popped, and I was free.

Tears sprang to my eyes, not just because of the

sharp pain on my ankles and the dull throbbing of my wrists, but out of joy for being free.

I stood and held my arms out, slowly stepping on rocks and stones until I found a wall. It was cool to the touch and hard. My first instinct was to follow the wall to see where it would lead me, but if I was in a cave, I might end up going in circles and not know it. I tried scratching the wall, but it simply tore at my nails. I bent down and fumbled for a rock. The ground was littered with them, but I needed one with a sharp enough edge to make a deep enough mark in the wall that I could feel it in the dark. I tried a couple of different ones. My arms grew tired from pressing into the wall, but finally, I was able to make a small arrow pointing in the direction I wanted to go.

Relieved, I kept the rock in my hand and followed the wall. I had to go stupidly slow as I'd already stubbed my toe on a large rock, and then there were the even larger rocks to crawl over if I wanted to keep my hand on the wall.

Suddenly the rocks cleared away, and I came across wood. I felt the edges, and my heart sank. It was a door. Finding the handle, I tried to open it, but it was solidly locked. So much for escaping. I sank to the ground, hugged my knees, my dress floating around me, and tried not to cry. It was cold, and I realized I was shivering. I tried to sit on my feet to keep them warm.

Paul and whoever had put me here would have to come back, right?

I supposed they didn't have to come back. I could pretty much die down here. Except I knew Rex wouldn't let that happen. Maybe even Mal or

Mella would help to find me. It was a comforting thought, as long as I didn't freeze to death first.

Then I realized I wasn't being smart. If my captors came back now, I didn't have any way to protect myself. The marking rock was sharp enough to hurt, but not big enough to do any damage. Scrambling around, I searched for a rock that was big enough to hurt someone. I found one that took two hands to lift, then made my way back to the wall and sat on the side of the door opposite the handle.

If anyone walked in, I could hit them with the big rock and then run. Luckily my dress had pockets. I slipped the marking rock into my pocket so that if I did get to run, I could stop and make marks and not get lost in the tunnels.

I sat with my back to the wall and listened to the sound of my own breathing. My mind went back to Rex. I was an idiot. It wasn't that I didn't want to get married—eventually. He had just taken me by surprise. I had latched on to his mention of Harry as a reason to escape the situation. If I got out of this current mess, I vowed to tell Rex I was sorry, and that yes, I wanted to marry him and maybe, in time, start a family. That, too, was something we hadn't talked about. So many things we needed to discuss before we got married. So many things I needed to know about myself. Did I want kids? Did I want to grow old with Rex? Was I willing to take his name? Whose house would we live in? How would our finances work? Yes, there was certainly a lot to think about, as I sat in the dark trying desperately not to think about dying alone of thirst and hunger.

* * *

I must have fallen asleep. A sound woke me, and a dim light shone under the door, piercing the darkness. Standing, I realized I was extremely stiff and sore. How long had it been?

The lock clicked, and the door slowly crept open. A small flashlight light pierced the darkness in a tiny beam that didn't go back far enough to shine on the sack that had been on my head. A person stepped quietly through the door. I took a step and raised the rock with both hands. I was about to come down hard when the light swung my way, exposing the person's face.

"Carol?" I froze, rock still held high in both hands. Was Carol a part of the kidnapping plot?

"Oh, Allie, thank goodness I found you!" Carol said in a stage whisper. "I've been searching all day ever since I heard them bring in another person last night. I knew it had to be you. You must have figured them out, too." She reached up and pulled my arm down. "Come on, let's get you to a safe place."

She pulled on me, and I followed. I didn't drop the rock, and my feet protested the rock-strewn floor, but she did lead me out of the room. "Hang on, I need to lock this so they don't get suspicious."

"Carol, what's going on? Who are 'they'?" I whispered.

"Shhh, no time for that now. Follow me." She started down a tunnel.

"They took my shoes," I said as I tiptoed behind her.

"Oh, that's just mean," she said. "Try to keep

up." She moved straight ahead. At the first turn, I stopped and quickly marked the wall. If Carol was a part of this, then I needed to be able to find my way back on my own. I hurried toward her light.

We turned another corner, and I marked another arrow, and then she stopped at a door, took out a skeleton key, and placed it in the lock. With a *chi-chunk* sound, the door swung open, and she pulled me inside. There was a small landing with a staircase that went straight up, sort of like the one in her home.

"Now, when we get to the top, be very quiet," she said. "They have me locked in a basement room, but they don't know about this entry to the tunnels."

"Won't they wonder how I got inside your room?" I whispered.

"Oh, no, they only come in to give me food and water three times a day, and then they barely open the door. If you stand behind the door, they won't even know you're there."

I took her at face value and followed her up the stairs. She opened the trapdoor, and we were, indeed, in a small basement room. There was a mat with blankets on the floor and a toilet in the corner. It also held some shelves with old empty canning jars and boxes.

"Welcome to my abode," Carol said as I climbed up into the room. "They gave me a flashlight because I kept complaining about the dark, but I mostly keep it off unless I'm wandering through the tunnels."

I followed her over to the mat, where she huffed and sat down. "You can share the mat." She patted the blanket. I sat down next to her. There was a pillow and a blanket on the thin mat, but that was all there was.

"I found Evan and Dwayne," I said. "Yesterday or maybe the day before. I have no idea how long I was down there."

"Good," she said. "Those boys weren't cut out to survive a kidnapping plot."

"You called me," I said.

"Yes, I got this phone off of one of them." She pulled a small cell phone out from under her pillow.

"Is the battery still working?" I asked, keeping my voice low. "I need to call Rex."

"I think so," Carol said. "Go ahead and call him, but I have no real idea where we are."

"But you've been in the tunnels," I said. "Surely you could have escaped."

"I've been looking for other ways out," she explained. "But so far I've only run into walls with no stairs. I'm not sure this is connected to the other tunnels."

"You mean the ones that run under your house," I said.

"You found that, did you?" she said. "I'd completely forgotten about it until they put me in here. Then I heard them talking about putting Evan and Dwayne in a tunnel room to keep them separate from me. I wondered how they were getting to the tunnels, and well, I had a lot of time in here, so I just nosed about until I found the hatch. I think they would put something in my dinner to make me sleep and sneak down there, but I haven't been able to find the way they get out."

"Carol, who are they?"

"You haven't figured it out yet?" she asked.

"Well, I know Paul is one of them, although I found him when he was attacked, so I don't know how he's connected . . ."

"Paul and his girlfriend," Carol said. "You see, I suspected Paul. I was about to show Evan and Dwayne why I suspected him when Paul and Cathy ambushed us. They had masks on, so I didn't know who they were, but they've gotten pretty confident the last few days and I'd pretend to be asleep, so they showed their faces when they dropped off the food and water. I heard them talking about how old and pathetic I was. *Hmph*, little did they know."

"Paul and Cathy? Do I know Cathy?"

"Sure, she was the fair coordinator," Carol said. "She's from St. Ignace. I think she's still married. In fact, I think it was her husband who attacked Paul. That's what I heard, anyway."

"Were they talking in the basement?" I queried.

"No, I can hear them through the heating duct," Carol said, then pointed the flashlight over to the furnace and the ductwork that went out of the furnace and out to the upper floors.

I was quiet and listened, but there wasn't any sound.

"It's night," Carol explained. "They usually are asleep at this time."

"How can you even tell what time it is?" I asked. "Oh wait, the phone tells you."

"Oh, honey, I'm a senior citizen," she explained. "I don't need to look at a phone. I'm asleep by eight p.m. and up early in the morning. That doesn't change no matter how dark it is."

"Right," I muttered. "Can I have the phone?"

"Sure," she said.

"Just a question," I said as I took the phone. "What?"

"When you called me, why didn't you tell me who took you?"

"Well, I thought you'd already figured that out," she said. "But we're not at Paul's place. So, sending you there wouldn't have done any good."

"I see, I think?" I checked the phone and saw there was only one bar. "How were you able to call? There isn't any service in this basement." I held the phone in the air and tried to find a spot with better service.

"Oh, there's a little window behind this set of shelves." Carol walked me over to the shelves and pointed at a spot near the ceiling.

There was, indeed, a window there, and it appeared to open from the inside. "Why didn't you just climb out the window?" I asked.

"To begin with, I'm too short and too stout—don't tell anyone I admitted that," Carol said. "Even if I could stack up some boxes, I don't have the arm strength to get up there. I tried." She crossed her arms. "But really, I just wondered what they intended to do with me. I mean, if I was enough of a threat for them to kidnap me, then why not kill me?"

"That is a good question," I said as I dragged a box over to the window. "But I don't think I'd have stuck around to find out the answer. I mean, I have no idea why they kidnapped me. Did they plan on just leaving me to die in the tunnel?"

"I heard them talking," Carol said while I climbed up on the box and unlocked the window. "Paul told Cathy you knew about the embezzlement, and they needed you out of the way long enough to plan their escape. You see, they're heading for Canada the moment Paul has access to the money in the bank accounts."

"Is that why he let me see him in the alley? He figured they'd be gone before I was found?"

"I can't say for sure, but it makes sense to me," Carol said.

The window tilted in toward the basement, which made it difficult to climb through from the inside. I stuck the phone outside the window and saw it had enough bars to call, so I dialed Rex's number.

"Manning," he answered, his voice tense.

"Rex," I said. "It's Allie. I've been kidnapped."

"Allie, where are you? I went to your door and Mal barked, but you didn't answer. I thought . . . Where are you?"

"I don't know for sure. We're in a basement, and it's too dark to see anything out of this window. But Paul Patterson and Cathy—"

"Lund," Carol said. "Cathy Lund."

"Cathy Lund kidnapped me and Carol," I said. "We believe Paul killed Mike, and Carol says Paul and Cathy are planning an escape to Canada. So, go get them. We're fine here for now. Get them, and we'll stay put."

"Allie, don't try anything, okay? I've got the whole squad on this. We'll get them and get to you. Stay safe."

"Quick—get down and hide," Carol said. "Someone's coming."

I ended the call, stuffed the phone into the pocket of my skirt, jumped off the box, and crawled to the darkest corner. Carol hurried to the makeshift bed, pulled the covers over her body, and went very quiet.

The door to the basement room opened, and I

realized suddenly that I'd left the window open. Darn it. What if they noticed? The shelves helped to hide it, but one wrong breeze and the door to the room could slam. I eased under a workbench and squeezed tight into a ball.

Whoever came in was in shadow. They left what looked like a tray on the floor by Carol and then went back to the door. Suddenly a noise came in through the window. The person stopped and looked over my way. I held my breath.

They walked purposefully toward the shelves, and I knew we were about to be found out. I leapt out from under the workbench and tackled them. We both went down with a thud and a grunt. It was a woman. I grappled with jeans-clad legs and held them tight as she tried to kick me off. She grabbed my hair and pulled it so hard my eyes watered. I let go of her legs and got her in the jaw with my elbow. She grunted and let go as I leapt on top of her and held her arms down with my knees.

"Carol, turn on the flashlight!" I shouted.

I heard Carol scuffle, and the dim bulb flared to light. "Christine!"

"Get off me!" Christine struggled.

"No," I said. "Carol, get me something to restrain her."

"Will this do?" Carol handed me a length of cording.

"Perfect." I kept my seat on Christine's chest and grabbed her hands, tying them tightly together. "Now, don't try anything," I warned Christine. "Rex knows where we are, and he's coming to get us."

"He is?" Carol asked.

"Yes," I said and used my eyes to emphasize my words. "He is."

"Oh, right, that's right," Carol said.

I rolled off Christine and grabbed her by the arm, pulling her up. "I don't know how you fit into all this, but we're going to find out."

"She's Paul's mom," Carol said.

"I know that," I said and dragged Christine through the open door into another room with a staircase that led to the ground level.

"Paul and Cathy are up there," Christine said. "You won't get away with this."

"Let them try something," Carol said and lifted her arm. "I've got this nice hammer here, and I can and will inflict damage if I have to."

I pushed Christine up the stairs first and followed closely behind with my hands on her forearms in case she tried to escape.

The door opened into a kitchen, where the light from the sunrise shone through the window. The house was quiet. Behind me, Carol emerged from the basement with the hammer in hand and went straight to the back door, unlocking it and stepping out onto the back porch.

I followed with Christine in tow. We walked the short distance across the lawn to the street. "Take her," I said to Carol.

"Gladly," Carol said.

I pulled out the phone and hit *Redial.*

"Manning."

"Rex, It's Allie. Carol and I are out safe. We have Christine Keller tied up. We need the police at Christine's house."

"On it!" he said. "Stay on the phone."

Christine suddenly jerked away from Carol and made a run for it, but Carol was faster and tackled her to the ground. Both ladies were momentarily out of commission. I hurried over and grabbed Christine. "Don't make me sit on you again."

"You both think you're so clever, but I know you cheated at the fair!" Christine swore.

"We did not cheat," I said. "We both beat you fair and square."

"All those people who put up Team Christine signs are going to be taking them down once this all comes out," Carol said. "And you will be going to jail."

"Not if my son gets to me before the cops do," Christine said.

"Rex," I spoke into the phone, "Christine says Paul and Cathy are on their way to save her from us."

"Tell her I just got confirmation that they are both in custody," Rex said.

"Hold on." I put the phone on speaker. "Say that again, please."

"Both Paul Patterson and Cathy Lund are in police custody. We found them trying to steal a boat from the marina."

"See," I said to Christine. "Now, sit still and wait."

"They are threatening me with a hammer!" Christine shouted toward the phone.

One of the neighbors, out walking her dog, turned her head and looked at us. She stepped over to the wrought-iron fence. "Christine, are you okay?" she asked.

"You should be asking me that, Nadine," Carol said. "Christine was holding me hostage in her basement. If it hadn't been for Allie, I could have died."

"Nonsense," Christine said. "I brought you food and water three times a day."

"See," Carol said. "She admits it."

"Well!" Nadine declared, and she and her dog went off in a huff. Hopefully to start the gossip mill about Christine.

"We're here," I heard Rex say over the phone, and I looked up to see him and Charles riding toward us. They stopped short, hit their kickstands, and entered the wrought-iron gate. I hung up the phone. "Allie, are you okay?" he asked.

"Did you know you can break a zip tie if you try hard enough?" I asked, then threw my arms around him and hugged him tight. "I'm so glad to see you!"

He held me close to him. "I'm so glad you are okay."

"Wow, I wish I had that kind of reception," Carol said. But as she said it, her husband, Barry, rounded the corner on foot. "Oh, Barry, you're here!" She ran toward him, and he put his arms around her.

I smiled and then looked up at Rex. "We need to talk about last night," I said.

He pulled my arms down and studied the red swollen welts the zip ties had left, along with the scabbed-over places where I'd put the most pressure. "We need to get you looked at."

"I'm fine," I said. "Carol found me, actually."

"Carol?" He glanced over at her. "But I thought she was being held captive."

"In Christine's basement," Carol said. "I found a smugglers' tunnel entrance and was trying to find a way out."

Charles walked Christine out of the yard and down toward the administration building. She griped the whole way about how we had it all wrong. She shouldn't be restrained. She was simply ensuring that Carol lived.

"Come on," Rex said. "Let's get you two over to the clinic and make sure your wrists and ankles are looked after."

"Are you going to check out the basement where they held Carol captive?" I asked.

"Shane is on his way," Rex said. Office Lasko rode her bike up along with Officer Hendricks. "In the meantime, these two will ensure no one goes in or out of the house and all evidence is properly collected."

Rex instructed the two to watch the doors and wait for Shane. Then he and Barry walked Carol and me to the clinic.

"I'm sorry about last night," I said as I leaned into him.

"No, I'm sorry," he said. "I should have never sprung that on you. We should talk everything through before we become engaged. Maybe even get some counseling, if you're okay with it. I know I have a lot of baggage."

"I'm okay with that," I said. "Just as long as we go slow."

"It's a deal."

Chapter 32

"How are you feeling?" Jenn asked me as I entered the McMurphy after my trip to the clinic, where they'd cleaned and bandaged up my wrists and ankles.

"Exhausted," I admitted. Mal jumped on me, and I picked her up. She licked my face. Mella sat on Frances's reception desk, her tail twitching. "Thank you for watching over my babies while I was gone."

"As soon as Rex called to ask if I'd heard from you, I knew something was wrong," Jenn said. "I came over straightaway and took care of Mal and Mella. I knew something had to have happened because you would never miss talking to me after a fancy dinner date."

"Especially *this* dinner date," I said. "I left in a huff before we even started our appetizer."

"Wait, why?" Jenn asked.

"Rex asked me to marry him," I said.

"And you left in a huff? Girl, you need to explain that to me," she said and crossed her arms.

"I'm interested, too," Frances said from behind her computer.

"He surprised me, and I didn't know what to say. And then he kept talking and he said he knew Harry Winston was pressing me to go out with him and that he was concerned about that."

"Uh-oh," Jenn said.

"Are you telling me Rex proposed to you only because he was worried about Harry being interested in you?" Frances asked.

"That's how I took it," I said. "And I stormed off."

"I would have stormed off, too," Jenn said. "What was he thinking?"

"He wasn't thinking," Frances said.

"I know, right?" I leaned against the reception desk. "He didn't have any plans, really. He didn't get down on one knee, and he certainly didn't have a ring. I think he just overheard Harry talking to me and decided he needed to propose."

"A rookie mistake," Douglas said as he came around the corner.

"Rex is no rookie," I said. "He's been married twice before. I would think he'd get it right this time."

"Well, we'll talk about Rex later," Jenn said. "How did you get kidnapped?"

I explained what happened.

"They drugged you?" Jenn said, horrified. "What if you were pregnant? Drugs could have hurt the baby!"

"First off, I'm not pregnant," I said, slightly scared by that thought. "Second, I don't think they were thinking about my health and safety. I'm just lucky that Carol found me. I really think they were going to leave me there to die."

"I'm glad you figured it out and Rex caught them. How is Carol, by the way?" Frances asked.

"I think Carol is in better shape than I am," I said. "She seemed to be having fun."

Frances shook her head. "That sounds like Carol."

"And Christine was mixed up in all that?" Jenn asked.

"Yes, she was holding Carol in her basement." I hugged Mal, and she squeaked. "There's just one thing, well, more than one thing."

"What?" Jenn asked.

"I couldn't figure out why they didn't kill Carol, and why they did kill Hazel."

"You think they killed Hazel?" Frances asked.

"I'm pretty sure."

"Well, those are definitely questions for Rex," Jenn said. "Also, I'm going to have Shane have a talk with him about his romantic blunders. You're right, he really should be better at this by now."

I yawned. "Goodness, I need to go lie down. I didn't get much sleep last night."

"Take a shower first," Jenn said and brushed a wild strand of my hair behind my ear. "You look like heck."

"Right," I said and put Mal down. "Thanks."

Hours later, the sun was going down. I'd gotten a shower and a good five hours of sleep and was brewing an herbal tea when there was a knock on my back door. I peeked out the peephole and saw it was Rex. He had a paper bag in his hand. "Hello," I said and gave him a quick kiss.

"Have you had dinner yet?" he asked.

"No, I was just making some tea," I said. "Come on in."

"I hope you don't mind, but I brought last night's dinner." He stepped inside. The galley kitchen always seemed so small when he entered.

"No, that's great," I said. "Leave it on the counter. Can I get you something to drink?"

"Do you have a beer? If not, some of that tea will do." He took off his shoes, then went around the counter bar and leaned on it to give me space to maneuver.

"I have a couple of beers," I said. "I'll get some glasses."

"You look amazing," he said, and his blue gaze grew warm.

"Thanks." I had to work hard not to say how wrong he was. I knew my hair was a frizzy mess, and I wore cut-off blue jeans and a V-neck T-shirt. There were dark circles under my eyes, and my wrists were still bandaged. Instead, I pulled two beers out of the fridge, popped off the tops, and poured them into tilted glasses to settle the foam. "Here." I handed him a drink.

"Cheers," he said, and we touched glasses before we both took a swallow. He put down his glass and studied me.

"What?" I asked.

"I'm not good at apologies," he started. "But I

want to apologize for yesterday. I should never have tried to do that last-minute. We should talk first. Getting married is a big decision and we—er, I—need to work on my communication skills. So, yeah, I'm sorry."

"Apology accepted," I said. We both took another drink of the beer, and I set my glass down. "I can warm this food up, and we can eat at the couch."

"Sounds good," he said. "How can I help?"

"Get plates, I guess, and start distributing the cold stuff while I try to figure out how not to ruin it in the microwave."

"Oh, I almost forgot." He came around to stand beside me and reached into the bag, pulling out a piece of paper. "Ramsey added chef's directions on how to heat up the leftovers."

"Wow, that's great." I read the instructions and followed them while Rex worked beside me, filling plates with the cold sides. I added the rest when it was warmed appropriately, and we took our plates and silverware over to the coffee table and couch. Rex sat on the couch, and I curled up in the easy chair. "It smells delicious."

"Yeah," he agreed. "I don't usually eat this well."

I let that comment sit for a moment. "I know you were trying to be romantic."

"It was such a disaster." He shook his head.

"It was almost funny," I said and took a sip of beer. "But I think the beer is better than the champagne."

"I should have gone after you," he said. "I just stood there like a dope, not knowing what to do. I mean, the chef had already fixed up this meal, and so I had Ramsey box it up. I figured I'd give you a few moments to work through your thoughts. But by the time I arrived here, they'd already taken you."

"They took away my phone, and I couldn't call." I put down my plate and leaned back in the chair. Mella's tail caressed my shoulders while Mal studied my plate intently.

"I should have walked you home," he repeated. "I figured you were just mad and not answering, and I thought I'd give you some time to cool off. But when I came back, you still weren't answering the door, and so I called Jenn."

"Jenn figured out what happened, didn't she?"

"Yes," he said, then put his fork down on his clean plate and leaned back. "I immediately had people searching the island. I couldn't lose you."

I held out my hand, and he took it in his and rubbed the back of my hand with his thumb.

"I'm glad Carol found you," he said.

"Me, too," I said. "When I realized I was in the tunnels, all I could do was hope that your spelunkers had mapped the entire system so you could find me."

"Unfortunately, they hadn't mapped the part that came up into Christine's house. It seems that bit was cut off by a cave-in decades ago."

"That must be why Carol couldn't find a way out," I said. "But it doesn't explain how Paul and Carol were able to come and go through there."

"I've contacted the local archaeology group," Rex said. "They are going to write a proposal for a grant to map all the tunnels since they are an important part of the island's history."

"That's a really great idea," I said.

He stood, picked up his plate and mine, and put them in the sink.

"I still have questions," I said, turning to watch him come back to the couch.

He took my hand and gently pulled me out of the chair. "Sit with me on the couch." He kissed my hand.

"Okay," I said, wondering if I was going to be hit with yet another relationship surprise.

He put his arm around me, and I snuggled in, listening to the sound of his heartbeat. "What are your questions?"

"Oh." I sat up to look at him. "Well, first off, who killed Mike? Paul or Cathy? Who was embezzling from their company? Did Christine know all along? Was Hazel killed by those three or someone else? And why kill Hazel, but not kill Carol or me or Evan and Dwayne? And if Paul was the killer, who attacked him?"

"Just a few questions, I see," he teased, his blue gaze twinkling. "Sit back, and I'll tell you everything I know."

I snuggled back in. Mal jumped up on my lap and snuggled in, too. Not to be outdone, Mella sat on the top of the couch, her tail resting on my shoulder.

"It took a few hours, but Cathy finally cracked," Rex said. "When I told her she was facing life in prison, she said she wanted a deal. We agreed to do our best to keep a life sentence out of the picture."

"Wait, she wasn't in on Mike's murder? Was she in on Hazel's?"

"I'm the one telling the story," Rex said with a chuckle. "Let me tell it."

"Right, proceed." I snuggled back down.

"Cathy said that the day Mike died, she went over to comfort Paul. He was inconsolable. She stayed with him for a day or two to try to help him."

"Okay."

"There's just one thing," Rex said. "Cathy's married."

"And so she was having an affair with Paul?" I lifted my head to look Rex in the eye. "Was it Cathy's husband who attacked Paul?"

"I'm getting to that."

"Right," I said and leaned my head against him again.

"Well, then when Hazel died, Cathy was worried for Paul's safety."

"Like I was."

"Yes, like you were," Rex said and kissed the top of my head. "But Paul was even more distraught and had been drinking. It was then that he told Cathy about the embezzlement, and that he and Mike had had a terrible fight and he'd killed Mike."

"Oh, no, Cathy knew about Mike after Hazel died and didn't tell anyone?"

"Cathy claims she feared for her life," Rex said. "You see, Paul was drunk and told her that Hazel had been on the rooftop of the business where Christine worked and overheard Paul admit to his mother what he'd done. Christine immediately went into action, telling her son what he needed to do to get away with it. But then Hazel made a noise, and Paul ran out and chased her down. He killed her and then tossed her off your roof to make it look like an accident—and also to get people to stay away from the McMurphy. You see, he knew his mom was furious about you winning the prize, and he thought she would approve."

"And still, after knowing all this, Cathy didn't come forward?"

"Like I said, she claims she feared that if she didn't go along with Paul, he would kill her, as well. It was actually Christine's idea to attack Paul to draw suspicion away from him. It seems she'd been paying attention to your last investigation and copied that bit."

"You mean, when Michelle faked her attack," I said.

"Yes." He nodded.

"Christine actually put her own son in the hospital?"

"According to Cathy, yes," Rex said. "Cathy says she was in over her head, and when Christine heard Carol telling everyone she had a big clue as to who was the killer, well, she sent Cathy and Paul out to get Carol. But Cathy told Paul she wouldn't have anything to do with murder and she would only help if no one died."

"And Paul and Christine listened?"

"Paul agreed. He'd had enough of murder. They went to kidnap Carol, but the two podcasters were there, too, so they kidnapped all three."

"How?"

"Cathy's husband is a dentist."

"Ah, so she had access to drugs," I deduced.

"She had gotten ahold of propofol," Rex confirmed. "Once injected, it puts you out pretty quickly, but you wake up with very few side effects."

"How did they get everyone out of Carol's house?"

"They went down the tunnels," Rex said. "With all three hostages in the tunnel, Cathy climbed back up and padlocked the wooden cover, and she said she heard you come in just as she was leaving out the back."

"Then I did almost catch her," I said.

"Cathy said the men were too heavy to move very far. That's why they locked them in a storage room in the tunnels and then they took Carol to Christine's house, where they locked her in the back basement room."

"As angry as Christine was with me and Carol, I'm surprised she didn't poison Carol when she had the chance."

"It seems she didn't have the stomach to do it herself," Rex said and splayed his fingers through mine. "Christine hatched a plan. As soon as the will was read, Paul would liquidate the businesses and take the money. Then he and Cathy would go to Canada."

"What about Carol? She couldn't spend the rest of her days in Christine's basement."

"The plan was to knock Carol out and release her in the woods the morning they were set to leave. Then Christine would close up the house and follow them."

"Okay, I'm following most of that, but why kidnap me?"

"That is where they made their biggest mistake," Rex said.

"I'd say," I agreed.

"You see, according to Cathy, Christine was growing more and more paranoid each day." Rex teased my palm with his thumb, sending chills up my spine. "It was Christine who was certain you knew everything because of your reputation, and she demanded that Paul and Cathy kidnap you. Not knowing what to do once they had you, they locked you in the storage room at the end of Christine's tunnel. The idea was that as soon as they left, they would leave an anonymous tip on where to find you."

"But if that tunnel system only goes to Christine's basement, how did they come and go? Also, I could have been down there for days without food or water."

"There was no other way out of Christine's tunnel access. It looks like it started out as a root cellar and got connected to an older tunnel before the cave-in. And at that point, they weren't thinking and got desperate."

"And if the only egress to where they put me was Christine's basement, where they were holding Carol, what? What did they do with Carol while they were taking me down there?"

"Christine watched Carol, who was pretending to be dead asleep while Paul hauled you down there."

"That's how Carol knew to find me," I said.

"That's how Carol knew," he agreed.

"Well, that wasn't very smart." I squeezed his hand.

"Thankfully, killers are rarely as smart as they think they are," Rex said.

"What about Christine and Paul?"

"They asked for a lawyer, and so far, neither one is talking."

"Then we only have Cathy's story." I ran my free hand over Mal's soft fur.

"And I think that's all we'll ever get," he said. "Now, enough about that. Let's talk about us."

"What about us?"

"Are we okay after the other night? You know I love you, right?"

"Yes, I think we're okay," I said. "I love you, too. But we need to talk about a few things before you propose again."

"Oh, you still think I'm going to propose again?"

I poked my elbow into his ribs. "Stop teasing."

He kissed me. "What kinds of things do we need to talk about?"

"Well, do you want children?"

"Yes, I told you that before. I want at least two."

I shifted. "And what if I don't?"

"Then we won't." He didn't seem upset by the question.

"And you're okay with that?"

"As long as I'm with you, I'm okay," he said.

"That's very romantic," I said. "But you need to really think about it."

He straightened. "Wait, you really don't want to have kids?"

I sighed. "Yes, I want kids. I want them to grow up in the McMurphy and love the island and make fudge and be happy."

"Then, marry me," he said.

"And still, he asks without getting down on one knee, without a ring, without anything special—"

He shut me up with a kiss. "You need to be prepared," he whispered. "Because I'm going to be asking you over and over until you say yes."

"We'll see about that," I quipped.

"Yes, we will."

And that was all the talking we did that night. With the killers in jail and my pets around me, I was happier than I'd ever been. Oh, and I planned on saying yes to his proposal. I was just going to do it on my terms and in my own sweet time.

Don't miss the next delightful Candy-Coated
Mystery by Nancy Coco:

Three Fudges and a Baby

Coming soon from Kensington Publishing Corp.

Keep reading to enjoy a tasty excerpt . . .

Chapter 1

Don't tell my boyfriend, Officer Rex Manning, but Mackinac Island might just be the love of my life. The month is April, and I'm prepping for my third season on the island. The Historic McMurphy Hotel and Fudge Shop had made it through another winter, and I felt pretty proud about the fact that I had made it my second season with flying colors.

Fudge shop sales had soared with last summer's Best in Show fudge flavor driving most of the on-line sales. Who knew dark chocolate mint would be so popular?

"Morning, Allie," my general manager, Frances Devaney, said as she walked into the hotel promptly at eight a.m. "It's going to be a gorgeous day. They say it might even get up to seventy degrees."

I glanced out the front window. "That would be a heat wave for this time of year." Main Street Mackinac was busy as more and more shop owners trickled back into town to open and ready for the "fudgie" season, as we loved to call the tourists who came to spend time in the beautiful parks, and the Victorian-era no-cars-allowed feel of the island. I saw my best friend, Jenn Carpenter, reaching for the door, so I opened it and waved her inside.

"Don't say I look positively radiant, or I will slug you," she said. Her cheeks were red as she waddled in. "This baby was supposed to come two weeks ago. I'm no longer worried about the pain of childbirth. I'd just like to see my toes again."

Jenn's pregnancy felt like it had gone on for years, but in fact, it was just over nine months. She was still gorgeous as she held her back and sat down in a wingback chair near the front door. It was a seating area with a wonderful view of Main Street and a cozy gas fireplace. The fire wasn't burning today.

"Hello, Jenn," Douglas Devaney, my curmud-geonly handyman and Frances's new husband, said as he walked toward the front door. "You look—"

"Don't say it," I warned and put up my hand in a stop gesture.

"What? I was going to say she looks—"

"Ready to pop?" Jenn said from her perch on the edge of the chair. She'd told me last week that if she sat back on a chair, she would never be able to get out of it due to her current low center of gravity.

"Lovely as ever," Douglas said. "What is wrong with that?"

"Nothing," I answered. "Absolutely nothing." I hurried to the coffee bar situated in the lobby be-hind the fudge shop and grabbed a bottle of water for Jenn.

"I'm sorry," Jenn said to Douglas. "I'm just so crabby these days."

"That's understandable," Douglas said and scooted the footstool over so she could prop her feet up. "Are you sure you should be working?"

"Sarah, my midwife, said it's good to move around as much as possible," Jenn said. "Although I feel more like I'm waddling than walking. That and I have to get out from under Shane. That man is driving me crazy hovering. Just last night I woke up to find him watching me with the 'go' bag at the foot of the bed."

"What's he do when he has to go to work in St. Ignace and leave you here on the island?" I asked.

"Oh, he's not going in to work. Oh, no, he's set up his own lab in our carriage house, complete with an evidence cage and chain-of-custody logs."

"That had to be expensive," I said and handed her the bottle of water.

"You don't want to know," she said with a sigh, then unscrewed the cap and took a sip. "But he got it okayed by the county, so there's that."

"How'd he manage that?" Frances asked.

Jenn shook her head. "His father is good buddies with the governor, so that might have helped him."

"Wait, does that mean you've definitely decided to have the baby on the island?" I asked.

"Yes," she said and rubbed her belly. "Sarah has permission to set up at the clinic, and I have a doula, Hannah Riversbend, who's been working with us through the birthing classes and such. In fact, she's supposed to be meeting me at the Coffee Bean for—" Jenn held up her hand. "Before you say anything, I'm not drinking coffee. They have this nice triple-berry herbal tea. Anyway, I'm supposed to head over there, but I thought I'd stop for a moment and take a load off."

"I'm done stocking the fudge shop," I said. "Why don't I go with you? I would love to meet your doula." I pulled off my hat and unbuttoned my chef's coat. "As long as you don't mind me going smelling of sugar."

"Sure," she said. "You know I love the smell of sugar. But I'm going to rest a bit, if you would feel better about changing first. I can text Hannah what's going on."

"Great," I said. "I'll just be a minute. Besides, that way if we run into Rex, I'll look less like the walking dead."

"You know he doesn't mind how you look," Douglas said.

I shook my head and scurried up the stairs, my bichon-poo pup, Mal, racing ahead of me. It took less than ten minutes for me to wash up and change. I even brushed out my wavy hair and pinned it up into a top bun, which I had heard was all the rage for busy women these days.

I came down wearing jeans, a pink polo with the McMurphy logo on it, and my favorite pair of black flats. Mal loved it when I hurried. She would dance around, picking up on my excitement.

"You can't come with us," I said to my pup as she raced down the stairs and watched me descend with my gray sweater in hand, her stub tail wagging. "It's still too cool for Jenn to be sitting outside, and they don't allow dogs inside."

Mal sat, cocked her head to the side, and just kept looking at me like I was spouting nonsense.

"Oh, let's take her," Jenn said as she rose awkwardly from the chair. "Sarah said sitting out in the sunshine was good for the baby. Plus, I have my sweater." She pointed to the blanket-like white-and-blue-striped sweater.

"Are you sure?"

"Positive." Jenn waddled toward us at the back of the lobby. "Grab her leash, we'll cut through the alley."

I slid Mal into her halter and leash and opened the door for Jenn. The back alley was Mal's favorite potty spot. There was a small strip of grass between the alley and the fence of the neighboring hotel. Mal did her business quickly, then forged ahead of us through the alley.

"How are you feeling, really?" I asked as Jenn stepped out into the sun and the door closed tight behind us.

"Do I look that bad?" Jenn asked as she held her low back and walked slower than I'd ever seen her walk.

"Hey, only child here." I waved my hand. "I have no idea what you should look like at this stage of pregnancy. I was asking because you don't complain about anything."

"Oh, I complain plenty," she said. "But only Shane gets to hear it because he helped create this whole situation." She gestured toward her belly. "Not that I'm not excited for the baby."

"Oh, I know you're excited. You had your nursery done in October." We exited the alley, and Mal turned left, not right toward the Coffee Bean.

"This way, silly," I said and pulled her toward us, but Mal insisted that we go left toward Main Street. "I'm sorry," I said to Jenn. "She must want to go for a longer walk."

Jenn glanced down at her phone. "I texted Hannah we'd be running late, and she didn't get back to me. So, I see no harm in taking a detour. Maybe I can walk this baby out."

"Fine, we'll go around the block to the coffee place," I said. "You might want to text her and let her know where we are."

"Got it." Jenn paused and thumbed in her message, then hit *Send*, and we let Mal lead us to Main Street. The street itself held the usual bustle of repair people and shopkeepers, touching up paint and washing windows and prepping things for the upcoming season.

Mal seemed to know which way we wanted to go and led us again to the right. Joann's Fudge Shop hadn't opened yet. The ticket booth where people paid for horse-drawn tours around the island was also closed with a note that tickets were available at the Visitor's Center.

It was a pleasant walk as we turned right again and headed toward Market Street. Jenn paused and pulled out her phone.

"Is she there?" I asked.

"I don't know, she hasn't answered yet."

"Huh," I said. "Maybe her phone died."

Jenn frowned at me. "She's a doula. Babies come at any time of the day, so she needs her phone to always be working."

"Okay, well, hold on a second. Let me text Helen and see if she's at the Coffee Bean waiting on us. If she's there, then Helen can let her know we got delayed." Helen was the manager of the coffee shop, and unlike me, she knew everyone on the island.

"Okay," Jenn said and sat down on a small bench in front of a restaurant on the corner. "I need to sit a moment, anyway. It sucks being as big as a whale."

I texted Helen, and she got right back to me.

I haven't seen Hannah Riversbend today, Helen texted. *But if I do, I'll let her know you got delayed.*

Thanks, I texted back, then glanced at Jenn, who looked tired from our two-thirds-block walk. "She's not there yet, so we're fine."

Jenn frowned. "None of this make sense. Hannah has always been so reliable. She should have been there, like, twenty minutes ago."

"Maybe she got waylaid, or maybe she overslept," I suggested. It was only eight forty-five in the morning.

"Hannah does not oversleep," Jenn said. "Her job is to be on call twenty-four/seven. I mean, what if I was going into labor now?"

"Are you going into labor?" I asked, trying not to sound scared.

"No," Jenn said and sighed. She heaved herself out of the bench. "Hannah doesn't live far—just the next block over. I say we go check on her."

"Are you up to it?" I asked. "Because I can totally go check while you go to the Coffee Bean."

"No, no, no," she said. "I'm going, too. I think something's wrong. She lives above a shop on Market Street. We can cut down the alley behind it and check her back door."

Just then, a man wearing a hoodie barreled between us. "Hey!" I shouted. "Watch out for the pregnant woman." Mal barked fiercely, and the man glanced over his shoulder for a second, then continued on his way. "Are you okay?" I asked Jenn.

"Yep," she said as she clung to the bench armrest. "I caught myself in time."

"Who was that? I mean, that was really rude. I want to follow him and give him a piece of my mind." I helped her straighten.

"Are you girls alright?" It was Melanie Grazer, the owner of a nearby whatnot shop. "I saw him nearly push you to the ground."

"I'm fine," Jenn said and sent us a reassuring smile. I still had ahold of her elbow.

"Do you know who that was?" I asked Melanie.

Melanie and I had met at a Chamber of Commerce meeting last month. She had retired from a corporate marketing job and bought the shop last fall. She'd just returned to the island for the season. Her brown eyes showed concern, as if Jenn weren't telling the truth. "I think it was Vincent Trowski. I swear that man gets ruder and ruder every time I see him. Are you sure you girls are okay?"

"We're sure," Jenn said. She glanced at her phone. "Still no answer from Hannah. I'm getting worried."

"Are you looking for Hannah Riversbend?" Melanie asked.

"Yes, she's my doula, and she hasn't been answering my texts," Jenn said.

"I saw her just a bit ago," Melanie said. "She was arguing with Mathew Jones. I have no idea what it was about, but it was pretty animated."

"Mathew Jones?" I asked.

Jenn shrugged. "He works on the ferries. Shane knows him from their softball league."

"Wait, Shane plays softball?" I asked. Jenn's husband was a skinny, science type with round glasses.

"Why do you say it like that?" Jenn asked. "He's a really good pitcher."

"How did I not know this?" I asked.

"Because you spend a lot of your time making fudge and running the hotel." Jenn patted me on the shoulder. "It's okay that some of us have a life."

I frowned at her, and her eyes twinkled at me. I couldn't be upset because she looked so happy when she teased me.

"Listen, you girls might be able to catch her," Melanie said. "When she saw me, she stormed down the alley toward her place. It wasn't that long ago."

Mal whined and pulled on her leash, telling me she was done talking and was ready to keep walking. "Thanks," I said, and Jenn and I followed Mal down the sidewalk and into the alley. The shops along Main Street and Market Street often had two stories, with the shop underneath and an apartment or two above. Like my apartment, they often had exits facing the alley, keeping the street view of the shop from being marred by stairs.

Mal sped up as we entered the alley, dragging me behind. "Hey, slow down," I said. "Jenn can't walk that fast."

"Watch me," Jenn said and stepped up her waddle. "Is that Mella?" she asked and pointed to a calico cat sitting on the top of a set of wire stairs that led to an upstairs apartment.

"Looks like it," I said as we approached.

"Wait. Stop." Jenn grabbed my arm just steps from the staircase.

"Are you okay?" I asked.

"Yes, I'm okay," she said, "but he's not." She pointed with her chin toward the bottom of the stairs while Mal strained at the end of her leash.

On the gray rocky alley floor was a young man, lying in a widening pool of blood. "Oh, dear," I said.

" 'Oh, dear' is right," Jenn said. "Hannah? Are you okay?"

A woman sat two steps up from the man and two steps down from where my cat, Mella, sat licking her paws.

"No," Hannah said and looked up at us. I saw a gun in her right hand, which rested on her lap as if she didn't realize what she held.

"Here." I handed Jenn Mal's leash. "I need you to get as far down the alley as you can."

"But Hannah—" Jenn balked as she took Mal's leash.

"Has a gun," I said as calmly as I could. I glanced down at Mal. "Mal, take Jenn to safety."

Mal turned and immediately pulled Jenn toward the end of the alley we'd just turned down.

Jenn looked like she wanted to protest, but Mal jerked hard, and Jenn took a step, turned, and hurried down the alley.

"Hannah," I said calmly. "You need to put the gun down."

She looked at me blankly. "What?"

"The gun in your hand," I said and slowly stepped toward her. "You need to put it down."

"Gun?" She didn't seem to register my words.

Mella moved two slow steps down and wormed her way into Hannah's lap, knocking the gun out of her hand. The metal object rattled thickly across the end of the step and fell to the ground.

For a brief moment, I held my breath that it didn't go off. When it hit the ground without discharging, I leapt into motion, diving under the stairs and grabbing the gun with the hem of my long sweater. I rolled to the other side of the stairs and lay there a moment. Hannah sat staring blankly, petting Mella, who had taken up residence in her lap. I got up and brushed the dust off my clothes, then carefully placed the gun in the deep pocket of my sweater.

Now, I wasn't familiar with handguns, but this was a stocky weapon with a ridged grip and big enough that the handle stuck out of my pocket. Carefully, so as not to startle Hannah, I walked over to the man on the ground. His head turned away from the stairs, and the pool of blood widened around him. I squatted down to check for a pulse. I didn't feel one, and he was already starting to go cold.

Rex and Officer Charles Brown came dashing down the alley on their bikes. They stood them next to the building and studied the scene.

"I've called the EMTs," Rex said as he approached in his calm, steady strides.

"I don't think they can help," I said. Then I straightened and added, "I have a gun that may be involved." Pointing to my pocket, I watched as he slipped on gloves, then squatted down much like I had, careful to avoid the blood. With a shake of his head, he silently communicated to Charles that they had another murder on their hands. Charles immediately went to a kit on his bike and began to secure the scene with crime scene tape.

Rex studied the man, careful not to miss any clues. Then he rose and walked over to me. "You picked up the gun? Why?" His blue eyes went flat cop, where everyone and everything was suspect—even me.

I swallowed as my heart rose in my chest. I held the pocket of my sweater open, careful not to touch the gun. "Hannah was holding it when we got here."

He glanced at the woman who stared into space and kept absently petting Mella. "You said 'we.' Do you mean you and Jenn?" he asked as he carefully took the gun from my pocket and examined it.

"Yes."

"Did you touch it?" he asked and sniffed it. It had definitely been fired.

"I used the hem of my sweater to pick it up after she dropped it," I explained. "I wasn't sure of her state of mind, and so I thought it was best not to leave the gun within her reach."

He grunted as if to acknowledge what I said but not agree or disagree with my thinking. You would think I'd be used to this by now, but it still shocked me to be treated as part of a crime scene, especially by the man I was in love with.

Charles came up with an evidence bag and took the gun from Rex. "We passed Jenn at the entrance to the alley," he said. "I imagine she's called nine-one-one."

"And Shane," I agreed with Charles and hugged myself.

Rex had gone to try to talk to Hannah, who appeared to be in a state of shock and unable to tell him anything.

"Maybe it's a good thing we called for George," Charles said as the sirens of the ambulance—one of the few motor vehicles allowed on the island—indicated its arrival as it pulled in from the opposite mouth to the alley.

I became aware of a small crowd of locals that stood at the edges of the crime scene tape and the curtains moving in a neighboring window. "You might have a better witness than me," I said and nudged my chin in the direction of the window. "They had to have heard the shot."

"Did you hear the shot?" he asked.

"No," I replied.

He looked at the gun. "Huh, that surprises me," Charles said. "Stay put and I'll get your statement in a few minutes."

I nodded and watched as the island's EMTs, George Marron and Kathy Bates, pulled a stretcher under the crime scene tape. Charles intercepted them, and they turned their attention to Hannah. The alley was warming up as the sun grew higher in the sky. My phone buzzed, and I saw it was Frances. "Hello?" I asked after hitting the *Answer* button.

"I heard sirens and saw Shane riding fast down Main Street," Frances said. "Are you and Jenn alright? Did she go into labor?"

That thought made me smile. "Yes, we're fine. No, she didn't go into labor. We have a bit of a situation."

"Oh, dear," Frances said. "Another murder?"

"Yes, but this time it looks like we have the killer," I said and glanced over to see Rex take Mella out of Hannah's lap and let George and Kathy do their work.

"Oh, good," Frances said with relief.

"Not so good," I said.

"Why?"

"It's Hannah Riversbend." I spoke so low it was near a whisper.

"Oh, dear, the doula's dead?" Frances asked.

"No," I said. "Worse. We found her with the smoking gun."